Acknowledgements

A sincere "thank you" goes to my many editors who combed early novel drafts to ensure grammatical correctness and that the story properly reflected life in America and Vietnam during the era described. Oversights that remain are mine alone.

And a note of appreciation to the men and women of our armed forces who served in uniform during the troubled and confused times described in the story.

Stephen J. Dennis

The Girl With the Cinnamon Twist

Stephen J. Dennis

Stephen J. Dennis

ISBN-10: 0615887589
ISBN-13: 9780615887586

Chapter One

March 1, 1969, Colorado Springs
Hunk,
    I made it! As of February 16, 1969 I'm officially an Air Force officer with gold bars to prove it. You won't believe the assignment; Colorado Springs, Colorado. Arrived last night and have no idea what I'll be doing. Whatever it is it'll be better than jungle humping like you.
    Just think, I'm in Colorado, the home of Coors beer! Life is good (so far.)
    Can you believe a year ago we were busy planning the senior class weekend? Now our class is so scattered you're about the only one I've kept track of.
    Had two weeks leave before I came here so went to Seattle to see the folks and pick up the car. After a week I was ready to go. Mom, God love her, was just too 'mommish,' if you know what I mean. She kept wanting me to put on my uniform so she could parade me around to see her friends.
    Your wife may have told you I escaped for a day to see her and your kid. Sally looked great and little Jeff is a giant for a one month old.
    When I settle in I'll send an address. For now use the Seattle one. Take care and keep your fat head down. Sally and Jeff Jr. want you home in one piece.
Rog

***

It happened so fast my head was still spinning. I remember flinging the door open and lunging from the car. Next I found myself lying on the ice glazed asphalt looking up at a girl, with a floppy wide brimmed hat, kneeling beside me.

"Oh, I'm so sorry. Like, it was all my fault. Are you all right?"

I tried to focus. My vision was confused by star-like flashes of light and the throbbing of the back of my head. Faces

1

and shadowed forms hovered behind the floppy hat girl as they leaned forward to examine the prostrate me. Their voices merged into a single jumble with random words leaking out.

"… didn't see it…"

"… slipped on ice and hit with quite a thud…"

"… think she ran into him…"

"… get a doctor…?"

I blinked and tried to sit up, conscious of her gloved hand pressing lightly on my neck. Then, with the aid of the shadow people, I made it to my feet and was eased back onto the still warm seat of my car.

"You OK now?" said a voice.

"Think we need a doctor?" said another.

"Huh? No, I'm fine," I mumbled, staring at the jumble of feet on the ground before me. "Really, I'm fine."

Actually, sitting there with swirling snow piling on my lap and drifting into the car, I was confused as hell and my head felt like I'd been whacked with a cast iron skillet.

"Let me try something," rumbled a male voice. "How many fingers do you see?"

A gloved hand was thrust down, a foot from my chilled nose. "Two," I mumbled.

"What's the date?" he continued.

"March something."

"Year?"

Annoyed by the persistence of my interrogator, I lifted my gaze and was greeted by the sight of a tall Army officer, in dress greens. The snow-covered colonel's eagles on his shoulders seemed to snap me back to reality.

"Ah, 69; 1969 …sir." The "sir" just slipped out. But it seemed right. At least Officer's Training School had taught me to recognize a senior officer when I saw one.

"He's looking a little better," said a woman's voice. "I'll stay with him. Thanks for your help."

Again, staring at the ground, I saw feet shuffle away until I was looking at a single pair of fur topped snow boots. "How you doing?" said the voice in the boots, squatting beside me with a green-gloved hand resting on my knee.

"Me? Better, I guess," I said raising my head to see Miss

Floppy Hat gazing at me with an earnest look of concern. "Where am I?"

"You're in the Dunkin' Donuts parking lot."

Like a puzzle I tried to fit that piece of information into a larger picture. "Man, what hit me?"

"I'm afraid that I did and I'm terribly sorry. You see when I tapped the brakes, nothing happened. I just kept sliding until...."

I followed her gaze to the rear and there, resting firmly against my Camaro, was a brilliant yellow VW with the driver's door hanging open and a dusting of Colorado Springs snow settling onto the front seat. "You've wrecked my car. I can't believe it, you've wrecked my car." I tried to stand but a shot of neck pain dropped me back to the seat.

"Excuse me, but I didn't wreck your car. I just nudged you a bit." She stepped toward the rear and bent to examine the point of contact. "Don't think there's a scratch on either of them as near as I can tell," she said as she wiped snow off the bumpers. "Looks like our cars are very compatible; chrome to chrome so, to speak."

How could she be so casual? She'd just smacked into my new Camaro, my baby; I loved that car. I wanted to tell her how much it cost, how it cornered and how many coats of wax were on that bumper she'd just examined in a most cursory manner. And she was acting like it was no big deal and all the while my head throbbed and my car was filling with snow.

"Hey sailor, I am sorry you hit your head. I'll tell you what; why don't we go inside and you let me buy you a cup of coffee. It's the least I can do and maybe the warm air will do you good. You stay there and I'll park Sunny."

"Sunny?"

"Oh, that's what I call her," she laughed, patting her car on the roof. "I guess it's the color."

She retrieved a combination ice scraper and brush and bent to sweep the snow from the driver's seat. The girl was a study in contrasts. Her scarlet hat was pulled well down until it met a pink wool scarf wrapped around her neck with the tasseled ends tossed over her shoulders. A poofy orange down parka gave her a doughboy look while the thin, deliciously long, jean-clad

3

legs that emerged from beneath the parka and disappeared into fur-topped boots suggested a thin body hidden beneath the fluff.

Finally, seat cleared of snow, Sunny chugged to life and was maneuvered into a nearby parking space.

Returning, she took my hand and pulled me to my feet. "There, now let's get out of this cold."

I brushed the snow from my lap, resisted the temptation to inspect the bumper for myself and followed her into the store.

I'd never been in a Dunkin's before. That morning I'd told the desk clerk I needed a donut fix and he said, "Oh sir, that's easy. Try the Dunkin' place over on Circle Drive. Hot coffee and more kinds of donuts than you can imagine. Yes sir, Dunkin's is the place."

He was right. I was greeted by a display case packed with donuts of all shapes and sizes and the counter crew was slipping trays of even more choices into the case as we passed. But we didn't pause. She took my elbow and guided me through the counter crowd to a curved plastic booth in the dining area.

"Here you are. Grab a seat and I'll get us something to drink. I'll only be a minute." She tossed her hat and green gloves onto the table and returned to the crowded counter.

While the snow melted from her hat and gloves, forming a small puddle on the table, I surveyed my surroundings still feeling somewhat muddled. Outside the snow was swirling and my car was beginning to disappear beneath a thin blanket of white. Inside business was brisk with a constant stream of people coming and going and drinking and eating despite the weather and driving conditions. Colorado Springs was clearly a military town. It seemed that half the customers were in uniforms of some sort. There were Army greens, Air Force blues and several other uniforms I couldn't identify. I was in civilian garb. I could just observe.

"Here you go," she said, slipping carefully into the booth. "Two black coffees, two dunkin' donuts and a couple of cinnamon twists. Take either one. It's just that I thought you might need a little something to eat."

"That one looks like it had a bad morning too; it's a bit deformed," I said, pointing at the dunkin'. "It looks more like a ping pong paddle."

4

"Haven't you seen one before? That's the handle for dunking. Try it."

While she pulled napkins from the table top dispenser I reached for the donut handle and followed her advice. It was very dunkable.

"By the way, I'm Maggie; Maggie Meyers."

"Roger Munson."

"Army or Air Force?"

"You think I'm military?"

"Roger, this is a military town," she said as she pulled the cinnamon twist apart, dropping crumbled frosting on her napkin..

"That doesn't mean I'm..."

"OK. It's the haircut. No one would wear their hair that short unless ordered to," she said licking her fingers. "God, I love these things."

"Oh," I replied, running my hand through the stubble on my head, the result of an Officer's Training School haircut that cost me all of twenty-five cents. "I don't usually wear it this short...," I said, with none of the suave demeanor I was noted for during my fraternity days.

"I'm sorry," she began, reaching across the table to grasp my arm. "I didn't mean it looked bad or anything; it looks great. It's just that it looks military if you know what I mean. There are lots of guys in this town with the same style," she said, flashing a captivating smile.

"So you've broken my cover. I guess I wouldn't make a very good spy. I'm actually Lieutenant Roger Munson, United States Air Force, commissioned February 16, 1969. I just rolled in last night."

"Really, you've only been an officer two weeks? So this is your first assignment. Well, welcome to the Springs."

"You're incredibly perceptive. You're not an enemy agent or anything...?"

"No enemy would have me," she said with a laugh. "I'm too irresponsible. You just look eager and fresh somehow. Are you a flyer?"

"God, no. They won't let me near a plane. I'm a base engineer; strictly a ground pounder. I'm going to work in

Cheyenne Mountain," I replied, twisting a napkin into a knot.
    "Oh, then you'll be working for...; you'll be working underground."
    "I don't know what I'll be doing. I need to call in and let them know I'm in town."
    "Well, I'm sorry I welcomed you with such a bang. Good thing I was barely moving," she said looking toward her yellow VW parked next to my Camaro. "But that lot is like a skating rink and when I pressed the brake, nothing. So thank you for stopping me."
    Maybe it was my aching head. Maybe I was self-conscious about my hair. Whatever it was, I found her flippant attitude irritating. I was annoyed that she could treat the accident so casually and yet there was something refreshing about that very casualness. It was like, no big deal. I hit you. Now would you like a donut?
    To me it was a big deal. That car was my graduation present to myself. Armed with a fresh engineering degree, and a good job offer, I'd drained my bank account and bought my dream car. The silver skin and throaty rumble of the big V8 with dual exhausts turned heads wherever I drove. I loved driving that car. And the rich black naugahide bucket seats seemed to cling to you while doing crazy maneuvers. Mother thought it was, in her words, an overindulgence. Dad didn't say a word but, from the look in his eye when he took it for a spin, I think he was gripped with envy. There was no way his Buick could've cornered like that.
    "So where's home? Where did you go to school? Tell me about yourself," she said, interrupting my car fantasy.
    "You are a spy."
    "No, no, no, just curious about people."
    "OK, I'll give you the Readers Digest condensed version of my life. Born and raised in Seattle; one sister; no distinguishing physical features; University of Washington grad, class of 68; B.S. in Civil Engineering; aversion to tomatoes, olives and most cooked vegetables; blood type A positive. There, what have I left out?"
    "I deserved that," she said laughing with a twinkle in her eye. "I'm way too snoopy or curious or something. OK, no more

questions; I promise."

At least there was nothing intimidating about her. She was cute, in a granola sort of way. But she wasn't my type which minimized pressure to be charming and cool. She was a study in contrasts from her clothes to her questions. Even her hair was a surprise. I'd expected it to be long, in a hippy sort of way, but when the floppy hat came off I saw it stopped at the collar of her yellow turtleneck.

My reflection was interrupted when she spotted someone at the counter. "Oh look, there's Len. Len, we're over here. Join us."

***

"Len, meet Lt. Roger Munson. Roger, this is Len, one of my roommates."

I did not mistake Len for a military man. Much of his wild stringy hair had escaped the confines of a black knitted stocking cap and was tangled in greasy curls at his collar. A bushy mustache drooped beneath an over large nose and acne-scarred cheeks and two deep set eyes gave me a look that suggested disapproval. Everything except his pasty white skin was dark about the guy: his hair, his clothes, his sneering attitude.

And he was living with Maggie.

"You left early," he said, slipping into the booth beside her.

"I wanted to get to the photo lab before it got busy. Anyway, it's early for you too."

"Yes, well...," he grunted staring at his hairy hands wrapped around a steaming cup of coffee.

Charming guy, I thought.

"So, you're here to kill gooks?" he asked suddenly, looking me in the eye.

"Pardon me?"

"Now don't get pissy," Maggie said, hitting Len playfully on the arm. "It's too early for that."

"You see," she continued, turning to me, "he has some issues with this Vietnam thing. It's nothing personal..."

He frowned at her without reply.

"Well, I assumed he wasn't with the Chamber of

Commerce. Anyway, you can rest easy. I'm here to fight the
Russians. I'm Air Force."

"Same difference. Just a different color uniform."

And it really didn't matter to old Leonard. As the
conversation progressed it became clear he hated, in no
particular order, the military, the war, authority, his bourgeois
parents, John Wayne and President Nixon. The list could go on. I
could have challenged him on several topics but didn't have the
energy so let him spout his drivel without rebuttal.

We'd been having a nice conversation before he arrived
but somehow his presence seemed to suck the energy out of the
air. And God he was a slow drinker. He nursed his coffee while
creating table top designs with a small pile of donut crumbs.
Finally he took the last sip and slid his rumpled body from the
booth. "You coming to the meeting tonight?"

She gave him a "not likely" shrug.

He grunted and turned to go. "Nice to meet you Len," I
tossed after him.

He gave me a "go to hell" look and continued walking.

I figure you can tell a lot about a person by their car. His
was a perfect fit; an old Econoline van with rust spots on the
lower panels and anti-war stickers on the rear doors. The stickers
might have been all that was holding the doors together. Tires
spinning on the ice-glazed pavement, he backed from his space
and careened from the lot into traffic.

***

"Don't mind him," said Maggie. "He takes life too
seriously."

"Are you going with that guy?" That was none of my
business but the question was out and I couldn't reel it back.

"Me and Len? Hardly. I share a house with two girls,
Val Hanson and Susan Burns. As you might have guessed we're
all going to Colorado College. Anyway, Len knew Val, and
needed a place to live, so we rented him the attic room that no
one wanted."

"What's he studying?"

"Nothing at present. He works at a coffee and record
shop near campus and likes to hang with students but he's not
actually enrolled. He says he needs to devote his energies to the

8

'cause'."

"The cause?"

"Vietnam. As you could see he's quite into the Vietnam thing. But he's harmless and helps us cover the rent. I find it's easiest to just ignore him."

She thought he was harmless. Perhaps she was right. But, from our brief meeting I was also convinced he was a genuine prick. Yes, that fairly described him. A prick with an attitude.

"Oh-my-gosh; it's later than I thought," she continued, looking at her watch. "I've got to run. I really do need to get to the lab. And I'm so sorry about this car thing. Are you sure you're going to be all right?"

Without much thought I assured her I was, ignoring the soreness on the back of my head and neck.

"Well, welcome to Colorado Springs," she said, leaning over to squeeze my arm. "Maybe I'll see you around sometime."

Then she was gone, leaving only a shredded napkin and a small puddle on the table where her hat had rested. I watched as she walked gingerly across the lot to her yellow bug, brushed the snow from a small part of the windshield, climbed in and slid out of the lot driving much too fast for the conditions. Suddenly it occurred to me what a jerk I was. I hadn't really looked at the damage to my car. I didn't know how to contact her or her insurance company, if she had one. All I had to show for the morning was a donut, a cup of coffee and, potentially, a big bill from the body shop.

I pulled on my parka and scurried out to inspect the car. She'd been right. I couldn't see any damage. There was a little smudge on the chrome bumper but you had to look hard to see it. With the car covered with snow there could've been more but it looked like the Camaro had dodged a bullet.

And at least I'd found a great new place for donuts.

***

"Lieutenant Mills? Lieutenant Munson here."

"Roger, I've been expecting your call. Where are you?"

Lt. Cory Mills was my sponsor, assigned to help me adjust to my new assignment. He was sort of a one man military welcome wagon. Since he was also a second lieutenant I didn't

9

know if I needed to "sir him" or not. He answered that question
by moving to first names in a blink. Maybe things wouldn't be as
formal as I'd been taught at school.

"I'm on the pay phone in the lobby of the Visiting
Officers Quarters."

"The VOQ, great. Well here's a plan...."

Cory proceeded to suggest a plan for my day. No need to
come to his office in Cheyenne Mountain. That could wait until
Monday. I could use the day to look at apartments and then come
to dinner at his place. That was an easy sell. I needed to find a
place to live and I was looking forward to meeting anyone who
could tell me what to expect in my new assignment.

"That's about it," Cory concluded. "Oh, wait. The wife
had a few questions she insisted I ask. She'll kill me if I don't
get answers. Is there a wife?"

"Nope"

"Girlfriend?"

"Ah, no," I said, after an uncomfortable hesitation. "Are
you filling out a form or something?"

"No, nothing like that. Just a curious wife. I don't mean
to pry or anything so ..."

"That's OK. I still get the job don't I?"

"You can't get out of it. I'll see you tonight."

I hung up and wandered back to my room. It was
nothing fancy. Actually it was a little shabby around the edges.
There were cigarette burns on the night stand and the beige tile
floor. The walls seemed to beg for a fresh coat of beige paint.
But it offered a warm refuge and, as I wasn't anxious to venture
into the swirling snow, I picked up my copy of "The Godfather"
and settled into a well worn vinyl covered chair. Perhaps the
storm would let up and I could look at apartments in the
afternoon, I thought.

I tried to focus on the heavy tome but my mind kept
wandering back to Dunkin' Donuts and Maggie Meyers. I was
convinced she wasn't my type and yet there was something both
irritating and intriguing about her. I had a tendency to categorize
girls by type. There were sorority girls, bookworms, hippies,
jocks and so on. It was too early to firmly categorize Maggie but
I put her on the hippie end of the scale. Her eclectic attire,

commune lifestyle and knowing asshole Leonard all put her on that end. Yet there was something about her that didn't fit.

What did it matter anyway? I was best suited for the sorority type. Give me a girl in a tailored wool skirt, a nice sweater with a string of pearls, fake or not, and I was a happy man. I'd spent my early college years trying to get my hand under as many of those sweaters as possible.

That all changed my junior year when I hooked up with Penny Wright, a consummate sorority girl. From then on my wandering hands were confined to her sweaters. Everyone figured Penny and I would be together forever. So did I. We went to all the right parties together. She earned a degree in English literature; interesting but not terribly useful. I was a civil engineer, the son of a civil engineer. We were on our way. Marriage, kids, a job with my dad's firm and a home in the suburbs all seemed on the horizon. Then senior weekend intervened.

***

Senior weekend at the ocean was just last April but, thinking back, that weekend seems like ancient history, a scene from a past life in a distant place. A fraternity tradition, senior weekend was the last great party during our final spring quarter before we left school to face the world. Someone's parents had a beachfront Ocean Shores condo at the Tiki Sands. That became party headquarters. Our class officers stayed in the "headquarters" condo and their dates were set up in a nearby rental unit. Larry Burgess, Hunk Osman and I rented two one bedroom units but Larry's date flaked out so he stayed home and stuck Hunk and me with the bill for the two rooms. Good ol'brother Larry. We decided we'd make him pay either in cash or practical jokes and, in the end, he'd regret dumping on us.

In hindsight, I'm glad he didn't come.

My love life took a sharp turn at the rain-drenched Tiki Sands.

***

Compared to past frat parties this was mellow, in an occasionally boisterous sort of way. It was a senior event so there was none of the freshman whooping and hollering typically found at an all-house party. Seniors were a bit beyond that stage.

11

The rain was unrelenting so we moved the planned patio party into the recreation building next to the Tiki Sand's still winterized pool. Someone had set up their portable stereo on the kitchen counter and a stack of LP's was poised to drop, one after another, to keep us in music for the evening.

After spring break, brother Milo had returned from his Colorado home with two cases of Coors which he brought to the party. They were sucked down by the appreciative brothers and their dates. Hunk and I'd donated two cases of Olympia which lasted a bit further into the evening.

The punch bowl proved to be the biggest draw. Joe Murray and his fiancé were mixing "French 75's" and distributing them in little red plastic cups. The stuff was great; tasted like lemonade. But the ingredients were explosive: equal parts gin and pink champagne with a dash of lemon and sugar.

Penny, never a big beer fan, was drawn to the punch bowl finding it "very bubbly." To no avail, I tried to monitor her intake so she didn't embarrass herself. I knew that, if she did, I'd get blamed.

About 11:00 Hunk took me aside and asked, in a near whisper, "Ah, could you stay out of the room for a couple of hours. Sally and I would like to be alone, if you know what I mean. I'll put out the 'do not disturb' sign and pull it in when the coast is clear."

He seemed uncomfortable asking but it was none of my business what he and Sally chose to do. They were practically engaged and already acted like they were married.

I rejoined the crowd, watched Sally and Hunk ease out the side door and moved to save Penny from further embarrassment. She was alone in the dance area doing the twist to a slow Johnny Mathis song. It wasn't pretty. This was not the Penny we all knew but the crowd was egging her on.

To a chorus of boos and catcalls I joined her on the dance floor where she slumped into my arms and we began a slow dance more appropriate to the music tempo.

"Oh honey, I love you. Where have you been? I've been looking everywhere for you, honest I have," she cooed.

The French 75's were talking to me but yelling at her. She leaned close and nibbled my ear between words. Pressed

12

against me she felt delightful. She had a beautiful body and, at that moment, I could feel all the good parts. I wasn't certain whether her warm embrace was inspired by the love or the liquor but I was good with either.

As others joined in the "slow dance" I eased us toward the door seeking a bit of fresh air. While I was enjoying the loving Penny I suspected a bit of ocean air would be good for both of us. Her head lay on my shoulder as we weaved across the rain-splattered parking lot. Midway we slowed and began a French kiss contest pitting her delectable tongue against my able challenger. Feeling me rise against her she reached down and gave my weapon a gentle squeeze.

"Glad to see me?" she giggled. She'd never been there before. This was good.

We made our way to the stairs, climbing slowly, still clinging to each other. I fumbled for my key and then paused. The "do not disturb" sign reminded me of my promise to Hunk.

"Looks like someone does not want to be disturbed," she slurred. "But do not worry my dear. Your little Penny can handle this unfortunate situation."

She produced a room key from her pocket, held it to the light to read the number and then led me down the corridor checking each door until she found a number that matched her key. After a struggle to find the keyhole, she let us into her darkened room, pushed the door shut, took my hand and led me to the bedroom.

Memories of the rest of the night are a little fuzzy, like viewing a scene through a steamed-up window. By now I'm not sure I can separate what I think happened from what actually happened. I am pretty sure about all the important stuff.

Tongue to tongue we picked up where we'd left off in the parking lot. While taking a breath I managed to pull her sweater over her head, sending her carefully coiffed hair in several new directions. She responded by trying to remove my shirt in like fashion but was frustrated by the legion of tiny buttons. I helped with a couple and then simply pulled the shirt over my head.

She leaned back, running her curved nails across my chest, firm enough to leave marks but light enough not to draw blood. My hand drew a strap down and slipped beneath her lacy bra. I think we both gasped as I cupped her breast and leaned to kiss it's silky softness.

After a moment she twisted free and began a struggle with my belt and zipper. I eagerly assisted.

"I've never seen you...touched you," she panted.

I don't know what she expected but, when she worked the pants below my hips, there it was, sloping up, presenting itself for review. She grasped it with a sense of awe, not realizing how crazy I found her touch.

I dropped to my knees and kissed her stomach while I made short work of her slacks which joined mine in a heap on the floor. My hand slipped into her panties, finding her moist and ready. She pressed her hand to mine as if willing me to go deeper. Then she stepped away, wiggled from her panties and pulled me to her on the narrow bed.

I buried my head in her breasts as she arched her back and pulsed toward me. Without thought or control I eased up her lithe body and my erect shaft slipped into her ready warmth. Regrettably I exploded into her almost instantly. I wanted to give her more. She was still pulsing with a beautiful rhythm and repeating, "yes, yes, oh yes, God yes...."

Then a fog set in; my memory fuzzes further. I recall sliding off and resting against her while doing finger designs on her breasts. I'd never had such unconstrained access to look, touch and kiss. Usually a center console or some too tight blouse would inhibit my access.

I must have drifted off for my next recollection was seeing her kneeling beside me on the bed studying and gently stroking my little soldier which was coming to attention nicely.

"I like your little friend and, oh my, I think it likes me."

"Oh, it likes what you're doing very much."

She ran her hand up my stomach, around my nipple and then, with a single motion straddled me, covering my lips with hers. "Kiss my breasts. I'd like you to kiss my breasts."

As her breathing picked up she reached down, found my guy and guided it deep within her. This time she set the pace, slowly at first with measured deep thrusts. Then her hips became alive as she leaped and plunged with an increasing needy

14

rhythm. It was like she was riding a bronco. I feared I would come too soon but my body held back its final explosion until I feared she would drive me through the bed. She gave a final plunge and muffled a cry before settling back with tears streaming down her face.

"You O.K?" was my best response.

"Yes, oh yes," she gasped.

***

Thinking back it's clear our relationship peaked that night. Was she angry about what we'd done or what I'd done or what she let me do? She never said and didn't want to talk about it. But she pulled back and grew cooler from that night on. Of course we both suffered those two weeks of Hell waiting for her period. At first she was sure she was pregnant. Then someone convinced her you couldn't get pregnant the first time you had sex. Another classmate assured her she was safe if she was on top. I'm not sure she actually believed those tales or just wanted to believe them but I'd never heard two more beautiful words than "it came" when she called me at the house one night.

Unprotected sex; how dumb was that? I'm still not sure if we were in love, in heat or under the influence of the French 75's. For me it was a blurry, blissful and educational night; we dodged the baby bullet and began drifting apart.

Penny took pride in her self-control. She knew she'd lost it that night and I suspect it rankled her no end. She never said. Our relationship didn't actually die that night but the flame was turned way down. The summer breakup came as no surprise and, frankly, with a sense of relief.

She was married by year end and on her way up the social ladder.

Hunk and Sally apparently had a great night too but failed to dodge the baby bullet.

***

If asked, I'm not sure how I'd describe my Penny relationship. In many ways we'd become little more than a habit, dependable partners when there was a party or a dance. Oh, I had feelings for her and missed her when I went off to Officer's Training School. But then, most habits are hard to break. We exchanged a few letters but the passion was gone. It was like writing my sister.

So when Cory asked about "a girlfriend" I could say I was a free man. Tall and trim I'd been described by friends as "nice looking," whatever that meant. In any case, I'd never had trouble getting dates. But I planned to approach the dating scene with more caution this time. I think George Washington warned our young country to avoid foreign entanglements. That was good advice. Though I didn't plan to be celibate forever, I didn't need serious romantic entanglements for now. I didn't need another "Penny" just yet.

In the meantime I needed a place to live and a decent head of hair. But there was something about Maggie ....

***

Old Colorado Springs was laid out in a nice predictable grid with streets running north-south, parallel to the mountains, or east-west, aiming right at Pikes Peak. The orderly layout made getting around easy, except for the icy streets and the snow encrusted street signs.

It was nearly 6:30 when I found the Bijou Apartments, home of Cory Mills, and pulled into a spot near building A. The Bijou was a slick looking, glass and aluminum three story box surrounded by parking and snow piles. A little slick for my taste but it looked better than the three empty apartments I'd toured that afternoon. The first two had been just OK and the third should have been condemned, with its moldy cupboards and worn carpet.

Carrying a bouquet of grocery store flowers I slipped into the lobby, relishing its steamy warmth, and made my way up to their floor. I was surprised to find flowers in March but they looked fresh to my untrained eyes and I didn't know what else to bring.

"Welcome to our humble abode," Cory exclaimed, responding to my knock. Then, while shaking my hand he leaned forward and almost whispered, "Hey man, I need to warn you. Jessie has ..."

"Oh, you're here!" said the enthusiastic woman I assumed to be his wife, who was fast approaching while wiping her hands on a grandmotherly cotton apron. Cory was short and stocky. She was shorter and plumper, the type a fairy tale witch

16

would love to push into an oven. She walked with a decided waddle and exuded an electric energy as she pumped my hand. "I'm Jessie and this is Marie. Come here you," she said turning to a second woman, just now exiting the kitchen. "Roger Munson, Marie Kalos."

Cory, pushed into the background, gave me the "I tried to warn you look," rolling his eyes and saying "I had nothing to do with this" with his upturned palms.

Marie Kalos made Jessie look trim. The same height, her pudgy wrists and arms suggested a "full figured" woman concealed beneath the muu muu like swath of bluish cotton fabric that concealed most of her merchandise.

I was escorted into the room while Jessie continued to chatter. "Oh, the flowers, how nice of you. Cory, will you put them in water while I get Roger settled. You see, Marie and I taught together until December when I quit to deal with this," she said patting the lump protruding beneath the apron which I hadn't noticed.

"It's not due until the first of June but the doctor wanted me to take it easy and my principal thought it unseemly to have a pregnant teacher on staff. Anyway, I've been meaning to have Marie over for dinner and thought tonight might be a good night for a foursome."

"It's a pleasure," I said, shaking Marie's sticky hand.

Shit, I thought! I'd been set up. I couldn't believe it. The Mills didn't even know me and they'd arranged a "foursome" as Jessie called it. God, I hated to be set up. I could get my own dates, thank you very much. My mother tried it a few times with daughters of friends and friends of friends and we had some wonderful post-dinner battles. She didn't quit playing cupid until Penny and I were a certified item and she figured I was out of circulation.

Marie was nice enough though she had a laugh like a wounded seagull. With her olive skin and black hair Marie reminded me of the owner of my favorite off-campus Seattle restaurant, the El Sombrero. It turned out Marie was a Greek from Omaha. I didn't ask how the family made it from Athens to the geographic center of the country. As we sat making small talk and sipping ice tea I tried to place her on my female typing chart. I could picture her in a dusty Mediterranean village, barefoot and surrounded by scruffy kids in some Anthony Quinn movie like "Zorba the Greek." But she was educated and articulate which belied that casting. I was still pondering the question when Jessie ordered us to dinner.

Reflecting their Kansas roots, the dinner was decidedly Midwestern in composition and execution: fried chicken, mashed potatoes with heavy brown gravy, Brown n' Serve buns and overcooked green beans which I don't care for over or undercooked. But the joy of having a home cooked meal overcame my reservations and my plate was quickly cleaned except for a scattering of green beans.

"Have some more chicken Roger," said Cory, noticing I'd finished my first helping. "This may be your last good meal in weeks if you cook as well as I do."

"Please do," added Jessie.

"I'm absolutely stuffed. Everything was so delicious. Tell me Cory, where did you find such a gorgeous woman who can cook like a pro?" I asked, wiping chicken grease from my fingers.

They beamed at each other as Cory reached across the table to squeeze her hand. Jessie wasn't really gorgeous nor the meal delicious but they were a very nice couple and I appreciated the company. Though I was still pissed about the set up attempt it was hard not to like the Mills. They were salt-of-the-earth Kansas-bred flag-waving Americans. My only serious regret was the discovery that their Baptist upbringing eschewed liquor, which accounted for the lack of beer or wine. The gallons of iced tea we downed were a poor substitute but I endured and never hinted at my desire for a malt based beverage.

"So, is this your first assignment Roger?" Marie asked as much to break the current silence as out of real curiosity.

"Sure is, and I only have three years and 50 weeks to go until I'm a free man again."

"Cory is thinking of making the Air Force a career," offered Jessie.

Blushing slightly he added, "Of course no decision has been made but here's how I figure it. I could stay 20 years, retire at half pay and then dust off my teaching certificate. I'd have two pensions and we could live well."

"Mmmm," I replied. I couldn't think of anything else to say. I owed the Air Force four years and planned to do a hell of a job but I'd never considered staying. Second, my friends didn't talk of pensions and retirement. That was much too far away to contemplate. It would take care of itself. Yet here was Cory talking about both. Maybe marriage made a person more responsible, I thought, as Jessie interrupted my reflection.

"Why don't you two boys scoot into the living room so Marie and I can clean up this mess? And put on that new album, honey. It's the soundtrack from 'The Graduate.' I just love it."

As directed we moved to the living room where Cory busied himself with his little stereo, which was balanced on a narrow book case made of cinder blocks and unpainted cedar planks. It was a small apartment and the living room was simply an extension of the dining area so the music easily filled the space and filtered into the kitchen where Jessie and Marie were prattling on.

Cory rose and plopped onto the sofa. "I'll have to give you the name of the furniture store where we got this stuff," he said patting the sofa cushion. "They had this three room group, living, dining and bed room for only $197. Can you believe it? Of course it's nothing fancy but I figure it will be destroyed after a few moves and we can get good stuff then."

I nodded in agreement. He had a point. The stuff looked pretty cheesy but then who really cared. And it went well with the bookcase. In any case, my furniture budget was parked outside in the lot. It would be a few months before I did much furniture shopping.

He glanced furtively toward the kitchen and then leaned forward, speaking in low tones. "Say, sorry about this Marie thing. I had no idea Jessie was going to …"

I lifted my hand to silence him. "Don't worry about it. She's a nice person and I'm an adult, at least I think I am. I was just a little surprised, that's all. Tell Jessie not to worry."

"Jessie worry? She doesn't have a clue. She loves to play cupid though she's never been successful as far as I know," he laughed.

"So forget it and tell me about the 4604th Support

Squadron. What do we support?" I asked.

"Oh, it's great duty. Cheyenne Mountain is top secret and top priority. It's a cherry assignment. I'm the squadron admin officer. As our Colonel Hahn says, the 4604th sweeps, feeds and guards the mountain. You see, it includes the engineers, where you're assigned, the food service troops and security police. Hahn is in charge of it all."

"The engineers sweep...?"

"That's just Hahn. You'll get used to him."

"OK you two," said Jessie as she joined us with a plate of homemade peanut butter cookies which threatened to overload the bargain coffee table. "Enough shop talk. I want to learn more about Roger."

Marie followed close behind with four coffee mugs balanced on a small wicker tray.

"So, how'd you spend your first day in town?"

Without touching the Dunkin' incident I told of my afternoon apartment shopping, embellishing the tale with an entertaining though overdone description of the moldy place. Jessie listened intently, laughed appropriately and then changed the subject. "Hon, did you tell Roger about the Morgans?"

"Oh yes, the Morgans," he replied.

"They're our upstairs neighbors, Army types," Jessie interjected. "Joe's got orders to Vietnam and Sue is moving back to Iowa. They need to break their lease and the landlord's giving them a bad time and ...."

The rest of the evening passed in a blizzard-like blur. Jessie called the Morgans and they invited me up to tour the apartment. I wasn't sure being an upstairs neighbor to the Mills would be a good idea but Jessie was right; it was a perfect set up.

And I liked the Morgans. They offered me a beer. I agreed to take over the lease, saving the Morgans big bucks. In a show of gratitude, they agreed to leave a bed, a table, a few chairs and a sofa all of which they'd picked up used. None of the stuff would make it in "Better Homes and Gardens," but having the dreaded apartment shopping out of the way was a relief. With the addition of a pan, plate and silverware, I'd be in business. My mother would be proud. It meant living in the VOQ a few weeks but I could take that. Life was looking good.

After a second beer, and an agreement to meet the landlord Sunday afternoon, I bid farewell and followed Cory back to his apartment. All evidence of the dinner party was gone, including Marie who had slipped away.

I gave Jessie a polite hug, trying to avoid their child, and eased myself toward the door. "Thanks again for dinner and for introducing me to the Morgans."

"It was truly a pleasure to meet you Roger. What did you think of Marie? Nice girl huh?" asked Jessie.

"Marie was very nice. It was a pleasure to meet her."

"Well, she's just a sample. I know lots more girls in this town. You just let us know what kind of girl you like and I'll see what I can do."

"Jessie," moaned Cory. "Let it go. I'm sure he's capable of meeting girls on his own."

She gave me a knowing wink, ignoring his remark.

"By the way," I said, starting down the stairs, "when do I need to show up on Monday?"

"I suggest you aim for an 0800 arrival at the mountain. It takes about 20 minutes from here. You'll need to get your security badge and then have them give me a call. I'll come out and escort you in."

I made my way across the slippery lot to my frigid car. For the first time I could make out the silhouette of Pikes Peak looming over the town under a star studded sky. It was hard to believe the day had started with a blizzard. And a productive day it had been. I had nearly ended up in the hospital. I had found the Dunkin' Donuts outlet. I'd met the Mills and I'd found an apartment complete with furniture, after a fashion.

And I'd met some other interesting people.

Chapter Two

March 2, 1969; Colo. Sp.
Hi Sis,

How are things in Eugene? Sorry I couldn't stop down on way here but afraid I'd hit snow driving to CO. Wanted to give myself a few extra days. (Remember, I'm an engineer!) Snow no issue and trip went well. Mom continues to worry about her "little girl" in school at that "left wing" university. Tried to assure her you'll do just fine. My big brother advice; behave yourself and/or don't tell her what you're up to!

The Pikes Peak picture on this card is accurate! That big sucker looms up west of town—very impressive. More later.

Your Favorite Brother

P.S. If I do come visit I'll not wear my uniform. Not sure your long haired U of O buddies would approve!

***

Saturday dawned clear and crisp. Pikes Peak, seen in outline the night before, now glowed, reflecting the brilliant sun against an unbroken blue sky.

"This is pretty typical winter weather, sir," my chatty desk clerk advised me when I returned from an aborted run. Airman Friday was a nice black kid from some southern state. Actually he was about my age. The chief difference between us, other than skin color, was that I had gold bars on my shoulders and he had two stripes on his sleeve. So he addressed me as "sir" and I addressed him as "airman."

"It's colder than a well digger's ass out there," I said, slapping gloved hands on my thighs for warmth.

"Low 20s I suspect Lieutenant. I wondered about you when you left but …."

"Well you were right to wonder. I'm not used to this kind of cold. And the ice in the shade is a killer. A guy could fall on his ass big time out there. Point me to the weight room, will you?"

So, under the watchful eye of Airman Friday I'd gone off to the weight room to burn just enough calories to justify a second trip to Dunkin's where I now sat, reading a second hand copy of the local newspaper I'd found in the booth. Forsaking the classic dunkin donut I'd selected a French cruller and a maple frosted donut to go along with my coffee. Mother would not approve of my breakfast choice but mother wasn't here. She believed All Bran and prune juice was the breakfast of champions and preached the gospel relentlessly. I was not converted.

My calendar for the day was blank and I toyed with my options. I was tempted to find some curvy mountain road where I could let the car stretch its legs a bit but the recent snow recommended against that. A tour of the nearby Air Force Academy was on the list as was a trip to the Base Exchange to purchase a few things for my new apartment. Since there was no need to rush the decision I nursed my coffee while reading an editorial suggesting that we should bomb the hell out of Hanoi to show them we meant business. This newspaper, The Gazette Telegraph, had a clear point of view.

As I closed the paper and picked up my remaining donut I glanced toward the display counter and was greeted by a most delicious sight. Annette Funicello, or a girl with her redeeming features, was walking my way balancing a cup of coffee and donut bag in one hand while gripping the shoulder strap of a large black handbag with the other. She had the "Annette" smile, the bouffant jet black hair held back by a shiny red head band and, as well as I could assess, the official "Annette" body. She was a live piece of art.

I don't know any American boy who wasn't, at one time or another, in love with Annette Funicello. I was a Mickey Mouse Club fan because of her. Sure Darlene, Cheryl and Karen were cute but there was only one Annette. When she gave up her Club tee shirt for a bikini, switched to movies and began running around California beaches with Frankie Avalon my unrequited passion only grew. Now her clone was walking toward me.

She stopped at the booth across the aisle, freed her hands

and removed her knee length wool coat which was folded carefully and placed on the seat in a motion that placed her plush ass in full view. It was exquisite, wrapped in a scant tweedy looking skirt that stopped just above the knee, a few inches from her leather boots which stopped just a few inches below. She turned and slipped into the booth giving me just a brief glance at her sweater-covered profile. She was all Annette.

Trying to appear casual I reopened the paper and did my best to appear engaged while running through a mental list of time-tested conversation starters. I also decided that my resolve to avoid new female relationships could be amended to include this lovely creature. I was about to make my move when ....

"Well hello sailor. Mind if I join you?"

It was Maggie and, without awaiting a reply, she tossed her scarlet hat on the bench and slid into the booth. I could see my chances with Annette, the girl of my dreams, slipping away, smothered by Maggie's presence.

"No, no, please join me," I stuttered, gathering up the paper and empty creamers.

As she squirmed out of her poofy parka my eyes were drawn to the outline of her unrestrained little breasts resting on the table edge, pressing against the fabric of her orange turtleneck. They were not in Annette's class but they still appeared delectable. When she settled back on the bench the view, but not the image, receded.

"It's nice to see you again. I thought I might. This isn't that big of a town," she chattered while I glanced across the aisle which looked much wider and uncrossable now that Maggie had arrived. "Now you'll think that all I do is eat donuts. It is my worst vice I suppose but...."

"Well, it doesn't show. You look nice and trim," I said cautiously, having more than once tried to complement a woman with unpredictable results. When I'd say "trim" they'd hear "skinny." When I'd say they looked "nice" they'd hear "plain" and so on. I think Humpty Dumpty once said words mean exactly what you want them to mean—neither more nor less. I think a woman must have written that line.

"I'm lucky. I'm young and seem to burn it off. But they say girls end up looking like their mothers and mine is a bit on the chunky side, loveable but chunky. Maybe I have my dad's thin genes."

"Is he thin?" I asked, satisfied that I hadn't put my foot in my mouth.

"He was. He was killed when I was five. I barely remember him."

"I'm sorry," I replied, trying to steal a glance at Annette.

"Oh don't be. That was a long time ago. He was killed in Korea doing what he loved to do, fly planes. So what's your mother like?"

Maggie was fast. She could change topics in a flash. I had to pay attention or I'd be left behind.

"My mom? Chunky, I guess. Yes, you could say she's chunky."

"No, I don't mean what she looks like. What's she like?"

"Are you interrogating me again? I thought you got that out of your system yesterday"

"Oh my, I don't mean to sound snoopy. I promise not to ask any more questions." She paused for an instant and pulled a piece from her cinnamon twist. "Now, tell me about your mother."

I couldn't help smiling; she'd slipped easily into the interrogation mode as she savored the first bite of her sticky pastry. "Hmm, well, she's a good Lutheran mother who does whatever the women's group does at church. She also plays bridge at her club one day a week and worries about me and my sister everyday."

"Who's the biggest worry, you or your sister?" she asked, licking her fingers in what I can only describe as a sensuous manner.

"Louise, or Lou as we call her, is the focus of mother's worry right now. She's a freshman at the University of Oregon which, according to mother, is the hotbed of cheap drugs and free love in the Pacific Northwest. But Lou's squared away. She'll do fine and then Mom can start worrying about me again."

"She sounds like a dear lady. It also sounds like you give her a bad time."

"Not really. Now what about your mother?"

"A clone of yours," she said with a laugh. "Maybe

they're sisters. Now, how about your father?"

"Ah, you're doing it again. Sorry, you've had your 30 questions for the day."

"Oops. Sorry. I'm just naturally curious."

"Tell me about yourself. What are you doing in school? Are you working? How did you vote in the last election? You know, all the normal stuff," I said.

"Wow, what a list. I'll go in reverse order. I didn't vote in the last election. Shame on me. I don't work and, as you know, I'm going to school at Colorado College."

"Degree?"

"Nothing yet, I'm a bit of a wanderer. I was in elementary ed at Boulder but decided I would make a lousy teacher. So now I'm doing art history and I'm still not sure what I want to do when I grow up."

She paused, as if catching herself talking too much, and then turned the conversation back to me.

"Well, do you have a busy day planned? Apartment shopping I suppose? Oops, there I go again, asking questions. I'll quit asking."

"Actually I was lucky with apartment shopping," I said, explaining how I was taking over the Morgan's unit.

"You're a lucky one."

"So now I can move to the other things on my to-do list. First I'm having coffee here and then I'm doing nothing. A young officer's life is full of excitement. I may go out to the officer's club later and start a brawl in the bar like they do in the movies."

As the last word slipped from my lips my Annette world was shattered like a fragile goblet. A guy, who looked like he stepped off of the cover of "Esquire" magazine, joined her in the booth, reached across the plastic table and squeezed her hands in a very familiar way. One thing was clear. Annette was not waiting for me.

"You OK?" asked Maggie.

"Huh? Yes, I'm fine. I was just wondering what he's eating," I said, nodding toward Mr. Esquire.

She took a quick look across the aisle. "That's an apple crumb; they're not as good as they look. Anyway, your bar brawl idea sounds exciting. Good luck with it."

We fell silent for a moment, surrounded by the clatter and chatter of the ever changing crowd. Then she continued while tearing a napkin in neat little strips.

"Hey, I've an idea but it does involve a question."

"Fire away."

"Today is Val's birthday; you remember I mentioned my roommate Val? A bunch of friends are coming by tonight for a little party. Nothing big and no gifts. It's just an excuse for a get together mainly. Most of them are students. You'll fit right in. Why don't you come by?"

"I don't know. I wouldn't know anyone and...?"

"Oh, come on. You know me and Len."

"I didn't think old Len and I hit it off too well at our first meeting."

"He's harmless. It's just that a nasty chip falls off his shoulder from time to time."

"I don't want to inspire his jealous streak or...."

"Good God," she said laughing. "Like I told you before, he's our attic rat. I don't think he even has a jealous streak."

I heard her but also remembered the look on his face when he saw her sitting in the booth with me. Perhaps she didn't think they were an item but that didn't mean Len didn't wish they were. Maybe guys see things different than women but I saw lust in his eyes and jealousy in his mood.

"....so anytime after eight. Here's the address and phone number," she concluded pushing a napkin scrap covered with red ink across the table to me. "If you don't show I'm calling the police because I'll assume something bad has happened to you. Gotta go. See you then."

And she was gone. Annette and Esquire followed her out the door.

***

I drove slowly down the darkened street looking for Maggie's address. The snow on the lawns reflected the meager available light helping me to see the nearly hidden address on an old two story house near the corner. I turned around and returned to claim a small parking space across the street from the party house.

I was still trying to decide why I'd come. A Coors evening at the officer's club or a quiet night at the VOQ with a good book were fair alternatives. But this Maggie person intrigued me. Where did she live? Who were her friends? What were they like? So, for whatever reason, there I was.

There appeared to be someone in the car behind the chosen space so I tried unsuccessfully to avoid tapping that car when I pulled in. It was a gentle tap but embarrassing for me with a witness in the car. I locked my door and walked to the rear spreading my hands in an 'I'm sorry' pose.

The driver rolled her window half way down and laughed, "No problem; it's a rental." I nodded and headed for Maggie's.

The sound of voices wrapped in the quiet background tunes of Simon and Garfunkel wafted through the heavy wooden front door. When no one responded to my knocks I pushed the unlatched door and let myself in. I should have turned right around.

I had entered another world, a world where I did not belong. I was wearing a V-necked blue wool sweater over a short sleeved dress shirt complete with a buttoned down collar. This was over a pair of well starched khaki cotton pants, white socks and penny loafers. There was no one, I mean no one, who was dressed anything like me.

I'd entered the world of Leonard Hoffman: dark, unwashed and ominous. It was a world of dark colors, tie dyes, beads and sandals. The lighting was provided by candles which occupied every flat surface in the room and the air was thick with the smell of incense or, I feared, some illegal burning leaf.

There was much talk of drugs when I was in school but, believe it or not, I'd never been around any—at least not that I knew of. We were beer drinkers and we accounted ourselves well in that department but pot—it just hadn't happened.

Great, I thought, now I'm going to be caught in a drug bust and I haven't even reported for duty.

I was about to step back toward the door when Maggie appeared out of the haze wearing a billowy dress that fell to her ankles. "Roger, you found us," she said as she approached, grabbed both hands and leaned up to kiss me on the cheek like an old friend.

"Good directions," I stuttered recovering from the surprise. "Say, I'm not sure this is a good fit for me. Perhaps..."

"Oh you funny man," she said, stepping back to survey my outfit. "I'll just tell everyone you thought it was a costume party and...."

"Oh shit; that makes me feel better."

Ignoring the response she took my hand and led me to a small group of people standing by the fireplace. "Val, I want to you meet the flyer I was telling you about. Roger, this is the birthday girl."

She was wearing a loose fitting top, which looked like burlap, over well patched jeans. I instantly classified Val as a 'hippie' on my female typing system. Her long hair and dangly beaded earrings reinforced my assessment.

"Welcome to my party. Help yourself to something in the kitchen. It's all good."

"Thanks and happy birthday."

"Roger thinks he's overdressed for the occasion," Maggie offered with a laugh.

"Oh, you didn't take me seriously," I replied feigning disbelief.

Val laughed. "Don't worry about this group. You look fine. This is Jerry's bath night," she said leaning on the guy she'd been speaking with. "You won't recognize him in the morning. He'll look just like you."

"Hey man," said Jerry, shifting a cigarette-like object into his left hand so he could shake with his right, "don't pay any attention to her. Welcome to our little celebration."

Jerry released my hand as Maggie pulled me toward the dining room. It may have been my imagination but it seemed there were ten pairs of eyes watching us as we left. I was feeling very conspicuous but there was a good chance some of the other guests weren't feeling anything at all.

Entering the narrow kitchen I nearly ran into Len as he emerged from the refrigerator. With a Coors in each hand he stepped back in surprise. "What the fuck is he doing here?"

"Len, really...," Maggie replied, taking a beer from his hand and offering it to me.

"Maybe that one was spoken for," I offered in a consolatory tone.

"Goddamned right it was spoken for warrior. Now Maggie, why did you…?"

"There's more in the fridge," she replied, pushing by him to retrieve the opener from the counter by the sink. "Really Len. Aren't you being a bit of an ass? He's my guest."

"Actually I think he's being a full fledged ass," I tossed out, glaring at Len.

"Shit," he responded, slamming his remaining beer on the counter before retrieving a replacement for the purloined one from the yellowed refrigerator. Without another word he fumbled opening both cans, tossed the opener into the sink and bumped past me into the dining room.

"I think he's warming up to me," I said as she took the church key and deftly opened a second Coors for herself.

"They say he takes some getting used to. Well, he's been here since the fall and I'm still not used to him. But it's a big house so I don't see him much. So, here's to Val," she said, raising her can in a toast.

I took a long draw and then examined the golden can in the dim light. "You know we can't get this stuff in Seattle. We had a Denver guy in my fraternity who used to bring back a couple of cases whenever he drove home on break. That was a big day in the house."

She looked at her can with less affection. "I'm not much of a beer drinker. They all taste the same to me. Come on, let's mingle."

As we left the kitchen we were nearly run down by a Ringo Starr looking guy on an apparent refrigerator run.

"Oh Luke, meet Roger here. He's new in town," she chirped, "and I wanted to …."

"Cool," he drawled, without pausing.

"Friendly sort," I offered as he passed from earshot.

"Yes, he is isn't he? Actually 'cool' is the only word I think I've heard him utter," she replied as she scanned the room for a conversation we could join.

I watched as Luke returned from the kitchen with two beers, delivering one to a skinny girl lounging on the sofa near the fireplace. For some reason Luke seemed out of place in this crowd. I couldn't put my finger on it. He was scruffy looking. But then so was everyone else. He had a droopy moustache and hadn't shaved for some time. But that could be said of half the guys in the room. There was just something about Luke....

The next hour passed with glacial speed. I tried to make conversation but could barely understand the language. Len's presence was everywhere. He never spoke; rather he stayed nearby so he could glare at me from a distance. The other party people were polite in a chilly sort of way. I met Susan, the third roommate. Val and Susan had been high school friends. Maggie was a friend of a friend and had hooked up when she needed a place to live in Colorado Springs. The whole connection was confusing.

Like Val, it appeared that Susan had done her clothes shopping at Burlap City if there was such a place. Unlike Maggie and Val, who were both thin bordering on skinny, Susan was built like Cass Elliott of the "Mamas and Papas." Full figured and full voiced, with a robust laugh, she commanded the room when she spoke.

At first Maggie stayed close, trying to ease me into conversations, acting like a good hostess. When she thought I could get along on my own, or perhaps just felt confident I wouldn't start a brawl, she left me alone with Jerry and another unwashed fellow called 'Doggy.' Without joining in I listened to a range of wild opinions I didn't share, but when they began calling the President, my commander-in-chief, a shit head and fascist, I decided it was time to slip out. I wasn't sure what I thought of Nixon but that was over the edge and I was growing uncomfortable with the whole scene.

"But it's so early," Maggie implored when she returned and I announced I was leaving.

"I know but ..."

"Feel a little out of place?"

"Well, just a bit."

Standing together in the narrow entryway, both walls lined with heavy coats on hooks she studied me as if assessing the situation. "Do you have a coat?"

"In the car," I replied.

"How about a walk? I'll grab a coat. I'll only be a minute."

Before I could respond she reappeared in her snow boots, poofy coat, gloves and scarlet floppy hat. As I followed her to the door Len appeared out of the haze, beer in hand.

"Where you off to, Mag?" he growled, crowding by me into the narrow hall.

"It's Maggie and I don't have to check out with you Len. Come on Roger," she said grabbing my hand.

I was about to toss a barbed comment at Len when our feet tangled causing me to stagger against the wall and Len to tumble back into the living room, sending his beer sailing to the middle of the room where it lay in a foamy golden puddle. Luke came charging across the room like he was going to take me apart.

"Easy Luke," grunted Leonard. "Leave it be."

Luke looked from me to Leonard and then back to me, nostrils flaring. Then I noticed what was different about Luke. Beneath his loose fitting clothes was a ball of muscle; he was built like a weight lifter.

Maggie stepped back into the hall, examined the scene, shook her head and then pulled me out the front door as Len glared after us from his prostrate position.

***

I retrieved my parka from the front seat of my frost covered car. The windows were still clear on the car behind and the two heads were outlined in shadow in the front seat. Get a room I thought. It was too cold to stay outside chasing a little front seat nooky.

Maggie met me in the middle of the street. With her hat pulled low for warmth and hands cocooned in the heavy gloves she steered me toward the far sidewalk. Only her long dress hanging below the coat seemed out of place.

"Sorry about in there. You looked a little uncomfortable," she said

"Me? No, I'm OK. I guess that's just not my kind of place," I replied, hands tucked firmly into the parka pockets.

"Some of them are a bit dark."

"Friends of yours?"

"I know a few of them. Being so close to campus the house has gotten to be a hangout for some of Len's buddies. Some of them creep me out. I try to avoid the place when they're there."

Following her lead we crossed a main street and veered onto the Colorado College campus. The pathway lighting reflecting off the snowy lawn gave the grounds a Currier and Ives quality. "Where do you spend your time," I asked. "when you're not at the house I mean?"

She pulled her collar up and walked along without responding.

"Hello in there," I said, stepping ahead and looking back at what little face was still exposed.

"Sorry," she replied with a laugh. "My mind seems to be wandering. Where do I spend my time? Here, mostly: on campus, in the library or the photo lab."

We walked silently to the porch of the library where she asked, "Did Len do something that I missed?"

"Little Leonard? Other than stand in the shadows and glare at me like a recently neutered cat, no, he didn't do anything. This may surprise you but I've concluded that Len and I will never become good friends. We're different kind of folks, as they say."

"Who's they?"

"Just an expression."

"Hmmmm," she said before falling silent again and steering me up the middle of the campus plaza.

This was a side of her I hadn't seen before. I'd only seen the effervescent and chatty Maggie. I drifted back a step where I could study this girl in the poofy down parka. She was an enigma. She lived on the edge of a musty world of pot smoking castoffs and yet didn't seem to be of that world. But she would have been a misfit at one of my old fraternity parties just like I stood out at Val's. We were from two different worlds and yet I enjoyed just talking, feeling no particular urge to get her into ....

As we walked in the fresh snow my mind drifted to a question long debated at the frat house. Could girls and boys just be friends? Some said no. The sexual tension would be too much. Others disagreed, citing girl friends that had stayed friends while they dated others. I'd never voted; my research continued.

Suddenly the old Maggie returned.

"This is Arnold Hall, the home of the art department. The photo lab is here and I'm, like having more fun with the class. Have you ever done any photography?"

"Nothing serious," I replied thinking of the Kodak Instamatic sitting back in my room. I'd purchased it during Officer Training so I could send a few photos home to my folks. It would not turn the head of a serious photographer.

"It's amazing what you can do in the lab. Gramps gave me this wonderful camera when I graduated from high school but I never knew the magic I could do with it until this quarter. I've taken some simple pictures and then with darkroom tricks I can make something wonderful out of them. I'm no painter but I sure have fun with photos."

"You'll have to show me," I said, trying to maintain the momentum.

Without a response she led us away from the building and fell silent until we reached the edge of the campus. Then ...

"What do you think about Vietnam?" she asked out of the blue.

"Vietnam?" I said, stopping and staring at her back.

She paused and turned. "I mean should we be there and all?"

"Well, we need to stop the communists somewhere."

I was sounding like my dad; that was his line. He and his friends all seemed to feel it was a good idea even though it was their sons who were being called to serve. That impressed me. Perhaps they knew something about war from having fought in the big one.

"The domino theory?"

"I guess. If Vietnam falls then Thailand, Laos and who knows what else will follow. Soon all of Asia will be under a red banner. Of course, I doubt Len would agree with that assessment."

"No, he wouldn't," she replied, turning to continue our walk.

"Why do you ask?"

She shrugged and seemed to sink even deeper into her parka. "I don't know. I just hate to see so many people getting killed. It seems like such a waste. I just don't get it."

What a shitty night this was turning out to be. First the party was a colossal bust and now our conversation was drifting into an equally black hole. I suddenly felt like eating a donut. It would have to wait.

We left the campus and headed down her street from the other direction. "I think I'll call it a night," I said as we approached my car.

Without a word she surprised me by turning and laying her head on my chest without taking her hands from her pockets. Instinctively my hands wrapped around her thin body and held her while the floppy hat pressed against my cheek.

After a pleasant interlude she shrugged back, placed a gloved hand on my left cheek and lightly kissed my right. As she turned toward the house all I could think of to say was, "Maybe I'll see you around." Now that was a weak line, I thought, as it left my lips.

She paused on the porch, turned and seemed to study me for a moment before replying. "I think I'd like that. And thanks for the walk."

Then she disappeared into the musty house.

Settling into the Camaro I fired up the big V-8, adjusted the heat to "high" and then sat, staring at the pulsating tachometer. What a confusing evening: Len, the whole party atmosphere, the anti-war talk and Maggie. It was all very disconcerting and had my mind twisting in a most uncomfortable way. Finally, when the first hint of heat settled on my feet, I shifted from neutral to first and pulled carefully out of my parking place so as not to disturb the lovers in the car behind.

I needed to get back to my world.

***

I'd never been in an officer's club. But since it was across the street from the VOQ and I felt a need to be around "normal" people I decided to wander over.

I didn't know what to expect. My image of officer's clubs came from the movies where a hero, like John Wayne, would always meet a gorgeous nurse at the club just before going off to battle. Or a group of lusty pilots would gather at a club bar and recount the krauts they'd shot down that day while drinking whiskey and smoking Chesterfields.

John Wayne wasn't there that night but the lusty pilots were.

The Ent Air Force Base Officer's Club, housed in an old barracks, had pretensions of grandeur, like an old woman trying to fool the world with too much makeup and too tight clothes. A coat of dark paint, trellises and a carved front door tried to hide the buildings origins. Inside the designer had more success with soft lights and plush carpets that gave the impression you were in a special place.

Acting nonchalant, I wandered into the lobby and followed the smoke and noise to the bar. Relieved to see I was dressed to blend into this crowd, I took a seat four stools from a group of boisterous young men that I correctly took to be pilots, just like the movies. From the loud conversation I deduced they had just flown in from a base in Idaho and, rather than brag about their sexploits or the number of bogies shot down, they were lamenting what a lousy place Idaho was for a single guy.

At the far end of the narrow room a pianist played Sinatra songs for a group of appreciative officers with their ladies.

The one thing missing was single ladies which, considering my dark mood, was fine with me. As I hunched over my second Coors I began to feel sorry for myself. The pilots were buddies, or so it seemed. The couples by the piano had each other. Maggie was in a house full of people. Cory and Jessie were likely tucked in a warm bed together. But no one knew or cared where I was or what I was doing. Instead of celebrating my freedom I was feeling lonely. Maybe it was the beer or the altitude or a combination of the two. Instead of reveling in my freedom I was sulking in my solitude.

Not counting the low life types at the party and the desk clerk, I could claim I knew four people in this town; Maggie, Marie, Cory and Jessie. I'd almost met Annette. When I went to work I would be a part of my new unit. That was something. But for now it was just Roger, nursing a beer, alone on a barstool. I was alone in the flat middle of the U. S. of A. and it was a strange and lonely feeling.

It was time to get back to the VOQ.

Chapter Three

Sunday, 3/2
Dear Mom and Dad,
Start work tomorrow in Cheyenne Mountain, this big underground command post. Not sure of job but should be interesting. More on that later. Address below is new address. Found apartment on Saturday. Great deal. Please forward any mail that comes your way.
Dad, photo on back is Broadmoor Golf Course. I hear it's a good one. It's covered with snow right now. You should plan a trip this way and you can pay my greens fees for a round. Remember, I'm just an underpaid 2nd lieutenant!
Love, Roger

***

I was nervous as hell. It was my first day on the job, my first real day in the role of an officer. To compound my anxiety some asshole in a hot Porsche nearly ran me off the pavement passing at a narrow spot on the mountain access road. Perhaps I'd get a chance to return the favor some time.

I pulled into the Cheyenne Mountain parking lot, killed the engine and sat for a moment, enjoying the view; it felt like you could see all the way to Kansas. The lot itself, nearly a thousand feet up the side of the mountain, was built from the tons of granite they'd blasted from the tunnels when they constructed the underground command post. At least that's what I'd read in an engineering journal. In any case, it was an impressive view.

Armed only with my virgin vinyl zippered folio—a gift from my folks—I plunged into the human flow of day-shift workers that was converging on a squat concrete block building across the lot. The folio contained my official orders, a pen and small tablet. Clutching it seemed to give me an unwarranted sense of security. As I approached the building entry I could see the black maw of the tunnel entrance looming behind a rugged looking barbed wire steel fence which sprouted from each side of the building and died at nearby vertical granite walls. Entering the building I stepped aside and watched the others flash ID cards, pass by a guard and then climb onto an official blue school bus that sat behind the building. When full, it rumbled to life and disappeared into the entry tunnel a short distance away.

Spotting an office labeled "Security Admin" I walked in and was greeted by a plump sergeant behind a counter.

"Excuse me but this is my first day here and...."

"Do you have your orders sir?"

I fumbled for a copy and handed it over the counter.

"Oh, Lt. Munson. We've been expecting you. Captain Lutz wants to see you but first let's take your picture and get your badge started. Bork," he said, turning to a nearby clerk, "take the lieutenant's picture and get his badge going."

I was directed to the corner of the room, placed my feet on the yellow line as instructed and tried to look officer-like while Airman Borkowski snapped my picture with a tripod mounted Polaroid camera. Then he pointed me to an open office door labeled "Captain Lutz, Security Police."

I tapped the open door and stepped in, snapping to attention and tossing off a crisp salute. "Excuse me sir, Lt. Munson reporting."

He seemed surprised by the interruption but returned the salute, closed his file, which was marked with a large red "secret," and rose to greet me. "Munson, good to meet you. It's Roger isn't it?"

He shook my hand and directed me to a gray metal chair opposite his gray metal desk in his beige office. I was getting used to gray and beige. Somewhere, sometime, someone had decreed that all Air Force furniture would be gray and the walls would be beige. Maybe it's because gray goes with everything or clashes with nothing and goes well with beige. Maybe the beige was selected by the same person. In any case, I was in a world of gray and beige.

Not much older than me, Capt. George Lutz came across as a brisk, no bullshit kind of officer. He wasn't a big man, maybe five foot six, but solid like a fire hydrant. His movements, his conversation and his office were all crisp and tidy. He still sported his officer training haircut, bald on the sides and stubble on the top. His uniform was impeccable with knife-edge creases where needed and wrinkles banished. His desk looked unused with all pencils at attention in a small coffee cup, an empty ashtray and the single file sitting perfectly square on the blotter. And he never said, "You can call me George."

He returned to his seat, swiveled toward me in his chair and studied me over steepled fingers.

"Home town?" he asked.

"Seattle."

"Hmmm, never been there. College?"

"University of Washington."

"Major?"

"Civil Engineering"

The interrogation or conversation or whatever it was continued through twenty questions as if he was seeking a fatal flaw. Then, like a prosecuting attorney, he changed the line of questions.

"What do you know about the mountain, this mountain?" he asked waving his hand toward the window and the granite face of the mountain beyond.

"Just what I've read, sir. I found an old "Newsweek" article that talked about what goes on here and an "Engineering News Record" article about the construction but that's about it."

"I hope you didn't learn too much from those magazines because if you can learn from them so can them Kremlin bastards. God, I hate those PR pissants at H.Q. I'm trying to keep our secrets in the mountain and the bad guys out and they want to be chatty with the press and ... oh well.

"Let me show you something," he continued, rising and pulling down a map like a window shade on the wall behind his desk. "See this? This is the DEW line, the distant early warning system. It stretches from Alaska to Greenland. All these radar stations send their information to this very mountain where we digest it and order out the cavalry. When the Ruskies come, they'll come from the north and we will see them coming and kick their sorry asses out of the sky.

"Shutting us down would be like poking our defensive eyes out. So what we do here in the 4604th is damned important.

Do you see that, Muncy?"

"It's Munson sir and yes, you make a very good point. I hadn't really thought about it quite that way."

In fact I hadn't really thought about it at all. The Newsweek article was pretty superficial and the Engineering News Record focused on the construction challenges. I knew it had been a gigantic tunneling job to carve a grid of three story tunnels 1000 feet into the hard granite mountain. I knew the underground command post was contained in 15 steel buildings supported by its own power plant and utility systems. And I had no idea where I fit in this top secret operation.

He returned to his desk, picking up an egg sized flat black stone. Rubbing the stone, like he was trying to remove the finish, he began pacing behind his chair.

"I look forward to working with you, Munson. We need some new blood around here and you look like the right sort."

The Lutz monologue was interrupted by Lt. Mills. "There you are," he said, walking into Lutz's office without knocking. "Are you about done with him, George? I need to give him a quick tour and then I've got to run into town."

Lutz glared at Cory without a greeting. "OK, he's all yours. His badge should be ready at the counter. Say, while you're here I need to talk to you about that kid you sent me as an admin clerk. I want him out of here. He's worthless as tits on a boar. Can't type for shit, he's sloppy as hell and Lawson says in four days he's been late three."

"Sorry George. You needed a clerk, I asked personnel for one and Borkowski is who they sent. Besides, if any unit could whip a slack trooper into shape I'd think it'd be yours. Think of it as a challenge. Turn Larson loose on him."

"You know that's bullshit. I run a security police unit, not a reform school. How'd he get in the Air Force anyway? I thought the Army got all the scum."

"Mention it to the colonel if you want but I doubt ..."

"Yes, I know. You doubt he'll do anything about it. So do I. Well," Lutz continued, turning to me, "welcome to the funny farm. It's good to have you on board."

Moments later, foregoing the bus, Cory and I were walking down a dimly lit tunnel into Cheyenne Mountain.

"You see, the engineers are like property managers for the mountain. They run the power plant, provide all the utilities, sewer, water and that sort of thing. The engineers are the biggest part of the 4604th, 120 guys under Captain, soon to be Major, Bob Kirkwood. Great guy, you'll like him," said Cory as we maintained a swift pace in the dimly lit tunnel. He paused to let a growling bus rumble by and then continued.

"Food service is run by Sgt. Baker and security by Lutz. That's the gang. Oh. there is also Andy Gruber in Engineering. Nearly forgot him. By the way, do you golf?"

"Not really. My dad took me out a few times but that's it."

"Good. Thursdays, weather permitting, the Colonel, Bob, Andy and I have a standing golf date. We need to ensure there's an officer around to mind the store, so to speak."

"What about Lutz?"

"George? He's in his own world. We never know what he's up to, chasing spies or something.

"Well, here we are," Cory concluded as we approached the first steel blast door, which looked like the truck sized entrance to an oversized bank vault. "You are about to enter the secret world of Cheyenne Mountain."

***

I laid the black ballpoint pen on the gray desk and stretched my cramped fingers. I'd spent the morning in my new office filling out official forms. Most looked like forms I'd filled out at Officers Training School but those were off in some distant file so new forms were needed. The pen was stamped with "Property U. S. Government" which struck me as mildly amusing. Everything in this room was the property of the U. S. Government: me, the others, the furniture, the manuals and files. It was all owned by Uncle Sam.

I'd arrived at my new office after a whirlwind tour of the underground complex with Cory. We saw his office, the command post, mess hall, computer room and lots of long beige corridors. I imagined it was like being on a ship. We were housed in three-story windowless steel boxes but, except for the steel walls and lack of windows, the offices were pretty normal.

Everyone he wanted to introduce me to was unavailable.

Sgt. Baker, who ran the mess hall, was the exception. He gave me a warm greeting and proudly showed me around his compact kitchen. I decided he would be a good man to know.

Ending the tour, Cory showed me my desk, introduced me to my roommates and ran off to a meeting.

I shared the office with Lt. Andy Gruber, two airman clerks and four non-commissioned officers or NCOs. The NCOs ran the engineering team. High ranking sergeants they each had over twenty years in the service and an uncanny ability to get things done if they chose to. They tolerated lieutenants because they had to. Half their age, I still outranked them.

My seven roommates had one thing in common; they all smoked. The NCOs favored cigars while the others stuck to cigarettes. Gruber was the worst. His fingers were yellowed from the constant presence of the Viceroys. At times he would light his next smoke off the butt of the previous so he was assured a continuous smoke. Gruber was a stubby, grubby, chubby little officer with an engineering degree and a firm belief that engineers should rule the world. As I soon learned, Gruber, like most engineers, was logical. Therefore it followed, according to him, that engineers were the logical ones to rule the country. Logic, rather than politics, made more sense to him.

It was the Gruber types I'd known in engineering school that made me question my career choice.

Our introductory conversation had been brief, revealing little about the man. "Welcome to the 4604th. It's a good unit. You'll like it here. Now if you'll excuse me I need to get this report done for this afternoon," he had said before turning back to his desk and lighting up a new cigarette.

Airman Lopez was chattier. "Here you are sir. I need two copies of the DD 235 and one of DD 407. You may have filled out the 778 but we need one for our files. This is for payroll and this will cover your rations."

The Air Force is very organized. All the forms had numbers and a purpose. I think the "DD" stood for Defense Department. We ordered supplies on "DD" forms. We kept track of people on "DD" forms. Even the new plastic coated security badge clipped to my shirt pocket was a "DD" form. And now, lying under my official black pen was my stack of newly filled out official "DD" forms ready for filing.

**

"Monday is staff meeting day," said Cory, as we set our trays on the conveyor belt by the kitchen. He'd rescued me from my smoke filled office just before noon and escorted me to the smoke filled mess hall for lunch. "Sometimes we meet in the morning and sometimes right after lunch. 1300 hours is the official start time but it takes a while to gather the troops."

He led me down the steel corridor from the mess hall and stuck me in the small conference room next to Hahn's office before slipping away to gather materials for the meeting. Lutz was first to arrive, taking a seat at one end of the table.

"Well, you get to attend your first staff meeting. Hope you had lots of black coffee at lunch."

"Why's that, sir?" I asked sitting on the table edge.

"You'll see. But first notice that it's 1300 hours and we're the only ones here. That should give you an idea of the tight ship Hahn runs."

Five minutes passed before Cory returned with a slightly built gray haired man close behind. "Colonel, this is Roger Munson, the new engineering officer I was telling you about."

This was the colonel. Without his jacket he bore no signs of rank. He looked more like a country parson than an Air Force Lieutenant Colonel. Remembering my 90 days of training, I jumped to my feet and fired off a salute. "Lt. Munson reporting for duty sir."

"Nicely done Lieutenant, nicely done," he said, giving me a lazy salute in return and reaching to shake my hand. "Welcome to the squadron. Cory, find a time Munson and I can have lunch real soon. Now where's that boss of yours?" he asked, looking toward me.

Col. Hahn set a blank tablet and yellow pencil on the table opposite Lutz, slumped into the chair and began fiddling with his unlit corncob pipe.

"Colonel," said Lutz, "I have a question about those VIP passes you requested for Gen. Winchester. The guests are Chinese and..."

"Oh for Christ's sake, George. You think Winchester is trying to sneak Mao in here or something? They're Taiwanese;

they're on our side."

"I'm sure they are sir," Lutz persisted, "But there is a procedure and when foreigners are involved I...."

"In this case we don't have time to follow procedures and I promised Winchester it would be taken care of," Hahn mumbled with his pipe clenched in his teeth.

The discussion was interrupted by the arrival of Lt. Gruber and a second officer I correctly assumed was my new boss.

"You may be right, Andy. So under load I should shift a little later on the power curve. I'll try that coming up the mountain tomorrow," he said, looking up and seeing me for the first time. "Oh, you must be Munson. I'm Bob Kirkwood. Welcome to the unit."

I started to salute but he intercepted and shook my hand without removing his tight fitting leather driving gloves, the kind with the little holes at the knuckles and joints. "Sorry about the gloves; they're new and I'm breaking them in."

"You'll have to be patient with Bob," Cory said to me. "He is the owner of a new Porsche 912 and he's quite into it. I try to tell him it's just a Volkswagen underneath but...."

"That's it. I was going to give you a ride but I'm taking your name off the list," said Kirkwood, sitting beside the colonel.

"By the way Bob," said Lutz, "I've had some complaints about you taking up two parking places and putting cones out so no one will park by you."

"Let'em complain. If anyone puts a mark on that car it's going to be me, not some airman in a hot Camaro with big doors."

Lutz glanced toward Hahn, as if seeking support for his position, but the colonel showed no sign of hearing as he made lazy doodles on his marked up meeting agenda.

I squirmed and the meeting began.

Lutz, first on the agenda, distributed a weekly incident report.

Hahn placed his reading glasses, hung librarian style from a chain around his neck, on the tip of his nose and skimmed the document. "Cripe George; I can't send this upstairs. It looks like it was typed by a dyslexic chimpanzee. You'll have to clean it up."

"Actually it's the work of my new clerk, sir."

"Oh yes, that Polack kid. Well, whip him into shape. This will never do."

George just smiled and we moved to the next agenda item. As a newcomer I watched the proceedings with a degree of detachment. It was Hahn's meeting but it was Lutz that kept it on track. They were easily distracted. They started on one topic and drifted to another. A report on electric generator down-time drifted to the price of gas in town. A report on progress of a construction project near the command post drifted to Hahn's new refrigerator. Each time it was Lutz that brought the group back on topic. All the while the colonel kept trying to light his pipe and Gruber kept smoking. Thoughts of Alice's tea party flashed through my head.

In the middle of Sgt. Baker's dining hall report Hahn, without a word, gathered his papers, rose and headed for the door.

"Excuse me Colonel, we haven't talked about security police staffing yet," said Lutz, rising and partially blocking Hahn's path. "Sir, you can't keep pushing me off on this. It's too important. We're going to have an incident and...."

"Now calm down, George," said the colonel, poking Lutz in the chest with the mouthpiece of his unlit pipe. "For the umpteenth time, according to the manning guidelines you are appropriately staffed. You just need to figure out how to use your people more effectively. Now I've got to run."

"God damn it sir," intoned George with his volume fading as he followed Hahn from the conference room. "Those regs were written for some base in a cow pasture in the middle of...."

A captain disagreeing with a colonel? I thought it noteworthy. The others ignored it. A short time later the meeting didn't end; it just deteriorated. Cory left for a dental appointment. Sgt Baker just left. Then, after Gruber and Kirkwood discussed a pending repair to the access road, we all wandered back to our offices.

***

By 1700 hours the office was empty. Except for the power plant crew most of the engineers worked a day shift. Late that afternoon Capt. Kirkwood had called me in to explain my new responsibilities. Gruber was switching to the operations officer slot and I was taking his position as maintenance officer. I wasn't sure what that meant but the heads of the roadway, carpentry, electrical, mechanical and plumbing shops now reported to me. According to Kirkwood, Gruber could help me learn the ropes.

I decided to stay in the mountain for dinner. The Italian menu looked good and my room at the VOQ held little appeal. The mess hall wasn't crowded but a steady stream of customers kept the place busy. With the command post manned 24 hours a day the mess hall was always open for business.

I picked a small table far from the food line and enjoyed my lasagna alone. Considering the place was a steel box, it wasn't bad looking. The ceiling and lights were office standard but heavy drapes lined the room concealing the steel walls. Artificial plants were spotted around for atmosphere.

It had been a day of learning. I learned you saluted in the tunnels but not in the building corridors. I learned it was hard to tell rank in the dimly lit tunnels so I decided to salute every officer I saw. As a 2nd lieutenant there were no officers of lower rank. I learned that Lutz seemed to be more involved in running the Squadron than Hahn. At least he appeared more serious about his work. I learned that Hahn was a passed over lieutenant colonel with 23 years of service who would never be promoted to full colonel. Were it not for the demands of the Vietnam war, he would have been eased out years ago. I learned that I had a lot to learn.

I finished up, said goodbye to Sgt. Baker, who was still on duty, and headed back to the empty office. Cory had explained how the phones worked. I could make long distance calls on the lines from the mountain at no charge to the government. Apparently the Air Force leased the lines and didn't get charged for individual calls. It seemed like a cheap way to keep in touch with home so...

***

"And you're eating well?"

"Mom, I've only been here four days."

"Are the other boys nice?" she continued.

"Boys?"

"The boys you work with; are they nice?" she asked again.

"This isn't a fraternity party Mom. This is the Air Force and I work with men and yes, they're nice."

"Of course dear. Your father wants to speak with you. Remember to get to bed at a decent time. I don't want you coming down with anything."

"Medical is free ...."

"Be serious Roger. Now here's Dad."

I shifted in my chair and placed my feet on the gray desk.

"Hi son...."

And so it went. We discussed gas mileage, tire rotation and the need to get my PE or Professional Engineer certification. Dad was all business all the time. Then I was alone in the empty office with only the hiss of the air passing through the yellowed ceiling grills.

I was a long way from home and I was beginning to think that was a good thing.

Chapter Four

1/20/69   In Beautiful Quan Binh
Rog,
  Have you heard? I'm a dad! My beautiful Sally
delivered eight pound Jeff Jr. on January 10th. No photos yet but
I hear he's handsome like his dad. God I wish there was a way
out of this rat hole so I could see my wife and baby. But the only
early way home is in a bag so I'll wait for R & R, maybe in the
Spring.
  Finally got my hands on a portable typewriter so you
don't have to decipher my scratch anymore. Belongs to a guy in
my hootch. I buy typewriter ribbons and give him a pack of
smokes each month and it's mine to use.
  By the time you receive this you'll have that butter bar
clipped to your shoulder. Don't let it go to your head. I still out-
rank you by six months.
  I'm anxious to hear where you're assigned. For all I
know you could be sitting on your ass over in Da Nang living the
cushy life of a rear area A. F. officer. I have to say I'm envious
of them from what I've seen. I don't envy the flight crews but the
ground jockeys mostly sit on their air base asses planning their
next trip to the local whorehouse.
  Do I sound bitter???
  After a few months in country I've reached one
overwhelming conclusion. Vietnam stinks! I mean really stinks!
The whole G. D. country has this earthy barnyard sort of smell.
You can't get away from it. Some say it's just the tropics. Others
say it's the shit (literally) they put on the fields. Of course, it's
worse when we're in the bush but it seems to permeate the
villages too. I just hope I can escape the stink when I escape the
country.
  Life here, if you can call it that, goes on. It's strange,
really. We studied engineering so we could build stuff and all I
do now is blow shit up. Not sure how I'll use my new skills when
I get back to the world but, I have to admit, I'm getting good at

*my job. I clear LZ's (landing zones to you flyboys) and blow up
captured bunkers. They give me all the green troops 'cause they
claim, "Lt. Osman is the best!" It'll look good on my resume I
guess.*

*Take care you sorry assed Air Force feather merchant
and let me know where you're assigned. Not sure when this will
catch up w/you. Hope it gets forwarded. Write when you can.
Hunk
FIGMO Countdown: 283 days
P.S. Your ol'buddy has earned a Purple Heart! Got nicked in an
LZ last week. A big band aid and I was back in action but a
wound is a wound. Don't, repeat, don't tell anyone. Sally doesn't
need to know for now. Ciao*

***

I eased out of my parking space and joined the flow of
cars out of the lot and down the winding Cheyenne Mountain
access road, my road since the maintenance crew now reported
to me. It was two weeks since my first visit to the mountain and
the time had flown by. I now knew my way around the place,
had met most of my troops and hadn't screwed up in any
noticeable manner.

Focused on work, my social life had taken a back seat. I
hadn't spoken to Maggie, the only girl I'd met, since the doomed
party at her place. Maybe I'd give her a call this weekend. I'd
only seen her a couple of times but she kept sneaking into my
thoughts. There was something intriguing about the girl. I could
talk with her. I enjoyed being with her. Perhaps knowing we
were so different relieved the tension that often comes with a
new relationship. Should I hold her hand? Should I try for a kiss?
Should I help her with her coat? None of that stuff was on the
table. She was just a girl, not a girlfriend. If we were anything,
we were more like buddies.

Frankly, other than Maggie and the nursing corps at the
base hospital, the social scene in Colorado Springs was looking
pretty grim. I'd been to the Officer's Club a few times. The food
was good but it was more of a couples place and I definitely
wasn't a couple. If I decided to seriously pursue the Colorado
Springs women, I'd have to do more research to determine

where the local mothers hid their virgin daughters.

But there was also a certain freedom in my life. My apartment was set up and, though spartan, very livable. Work was my only commitment. Otherwise I could come and go as I pleased, toss dirty clothes on the floor and leave the toilet seat up. I'd even developed an efficient system for managing the dish washing process. The few I owned would gather in the sink when dirty. When I ran out I loaded and ran the dishwasher. Then I'd take clean ones from the dishwasher as needed and place the dirties back in the sink. When the dishwasher was empty and the sink full the cycle was repeated. I thought the system very efficient as the dishes never touched the cupboards. Mother would not have approved.

There was something to be said for the bachelor life. And, as for tonight, this bachelor was going to get lost in a book.

***

Saturday I was greeted by another cold blue-sky Colorado day. I should have gone for a run but decided breakfast at Dunkins was a better, if not healthier, choice. To offset the ill effects of the donuts I decided to walk the three blocks and leave the Camaro behind. Not a calorie neutral choice but I felt better about it.

To be honest, the Dunkin decision was driven by two motives. First, of course, were the donuts. But lingering in my consciousness was the long shot that I might run into Maggie. I knew she didn't live at the place but there was a chance she would pop in. Calling her house might leave the impression that I was pursuing her, which I wasn't. Running into her would seem natural and the encounter could take its own course.

The morning sun was so intense the air felt warmer than the 20 degrees reported by the weatherman. I crunched along the sand covered sidewalks, dodging an occasional icy patch, until I could see Dunkins. I was in luck; a familiar yellow VW was parked near the door.

Deciding to be cool I walked in and kept my eyes on the display case, trying to look nonchalant, until I heard, "Hey sailor…."

I turned and truly was surprised by what I saw, the third Maggie. The first had been the snow hippy Maggie the day we met. Then there was the baggy dress Maggie at the party. Now I was looking at logger Maggie coming toward me clad in well-used leather hiking boots, heavy jeans rolled to a generous cuff and a too big plaid wool shirt with the sleeves rolled to the elbow revealing slender arms I'd never seen.

She looked warm and huggable.

In a familiar, but not too familiar, way she laid her hand on my arm and said, "I wondered if I'd ever see you again. Why don't you join me?"

A cinnamon twist and cup of coffee later we'd caught up like old friends. She heard about the mountain and I heard about her classes and any anxiety I might have felt about seeing her again had melted away.

"How's my buddy Leonard?" I asked, when our catch up wound down.

"I don't think he would use the word 'buddy' to describe you. I don't know what you did to him, but he gets real pissy when your name comes up."

"And my name comes up?" I asked, feeling flattered in a peculiar way.

"When he brings it up. Like every other day he asks me how you're doing. He seems to think we're an item or something. Can you imagine? So then, just to pull his chain, I'm real vague with my response so he can think anything he likes. I went to Denver last weekend and I'm sure he thinks I was with you. I haven't had this much fun with him since he moved in," she said with a laugh. "I don't understand why you inspire him so."

"What's happening in Denver?"

"Just family stuff."

There was an awkward pause as she stared out the window while tearing a new napkin into little strips.

"You know what I think? Len's jealous," I offered, breaking the silence.

"He's what?" she exclaimed, loud enough to turn the heads of customers in the booth across the aisle. "You've got to be kidding."

I sat my coffee down and cast a smile across the table. "It's a fact. I've studied him on two occasions and it is quite clear the boy is lusting after fair Maggie, the woman of the manor that is so close and yet never notices the lowly farmhand living nearby."

"Jane Austen?"

"No, Roger Munson."

"And Len is the lowly farmhand in this picture? Lt. Munson, I do believe you've been spending too much time alone. What have you been reading?"

Adopting a learned pose I continued. "Laugh if you will but I'm a student of lusty male behavior and, based on my exposure to Len, I believe he's the victim of repressed feelings toward you. He shows all the signs."

"God, you're impossible. Maybe he's lusting for Val but not old Maggie. But enough about Len."

She took on a contemplative look as she gathered the napkin scraps and dropped them into her empty cup. "Say, I have an idea. Are you busy today?"

"Are you asking me out?" I replied.

"In your dreams. No, I'm going on a photo shoot and thought you might enjoy the ride. Of course I'd expect you to lug my tripod and other gear so I can concentrate on the creative side of the business."

"What would I be, a key grip or something?"

"You can call yourself anything you wish. All I know is that I need the photos for a class project and I am, like, way behind on getting this done. Do you want to come?"

At that point I could think of nothing better than an afternoon lugging her photography gear. She was fun. She was relaxed. She was someone I could talk to. And my calendar for the weekend was quite clear.

"Hmmm, an offer I can't refuse. I guess I could do it. I'll need to cancel my afternoon date and be home for my dinner one but that should work. Where are we off to?"

"Cripple Creek. It's cool. You'll love it."

With little thought we tossed together a plan. Since I wasn't dressed to romp around in the mountains she would take me to the apartment to change. Then, since the camera gear was already in her car, she would drive.

We were just climbing into Sunny when someone yelled,

"Maggie Meyers, is that you?"

We both turned and saw a pimply little fellow in a dark brown wool coat, jeans and sandals stepping toward us from his rusty Plymouth Valiant. "Goddamn, it is you," he said as he approached. "How the hell are you?"

Maggie stepped behind her open door as if trying to keep it between herself and the newcomer. "Hi Jerry. What brings you to the Springs?"

He stopped, as if respecting the barrier she'd created. "The folks. Heading down to Pueblo to see the folks. But I'm coming through again tomorrow. Where you living?"

"Don't even think about it. I'm busy all weekend. Gotta run now, I'm really late."

The Maggie talking was not a Maggie I'd ever seen before. There was no humor. There was no smile. She was all "I don't want to talk to you; please leave me alone" in her movements and expression.

"OK, OK. Well, it was good to see you I guess," he said, stepping back from the car.

"Yes, well, later then," she replied before dropping into the car and closing the door.

I was still standing by my door, staring at "Jerry" and digesting the exchange when the engine chugged to life and the car jerked a little as she released the brake. He glanced at me, shrugged his shoulders and continued backing away. Not wanting to be left behind I slipped into the car and closed the door.

"Well, now where's your place?" she chirped as we pulled into traffic.

"What's with the guy?" I asked after giving her the directions.

She gripped the wheel and stared down the road. "Him? Nothing. I knew him once, in Boulder. He's not one of my favorite people."

"Oh," was the best I could come up with as we pulled into my apartment lot.

***

"Why's it called 'Cripple Creek'?" I asked as the heavily loaded VW struggled up Ute Pass at the base of Pikes Peak.

54

"Legend has it that an early prospector fell in the creek and broke a leg. I've also heard he fell in a mine shaft. In any case, someone broke something and named the creek accordingly. Then when gold was discovered a boom town grew up on its banks and the name stuck."

As she worked the gears to squeeze maximum speed from the little engine in the rear I studied my surroundings. The car was very 'Maggie.' First there was a certain Maggie fragrance in the air. It could have been lotion, perfume or something else. It was subtle outside the confines of the car but distinct in our cramped quarters. It was nice. The strings of brightly colored beads hanging from the mirror also seemed to fit. My seat area was tidy only because she'd stayed at the car while I changed clothes, clearing a place for me by scooping up papers and books and tossing them into the tight back seat which was already cluttered with similar stuff.

The car's rounded exterior was equally messy, yellow on top and muddy brown on the bottom, the result of driving on sanded winter roads.

"Oh that," she laughed when I commented on the mud. "I learned a lesson my first winter in Colorado. I washed my car on a sunny, cold day. The next morning the door locks were frozen solid. It took 25 feet of extension cord and a hair dryer to get me in the car. Never again. Now I wait until spring."

Looking at the passing cars it was clear she wasn't the only driver who disdained winter washing.

After an hour of climbing and winding we arrived at our goal, the nearly abandoned town of Cripple Creek. I could see why she'd come. The treeless snow covered hills were littered with mine structures, old buildings and other targets for a photographer's lens. The town itself was a relic from a robust past. According to a plaque set in stone in what passed for a plaza, the town was one of the largest in the state at the height of the gold rush. When gold prices fell the fortunes of the little city fell as well leaving just the shell of a once thriving little city.

Maggie spent the afternoon driving from place to place chattering about shapes, shadows and textures. We climbed hills, wandered around old mines and crisscrossed Main Street in our quest for the perfect set up. The camera found charm in odd places and rolls of exposed film accumulated in the bag I carried. By late afternoon, when we finally sat down on the porch of an old cabin, I was worn out by the chase.

"I'm exhausted," she said as she put away one of her big lenses.

I was glad to hear that it wasn't just me.

"Oh God," she continued. "What time do you have to be back?"

"No time, I'm at your disposal."

"What about your date?"

"Ah yes, my date," I said remembering my tale from the morning. "Well, you see, I might have overstated the complexity of my schedule today not wanting you to take pity on me thinking I was a total loser without a social life."

"So you don't have a date, you scoundrel. Well, maybe I do so we'd better get going."

With that we headed for the car and for home.

***

I relaxed my grip on the armrest when we pulled into my apartment parking lot. Her car struggled climbing hills but she could make it fly going down. The steep grade combined with her tendency to talk with her hands and look at me while speaking made for an exciting return trip.

"Well, this completes our Cripple Creek tour. I hope it met your expectations. Please call again and tell your friends about our services," she concluded as we jerked to a stop.

"I'm afraid I don't have too many friends but...."

"Nonsense. You have me; call anytime."

She was right. I did feel like I had a friend. "I'd like to tip the guide but I'm short of change. How about I fix you dinner instead?"

She paused, studying me with a furled brow. "OK, but I'll have to blow off another guy."

"Really?" I said, taking the bait.

"Yes, right. Come on, let's eat."

I grabbed my coat from the back seat and showed her the way.

Entering the sparsely furnished apartment we stepped over the jumble of old mail that had fallen from the coffee table and made our way to the compact kitchen where I tossed my jacket on a chair. She paused, crinkling her forehead as she examined the cluttered counters. "Looks like you maintain a horizontal pantry," she said with a laugh.

"Oh that," I replied, slightly embarrassed. "I suppose I could put the groceries in the cupboard but then I'd forget what I have. I guess it does look a little messy."

"Oh well, whatever works. Now, if you'll excuse me, I think I'll scrub some of this dust off. Is the bathroom safe to use?" she asked with a laugh.

"Well, don't trip. I've been using the floor as a laundry basket until I get around to buying one."

Alone in the kitchen I stuck my head in the refrigerator trying to come up with something that could serve as dinner for two. I was standing in the light of the open door when the sound of the door bell intervened.

"We thought we heard you clunking around up here. Hey man, you want to join us for dinner?" said Cory, standing in the hallway. "Jessie made this gigantic tuna casserole and if I don't have help eating it I'll see it for dinner every night next week."

Before I could reply Maggie came out of the bathroom still looking like the logger girl I'd first seen at Dunkins.

"Oh, I didn't realize you had company."

"No problem. Maggie, come meet Cory, that tough career officer I've been telling you about."

"It's a pleasure," she said extending a hand. "From what I hear, your food and advice have been keeping Roger out of trouble since he arrived."

"I was just inviting Roger down for dinner but now I'll withdraw that invitation and extend it to you. Would you like to come down? Jessie would enjoy meeting you and you could bring Roger if you like."

I looked at Maggie and we seemed to shrug simultaneously.

"Good, I'll take that as a yes. See you in about ten minutes."

***

As we climbed the stairs to my apartment, after dinner

57

and a rousing game of hearts, my mind skimmed over the evening. The time had flown. I couldn't believe it was past eleven. The simple dinner had gone well. Jessie and Maggie acted like long-lost sisters chattering about a range of topics from childbirth to fine china. After dinner Maggie joined Jessie in the kitchen and I have no idea what kept them so amused. Cory seemed to enjoy her unpretentious sense of humor and I enjoyed just watching Maggie be Maggie.

The more we were together the more I noticed her endearing quirks. She tossed her head back when she laughed. She rearranged her silverware whenever she sat down to eat. She tore paper napkins into little strips. She wore dangly earrings and never seemed to wear the same pair twice. She jerked her car whenever she shifted. And she was fun to be with.

The fact she got along so well with Jessie and Cory was a bonus. I hadn't expected that. Jessie seemed so domestic compared to Maggie that I wasn't sure how the evening would go. My apprehension was misplaced. Maggie had a chameleon like ability to adjust to her surroundings.

"We'd better grab your coat," I said, unlocking the apartment. "Did you bring anything else in?"

"No, I don't think so," she said as she walked to the window and silently gazed out at the faint outline of the mountains.

I stood beside her with the coat but she made no move to put it on.

Still staring into the outer blackness she turned to me, "Please don't take this wrong but could I stay here tonight? Len's having another one of his gatherings and I really don't want to be around the place. Some of his friends are so... oh I don't know. The sofa looks fine and I...."

Now my mind was really messed up. "...don't take this wrong but could I stay here tonight," was what I heard. Now my twisted tongue could form no words in response. Here she was, a beautiful girl—in a skinny, organic sort of way—asking to spend the night. Usually I could think of a dozen moves and responses for a situation like this but now, for some reason, none of them seemed right. I wanted to put my arm around her but feared I would break the shell of a fragile relationship. I was torn between breaking that shell and making the big move.

She turned toward me and continued, "I'm sorry. I can see how that might be awkward with your friends downstairs."

As she reached for the coat I found her wool shirt was every bit as alluring as the pearl covered sweaters of my fraternity days. "No, no, it's not a problem at all," I said, pulling the coat out of her reach. "But you can have the bedroom. I'll stay out here."

"No deal. It's the sofa or I'm out of here. I'll not toss you out of your bed."

And that is how Maggie Meyers, wearing my blue Air Force sweats came to spend the night on my swaybacked sofa, snug beneath my well used sleeping bag.

***

Sunday morning I studied my house guest as I passed through the living room. Maggie was sleeping on her side with just a hint of a relaxed smile on her face. Even with her hair scattered by a night on a pillow she looked good. The sleeping bag was in a heap on the floor but her modesty was protected by the ample fabric of my too big sweats.

I slipped quietly from the apartment on a morning pilgrimage to Dunkins. As I walked I tried to convince myself that last night turned out as it should. At first I feared I'd missed some come-on signals from her but, in replaying my mental tape of the evening, I couldn't recall any missed signs. Perhaps Colorado girls sent different messages but, if so, I was oblivious. I hoped she would be pleased with the way things went, not upset that I'd left her alone.

I'd come out of high school feeling like a stud on the run. Based on locker room conversations and limited experience I was sure I knew how to deal with girls. But by my sophomore year of college I was utterly confused. It seemed that if you pursued some girls too hard you risked being labeled aggressive. If you failed to pursue they assumed indifference, at best. And when you're dating sorority girls, who might compare notes, you'd better read all signals properly or end up a marked man, for better or worse.

Reggie, a fraternity brother, said not to worry. He espoused a theory that most college romances were disposable relationships. You would use them, like a paper towel, and then toss them away when you were done. I'd argued that the idea seemed unfair to the girls. But he rationalized that they were doing exactly the same thing. Since both sexes thought they were doing the tossing, no one got hurt.

My Penny relationship, lasting two years, had challenged his theory. But in the end maybe he was right. We just used our towels longer and then set them down gently rather than toss them. The outcome was the same.

Maybe Maggie wasn't or shouldn't be a disposable relationship. Maybe she was different. Maybe she was a friend who happened to be a girl so the theory didn't even apply. But then that went back to another frat house discussion: could you have a friend who was a girl without sex getting in the way?

I was soon back at the apartment with a Sunday Denver Post, two coffees, two French crullers and two twists in a paper bag. Entering the apartment my eyes were drawn to the empty sofa with a folded up sleep bag resting on the arm. Had she flown?

Then I heard the reassuring sounds of running water from the bathroom and moments later the logger Maggie joined me at the small kitchen table looking very much at home.

***

"Is there a way to eat a cinnamon twist without getting sticky?" I asked, rinsing my hands in the sink.

"Don't think so," she laughed. "Maybe that's why I like them. Licking the fingers is the best part."

I rejoined Maggie at the table where she sat gripping her cup with both hands as if trying to capture its warmth. While she was at the table her mind seemed to be elsewhere as she gazed out the window at nothing in particular.

'Who's Hunk?" she finally asked.

"Hunk?"

"Oh, I'm sorry. I didn't mean to be snoopy but I couldn't help but notice the letter from a 'Hunk' sitting on the coffee table. Is he a friend?"

"My best. We met in the fraternity and went through engineering school together. He's in Vietnam."

"Too bad," she said, still gazing at nothing.

"Which part? The fraternity, friend or...."

"The Vietnam part. He could get killed couldn't he? I mean, lots of people are getting killed over there."

That frank question set me back. I hadn't thought of it that way. Lots of guys had been killed. But no one I knew. With a few words she brought me to the reality that Hunk, my best friend, could get killed.

"Does he think it's worth the risk?" she continued. "Does he think it's a cause worth giving his life for?"

"Don't you? Don't you think it's a cause worth dying for? I mean, don't you think we have to stop the spread of communism somewhere?"

"Val thinks we're just propping up a corrupt government with our blood and money just to keep the defense industries humming."

"Val is spending too much time with Leonard. He's poisoned her mind. Anyway, Hunk and I aren't paid to make policy. We're on board to follow orders and do our job. We leave the strategy decisions to the big boys. I assume they have better intelligence than us lowly lieutenants.

"What do you think," I continued. "Do you think we should be defending the Vietnamese? I mean, from what I've read, the communists are not that kind to their own people after they take over a country."

After a pause she offered me a perplexed look. "You know, I don't know what to think. Friends say I can be wishy-washy. Maybe I need firmer opinions. I hear one side and then the other and don't know what to believe. I just hope your friend comes home OK for his sake and for his family's. I don't like to see anyone hurt."

Maggie gathered up the Dunkin' trash while I watched, waiting for her next thought. Finally she turned from the sink and said, "Sorry, I guess I'm being a bit morose for such a beautiful Sunday morning. Anyway, I should get out of your hair. I don't want to overstay my welcome and I do have lab work to finish."

She gave my shoulder a gentle squeeze, gathered her purse and walked slowly to the door. "Thanks sailor," she said, pausing at the front door. "I hope I wasn't too big of a pest. See you around."

I uttered a lame response, barely rising from the table. She gave me a pained smile and slipped from the apartment. I watched her as she crossed the lot, started Sunny and lurched onto the street. She was gone and I was facing the prospect of a long Sunday alone.

Chapter Five

Wednesday, March 12
Dear Son,

Hope things are good there and you are getting enough rest. If you get all tired out you'll likely catch something.

We are still looking for a letter. I know you must be busy with your new job but surely you could drop us a few lines. Your grandmother would like to hear from you as well.

Weather is a bit dampish; sun would be nice.

I put your new address in the church bulletin. Some of the ladies like to write to our servicemen. You have also been added to the serviceman's prayer chain. That has gotten more attention since the Martin boy was killed. I feel so bad for his family.

We'd like to send you a housewarming gift. Let me know if you need anything for your kitchen. I can order from Sears and have things mailed directly to you.

Father says hi. He's busy at work and says he could use you to handle some of the load.

All for now. Take care and write!
Love, Mother

***

As I wound my way up the access road, locked in Wednesday morning traffic, random thoughts tumbled through my mind. I was confused as hell. Nothing in my social or work life was turning out as I expected. My paradigms were being shattered.

On the social front my past weekend with Maggie seemed like a warm, distant memory. Saturday in Cripple Creek had been great fun. The Saturday night sleep-over still caused emotional confusion but I'd been too busy to focus on understanding why. Sunday morning had flown by all too quickly. Like an old married couple we read the newspaper together while enjoying our coffee and donuts. Then Maggie, bless her heart, tried to create some order in a cluttered kitchen that even I was a little embarrassed about. Mother would have been proud of her work. Then she was gone, to study she said. I couldn't seem to find a label for my Maggie feelings. But, for whatever reason, I couldn't get her out of my mind.

And life in the Air Force was turning out much differently than I'd anticipated. Considering the seriousness of our defense assignment, I'd expected a tightly run, efficient organization. It was well run in a quirky and ever surprising way. But the illogical often passed for logical and things that I found odd were ignored by the nonplussed veterans. Each day brought new surprises and left me wondering what other twists the coming days would offer.

I arrived at my office, striding with confidence in the vain hope that good intentions could ward off the wacky. "Good morning Lopez," I said as I passed my clerk's cluttered desk.

"Morning sir. Say, Capt. Kirkwood said he wanted to see you as soon as you came in."

That was good. Though he was my boss I'd seen little of him since I arrived. He was often out of the mountain and, when he was in, he seemed to spend his time schmoozing senior officers around the mess hall. He left the running of the engineering group to me and Gruber. Cory explained that Kirkwood wanted to make a good impression on as many high ranking officers as possible on the off chance that they might be on the promotion board when his name came up. He was a gregarious guy and the schmoozing seemed to come naturally.

When I reached the office I found him behind his desk straightening a framed piece of abstract art.

"Oh, hi Roger. What do you think of the new addition?" he asked, waving at the piece.

"It's…it's different," I offered, not sure what to make of the wide splotchy black stripe running diagonally across a stark white background.

"It was a bitch to hang. I almost had the welding crew come in and weld a hook to the wall. Then I noticed this little magnetic hook the wife had on the refrigerator door and I said to myself, 'that's it. Steel door; steel wall.' And bingo, the picture's hung. Do you know what you're looking at?"

"Abstract art?"

"Ha, that's a good one," he said, coming around the desk to examine the view from my side. "It's Michelin art; did it myself. Drove in the garage after washing the Porsche last week and noticed the bitchen tread marks the wet tires left on the floor. So I get some paints and art board and start to experiment. You're looking at the print my left front tire made when I coated the tread with paint and drove over the board. Pretty cool huh? This one was my sixth try; had to get the paint spread just right but it was worth the effort, don't you think?"

"Well I'll be damned. So it is," I said, finally recognizing the tread print for what it was. It was on one hand crazy and on the other creative.

"Oh gees, I'm running short of time. Gotta scoot. Have a seat. Here's why I called you in," he said, handing me a thick folder labeled 'Savings Bond Drive.' "You are hereby appointed the Savings Bond Officer for the squadron. The colonel concurs with the appointment. You'll be running our campaign as a part of the base-wide bond campaign."

"I'm flattered sir," I lied. I knew they dumped all these assignments on the most junior officer in the group. I suspected it was fruitless but I went on. "But surely there must be someone more qualified to run the campaign, Gruber, Mills or someone."

He smiled as he grabbed his hat and moved toward the door. "Ha, nice try but they've all done it. Don't worry. There's a training session coming up. You'll find the schedule in the packet. The key is participation. The more who sign up the better it looks on Hahn's record. So you better read this stuff and roll out a hot campaign because we're going to show the other units a thing or two about selling bonds."

With that he was gone for the day and I was the squadron's official Savings Bond Officer.

***

As I returned to my office Lopez greeted me with, "Phone call on line one sir. It's Lt. Mills."

When I picked up the receiver and punched the blinking "line one" Cory greeted me with, "Roger, do you know where Bob is? I understand you were just with him."

"He's left the mountain; didn't say where he was going."

"Shucks. Well, who does the grounds crew work for, you or Andy?"

"Me."

"OK then, the colonel needs to see you pronto."

I grabbed my vinyl folder and a pen and scurried toward Hahn's office. Cory greeted me when I arrived.

"Grab a seat buddy. Lutz beat you to the draw. They shouldn't be long."

Cory left for a meeting and I took over his desk, right outside Hahn's nearly closed office door. Sounds of a Lutz/Hahn confrontation assaulted my ears causing me to wonder if I should wait somewhere else. I was glad I stayed.

"I don't fix parking tickets," growled Lutz. "So don't even ask, sir."

It struck me that he fairly spit the word "sir" at the colonel.

"Now, now George, don't get so riled up. I'm just asking you to overlook the matter this one time. After all, the major is in a position too...."

"Colonel, that major is in a position to get his car towed if he insists on parking it in a fire lane. It's not the first time that smart ass has tried making parking places where none exist. And I'm not trying to make an example of the guy. Sure, I don't like the bastard but ...."

"Now George, there's no need for foul language. I'm just asking you to think about it, that's all."

"Right, I'm sure that's all. Is there anything else sir?"

"Well, yes there is," muttered Colonel Hahn. I could hear him shuffling papers before he began again. "I have my command post meeting notes here someplace. Yes, here they are. I'm getting some heat about the short staffing in the security building. It seems the lines are slow in the morning and...."

"They're slow because you won't give me staffing support. My men are spread pretty thin."

"There are rumors some of your men are doing assignments that take them away from the mountain. Is there any truth to those stories?"

"I have initiated several programs that directly relate to the security of this mountain. That's my job. Is there anything else sir? I'm late for a meeting."

There was a pause before the colonel responded. I would have loved to see his expression. "That's all George. But dammit, don't do anything that is going to embarrass this unit."

Following the last exchange the door flew open and Captain Lutz stormed out, without a backward glance.

When I approached the colonel's door I found him turned sideways, staring out the window.

"Is this a good time, sir?" I asked.

He glanced my way and waved me in. As I approached his desk I leaned forward to examine his view. Window my ass! There on his steel wall was a large poster of a double-hung, residential type window framing a garden view complete with spring flowers.

"You had me going there for a moment, sir. I thought you were...."

"... looking out a window. You're not the first one who's done a double take. I find the view relaxing," he said turning back to his desk and shuffling through a stack of papers. "Anyway, where's Bob?"

"Out of the mountain, sir. He didn't...."

"No matter." He pulled up his reading glasses and glanced at a pink telephone message slip. "Here's the problem. Your guys have created a big mess beside the access road and the general wants it cleaned up pronto."

"The general?"

"Jackson. He told his aide who told me and now I'm telling you. It shouldn't be a problem now should it?"

"No sir. I'll look into it."

"No, no, no Munson. You don't look into it. You get rid of it. The dirt pile goes. I don't want any more calls."

With that I was dismissed and headed back to my office, turning over the request in my mind. I was surprised that Jackson, the overall mountain commander, would take time to complain about a dirt pile. Frankly, I hadn't noticed it and had no idea what he was talking about.

"Hey Andy," I hailed when I walked into the office, "do you know any reason why we would have created a dirt pile down by the highway?"

He spun his chair to face me while lighting a fresh cigarette. "Water line repair. Saw them working on it yesterday. They have to replace a valve and it's buried deep. Why?"

I explained Hahn's order and Andy nearly exploded, exhaling a plume of blue smoke that engulfed me. "That's bullshit and doesn't sound like Jackson. He's a pretty square guy. He'd never call Hahn on a chickenshit thing like that."

"Actually the colonel said the general's aide made the call."

He tilted forward and slammed his fist on my desk. "That bastard, it sounds like something he'd pull. He's a major named Wiser; always trying to pull our chain. He thinks he wears the general's stars."

"So what do you suggest? Do I call the troops and have them fill the hole?"

Gruber leaned back, assuming a thoughtful pose. After blowing three smoke rings he smiled and swung around in his chair. "Lopez," he called.

"Yes sir?" said Airman Lopez, jumping to his feet.

"You still chasing the general's driver."

"Yes sir. Actually I've caught her. Been seeing a lot of each other lately."

"Good. Then here's what I want you to do."

"Begging the lieutenant's pardon but I've been listening to you and Lt. Munson. You want me to find out what went on in the car this morning, right?"

"Good man. When can you get on it?" asked Gruber.

"I'm having lunch with her."

So we sent our clerk off as a spy while I worried about following the colonel's order. He wanted the hole filled and I hadn't started any shoveling. I shouldn't have worried about it but I was still at the stage where I respected rank and the colonel had lots of it. I was only modestly relieved when Lopez reported in after lunch.

"So as they start up the access road the general looks out the window and says, 'I wonder what the engineers are up to over there…' and Wiser gets all worked up and calls Hahn. She didn't hear the call but it sounds like the thing was no big deal to the general," reported Lopez, leaning against my desk.

"Well, that's great," I said. "But I still have orders to get rid of the dirt. So now what?"

Gruber tilted back in his chair and took a thoughtful drag which I thought he would never exhale. Finally he issued a blue plume and turned back to me with a satisfied smirk. "It's your call Roger but, if I were you, I'd tell Sgt. Cavens the story and see if he has any ideas. His guys are doing the work and he knows the system as well as anyone. He'll come up with something."

And he did come up with something. When I drove down the mountain that evening three four-foot shrubs were growing out of the pile of dirt. After thinking about Hahn's order for a moment Sgt. Cavens had said, "We'll turn it from a pile of dirt into a landscape feature. I can borrow some shrubs from a nursery friend in town and return them when we refill the hole. He owes me a favor. Technically the dirt pile will be gone and the colonel should be happy."

I wasn't sure about the colonel but it made sense to me. And I'd learned another lesson about working the system.

***

I'm an engineer by training but that doesn't mean I'm anal retentive. I may prefer things more orderly than some but I think I roll with the punches as well as most. But I do like to plan my day and, if everything turns to shit, I can get a little edgy. The whole dirt pile incident dashed my plans and I felt I'd wasted the entire day. By the time I rolled into the apartment lot I'd decided to call Maggie and see if she would grab dinner with me somewhere. I figured she'd be good company and a nice diversion.

When I dialed her house Val answered. Maggie was out and Val had no idea when she'd return. She'd leave Maggie a note to call me.

That was it. Another plan gone sideways.

Undeterred, I hopped into the shower to get the smoky grime off and changed into jeans and a polo shirt. Then, grabbing a beer and some chips to tide me over until she called, I flipped on the evening news and slumped onto the sagging sofa. A student protest in Berkeley, a new offensive in a province called Trang or Dang or something and a bus driver strike in

Atlanta greeted me. Sports were boring but the weather forecast was encouraging. The news was soon replaced by a game show.

And Maggie didn't call.

At 7:30 I gave up and made myself a tuna fish sandwich on dry bread. Perhaps I'd been looking forward to seeing her more than I should. She didn't owe me anything. We were just friends, right? Finally, at a little after 10:00, the phone startled me.

"Hey, it's me, Maggie. What's up?"

I decided not to mention my dinner idea. She would either be disappointed or not. In either case I didn't see a reason to go there. "Nothing really. Just wanted to see how your week was going and see if you might want to grab a donut or something this weekend."

I could hear voices in the background and remembered the phone hung on the wall in her busy kitchen.

"Actually I'm going to be in Denver. Otherwise I'd love to. Another time maybe?"

We agreed to try again and then said our good byes.

Denver? What the hell was in Denver? Was she going alone? Who was she going to see? What difference did it make to me?

Then it struck me. I felt like a fool. Though I shouldn't, and had no right to, I believe I was feeling jealous. Of what and who I didn't know. Clearly I needed to get a life.

***

The next morning the new landscape feature looked good to me when I pulled from the highway onto the access road. Hahn wouldn't even be in today and perhaps he would have forgotten the dirt pile issue by Friday. Hahn, Gruber, Mills and Kirkwood were golfing for the first time this season and I would be the only squadron officer on duty in the mountain.

When I walked into the office it appeared the NCOs were trying to make up for Gruber's absence by cranking up giant cigars, filling the office with acrid smoke. "You just missed Sgt. Grady sir," said Lopez as I groped into the room. "He was passing out cigars; wife just had baby number four."

"Great," I acknowledged. I tossed my briefcase on the desk and was about to sit down when the door flew open and

Capt. Lutz burst in. "What the hell is going on in this loony bin? And where the fuck is everyone? No Hahn, no Kirkwood. Did someone declare a holiday and forget to give me the word?"

The NCOs slipped out of the office as he passed their desks and Lopez stuck his head in a file drawer, suddenly very busy. Lutz was rubbing the snuff off the black stone I'd last seen in his office. The way he held it I feared he was going to hurl it at me as he came to a stop at my desk.

"Where is everyone?"

"Golf day sir," I said, backing away.

"Oh shit. Has that started again? Well then, you're it. I need answers and I need them now. Who came up with the asinine idea to remove the security cameras from the tunnels?"

"Remove the security cameras?"

"Is there an echo in here Lieutenant?"

"Ah, no sir. I just don't know what you mean."

"You have a crew out at the south entrance preparing to remove the security camera. They told my guy they are planning to take them all down as a part of some project. Which side are you guys on anyway, ours or the Ruskies?"

He ranted on, slammed his hand against a metal cabinet and then stormed from the office with a parting comment. "I want you in my office by noon with some answers, is that clear?"

"Yes sir," I replied in my best military voice.

What the hell was that about, I thought as I sat down and digested the Lutz assault.

"Sir," came the voice of Airman Lopez from behind the file cabinet. "I might be able to help."

He climbed up on Gruber's tidy desk and sat facing me. "You see sir, the electrical shop maintains the camera system and they've had lots of downtime, faulty cameras and such. So two of them, Sneed and Collins, submitted a suggestion into the system to remove the cameras and rely on the guards for seeing what's happening. They figured we could save maybe ten grand a year in repair costs."

"Didn't anyone ask Lutz?"

"Don't know sir. I do know the suggestion came to Capt. Kirkwood for review and then he sent it on to the colonel for approval. The colonel is very big on the suggestion program. Thinks it's good to get ideas from the troops. Sneed and Collins split a $500 check for submitting the idea."

"And now I suppose the electricians are out pulling down cameras."

"I suspect so, sir. I suspect so."

"OK Lopez. You've been most helpful. Carry on." I said. I liked the sound of "carry on." It sounded like something an officer would say after speaking to his troops. "Carry on." I'd have to remember that one I thought as I headed for the electrical shop in search of answers.

***

"So that's all I know," I said, concluding my noon report to Lutz. "I've ordered the electricians to stop work and to replace the one camera they'd already removed. I'll let Capt. Kirkwood know about it in the morning."

Still rubbing his black stone he leaned across his desk and said, "And I'll take care of Hahn. I'll be in his fucking office at sun up and see if I can talk some sense into that old seized-up brain of his. Now, I mean no disrespect for the man but some of his decisions…."

While he went on about the colonel I was thinking about young Lt. Munson's sorry ass. I'd been on duty only three weeks and yet in the last two days I'd either disobeyed or overruled two direct orders from my squadron commander. I knew enough about military discipline to realize that was a bad idea.

A news bulletin flashing on the small TV screen on his credenza interrupted his rant. He turned up the sound and we both listened to an update on an anti-war protest at some New England school. When they cut to an advertisement he turned the sound down and swung back to me.

"Do you see the kind of stuff that's going on in this world today? The commies are behind it. They've got folks stirring the pot at all these campuses trying to make us look bad. They'd just love to get in this place and mess with us. So I have to be on the lookout for them and for the colonel's half wit ideas at the same time."

He set his rock down and turned to look out the window. "But I have this theory. It's easier to kill wasps in their nest than after they've flown. I may have found their nest. Now I need an excuse to neutralize them. Yep, that's the ticket, neutralize them."

I had no idea what he was talking about but was pleased that he'd calmed down.

During the pause Airman Borkowski, pushing hair from his eyes with a free hand, shuffled into the office, dropped mail into Lutz's "IN" basket and emptied his "OUT." When he turned to leave he exposed Lutz to a full view of his untucked uniform shirt tailing out behind. "Oh Borkowski, tell Sgt. Larson I'd like to see him ASAP," said Lutz.

"You bet."

"You bet, sir," snapped Lutz to the departing clerk.

"Oh yes, sorry. You bet sir," came the clerk's reply.

Lutz swung to face the window shaking his head in apparent disbelief. A tap on the door announced Larson's arrival.

"You wanted to see me sir?"

"Yes Charlie. Close the door and sit down."

Lutz remained silent until Larson was seated. Then he leaned forward, rested his elbows on the desk and studied the sergeant between steepled fingers. "When are you going to get that sorry assed clerk of ours whipped into shape. He's a disgrace to the whole f'ing unit."

"Bork? God sir, I have been busting my ass with him and nothing works. He can't type, can't file, can't make it to work on time, can't dress … he's just a goddamned slob. I've threatened him, restricted him and even walked him to the barber. He's a worthless son-of-a-bitch. It's not that he's got a bad attitude; he's a nice kid. He's just not cut out for the military."

Lutz leaned forward, and spoke slowly, placing emphasis on each word. "Well then, get rid of the sorry son-of-a-bitch. I don't care how you do it. Just get it done. Ship him off to some other outfit."

"I'm working on that, sir. But my buddy in personnel says no one wants him. He only has six months to go on his enlistment and they just want to tuck him away until they can send him back to the outside."

"Have you checked his record? Isn't there something we

can bust him on?"

"Accused of doing drugs, light stuff, in Nam. But nothing was pinned on him and he seems clean enough now. So, no sir, nothing. But I'll keep working on it. There's a chance I can get him into Transportation driving a truck, out of public view. Sgt. Greeley over there owes me big time. I'll keep working that angle but ..."

"Charlie, just get it done. It's frustrating as hell seeing him every time I go into this office. Get him out of here, the sooner the better."

"Roger that," said Larson, rising from the chair and escaping toward the door. "Good day to the two of you."

Lutz sat glaring at the door a moment longer and then turned to me with a charming smile. "Sorry about that interruption but I guess we were about wrapped up. By the way Lieutenant, you did a good job on this camera thing. It's a relief to have someone in the mountain I can depend on. Keep it up."

Chapter Six

2/10/69   Shit Bin, V.N. (aka Quan Binh)
Rog,

  Thought I'd answer your latest note. May help to get my mind out of this place for a bit. Just packed up the personal stuff for Mark, the owner of this typewriter. He bought it on yesterday's mindless escapade to a rotting valley no one cares about or can name to fulfill a mission of no consequence.

  Got to know him the past few weeks. Nice kid from Tacoma, 25, wife, one kid and one on the way. Son of a retired colonel who wanted to make his daddy proud. It makes no sense. Anyway, I'm keeping the typewriter. If I make it home I'll visit the wife and return it then. No one will care and it's less likely to get stolen if I carry it.

  I should ask how you're doing and tell you about the baby but my mind's all screwed up right now and, damn it all, I have yet to even see a picture of my baby.

  So, instead, I'll answer the question you asked in your letter. What do I do over here?

  I think I told you, last letter, that I blow things up. Last patrol was no exception. Some brass asshole wanted to look around this valley. Problem: no place to land. So they rappel my engineers into a likely LZ loaded with shit to blow things up, explosives and a couple of chain saws like you'd buy at Sears. Then, with a perimeter defense set, we begin wrapping det cord around these big-assed trees and lay 'em down. Between the det cord, chainsaws and my engineering skills we soon have created a suitable LZ for Mark and his patrol to settle into. That was the last time I saw him alive. He lands, we leave and then all hell broke loose. I guess our "clearing efforts" had not gone unnoticed by the local gooks and the patrol settled into deep doo doo. It took gunships and air support to pull them out.

  That's the usual routine when we are prepping an LZ. In December, my first mission, we had to stay with the patrol but they prefer to get us "specialists" out so we can do more dumb shit the next time they need an LZ. Personally I think they should just call in a B-52 strike. Those big bastards can clear an LZ in a heartbeat but I guess it's cheaper to use grunts.

Anyway, that's life in scenic Quan Binh. Write you bastard. I want to hear about your tough life at some cushy air base. Later
Hunk

FIGMO Countdown: 262 day

***

Out of sorts. That fairly described how I felt as I leaned back and placed my feet on the desk in my empty office. That was my grandmother's favorite response. "How you doing today, Grandma?" I would ask, by way of a greeting.

"Out of sorts," she would reply, laying the ever-present knitting in her lap.

The words never made sense to me, still don't. But she used them to describe everything from a simple cold to a broken arm. In the end, when the doctors said her heart was just shutting down, she would lie in her recliner and tell visitors, "I'm fine, just a little out of sorts."

Now, as I studied the smoke stained ceiling grills, I was feeling out of sorts.

It had been a week since the dirt pile incident and each day seemed to offer some unexpected challenge. Tomorrow might be worse; it was another Thursday golf day and I would be the only engineering officer on duty.

As expected, on Monday Lutz raised hell and the security camera project was put on hold. I'd have enjoyed sitting in on that discussion between Lutz and Hahn.

Tuesday the general's aide again rattled Hahn's chain about the dirt pile and I had to do my first bullshit dance explaining that the dirt pile was now a landscape feature. The colonel studied me with a cynical eye and then I was dismissed. I suspect I haven't heard the last of that.

During the dirt pile incident I'd even picked up some sound advice from Sgt. Cavens, a career airman and blue collar philosopher. "Don't sweat the small stuff, sir. The worst they can

76

do is ship you to 'Nam or Greenland and that's not likely. Too much paperwork."

Socially my life was a vacuum. I thought the free and independent life of a bachelor would be liberating. So far it had just been lonely. A bulky novel was proving to be a poor substitute for female companionship.

Saturday, in an effort to amp up my social life, I'd visited the officer's club and almost captured a nurse, just like in a John Wayne movie. Her name was 1st Lt. Rachel Lentz. She outranked me but that didn't matter at the bar. Her ankles were a little full but she was fair looking and nice enough. I prattled on in a most amusing manner and felt I was making progress. She even described her apartment in a most "would you like to come and see my etchings" sort of way. Nothing firm, mind you, but the hint was there.

There was something familiar about her and it took me two beers to spot it. She'd been a sorority girl at the University of Nebraska, like the predictable, pampered girls I'd left behind at college. I could have taken Rachel to any of the old fraternity parties. She was my kind of girl, if there was such a creature; Mother would approve. I sensed a relationship with a Rachel could hold promise in a most comfortable way.

Then her friend, Nurse Dillon, showed up. They were going to a movie. Did I want to join them? I declined.

Now as I leaned back and chewed on my black government pen I wasn't even sure I wanted a comfortable Nurse Lentz type of relationship.

Voices passing in the hall brought me back to reality. I pulled my feet from the desk and pondered my options: dinner at the mess hall or dinner at home in an empty apartment. I flicked the pen onto the desk and headed upstairs.

As I trudged up the stairs my mind wandered back to Saturday night.

I was still perplexed by the feeling I'd experienced leaving the club. I'd felt guilty about Maggie.

At that very moment she'd been off in Denver someplace, with someone, doing something and I'd been talking to a respectable nurse at a bar and I was the one feeling guilty. That made no sense. Maggie was, at best, an acquaintance.

Maybe she'd be elevated to "friend" status if we did a few more things but that was it. The guilt trip really confused me.

Maybe a good dinner would get me back in "sorts."

***

I arrived home and eased into my parking space as Pikes Peak hid the last rays of sunlight. It wasn't actually my parking space in the sense that it was assigned to me. But in the few weeks I'd lived there a parking etiquette had surfaced that, while not absolute, was generally adhered to. Most residents had a favorite space. It was polite to avoid those spaces. There were no signs; you just knew. I'd staked out a little used spot by an empty planter where I thought my doors would be safe from dings. Since it was some distance from the entry, and no one else seemed to use it regularly, I'd adopted it. A peaceful resident coexistence prevailed in the lot.

Now, I'm not a voyeur but as I walked around muddy snow piles to the entry I couldn't help but observe my neighbors who'd failed to draw their drapes. Two heads silhouetted by a flickering light in a darkened 301 suggested a TV was the center of their attention. The couple in 203 was still sitting at their table; I assumed dinner was in progress. The kids in 204 were busy sticking cut out snowflakes to the inside of the window as if there wasn't enough snow outside to satisfy them. The Mills had drawn their drapes.

As I fumbled for the mailbox key it struck me that I was perhaps the only person alone in their apartment that evening. Except, of course, for Mrs. Long, the widow in 101. Everyone knew and seemed to sympathize with her. With the apartment nearest the mailboxes she often popped out to initiate conversations when she heard someone in the hall. You hated to be rude but her conversations, or more rightly the monologues, were hard to break off. People learned to be very quiet in the hall.

Good God. Perhaps she and I had more in common than I cared to admit, I thought, as I tiptoed up the stairs. How lame was it that the highlight of my evening was going to be scoring a good parking space?

As I tossed the mail on the table my moribund reflections were interrupted by an impatient phone. What are they selling now, I thought? Since Mountain Bell connected the phone I'd had opportunities to buy steaks, the fruit-of-the-month, several kinds of insurance and a vacation home. I suspected the phone company made good money selling lists of new customers.

"It's Maggie. How you doing?" came the perky, guilt free voice on the phone.

After running off to Denver for the weekend how could she seem so casual? But then, I told myself, she owes me no explanation about the Denver trip any more than I needed to tell her about Nurse Lentz.

"Maggie, what's up," I said, balancing the receiver on my shoulder while I pried open a Coors.

We did the "how's school" and "how's work" phone ballet and covered the latest weather before she got to what I suspect was the reason for the call.

"I wanted to let you know about the art show on campus this weekend. I have some of my Cripple Creek photos in the photography exhibit and I thought you'd enjoy seeing the results. Some of them are fantastic, if I do say so myself."

"I think I could do that," I replied with just a hint in my voice that I would have to make some serious schedule adjustments to fit it in.

"Nine to five on Saturday. I'm working as a volunteer from nine to eleven so, if you can, why don't you stop by about eleven and I'll show you around."

We agreed and she was gone.

I walked to the window, beer in hand, and gazed blindly across the darkened lot. There was something Tinkerbellish about Maggie Meyers. She seemed to fly into my life, spread her fairy dust around and then disappear. And I always felt refreshed by our encounters.

***

"I hate to waste these bones. I wish I had a dog," I said, as I deposited the remnants of our T-bone steaks into the trash.

"Let me help you with the dishes," insisted Jessie as she pushed back from the table.

"Hold her down Cory. You're my guests tonight and you're not allowed in the kitchen. Besides, I'll wash dishes after you've gone," I said, rejoining them at the table.

My Friday night dinner party, the first in the apartment, had gone well. I'd invited the Mills up for the only meal I felt I could handle, steak with baked potato. Jessie supplied the green salad and apple cobbler and Cory the extra chair, since I only owned two. I felt I'd eaten with them so often I needed to reciprocate.

"OK Jessie, tell me about this delicious friend of yours," I said, picking up a conversation we'd begun during dinner.

"Well, Patti O'Neal is just a sweetheart, my best friend in high school. She was sort of my closet Catholic friend."

Cory laughed; I didn't get it.

"In the little town where we grew up there were two kinds of people, Catholics and everyone else," said Cory. "Jessie's folks saw no reason for her to spend time with the Catholic crowd when there were plenty of good Protestants to be with. So Jessie and Patti had to be ..."

"... closet friends," picked up Jessie. "That's just what we called ourselves. We found ways to shop and gossip and do things together and Mother never knew. She went off to the University of Montana but we've stayed in touch. Now she's just bumming around and will be in the Springs in a few weeks. You will come to dinner won't you? I think you'd really like her."

Cory seemed to sense my hesitation and changed the subject, much to my relief. "How about Maggie? Have you seen her lately?"

I looked at him, trying to determine how much he knew. One of the disadvantages of living above them was they knew my every move. They knew when I was pathetically spending another night home alone. They knew when I was away. But did they know Maggie spent the night? I couldn't tell and wasn't about to ask. There had been no hints one way or another.

"Cory," Jessie admonished, "What does that have to do with coming to dinner to meet Patti? I mean really ..."

"Look," I broke in, not wanting to bear witness to a domestic squabble, "you let me know when she's in town and I'll be there. At least if I'm not off on a secret mission, that is."

"Good, that's settled," said Jessie. "Now you can answer Cory's question. Have you seen Maggie lately?"

I explained how I'd been pretty busy and, that while Maggie was fun, she wasn't my type. Jessie listened intently but I suspected her bullshit filter was working and she wasn't buying my line. Finally, sounding almost like a confession, I told them about the next day's art show. That part of the story she seemed to believe.

"I wondered about you two. I don't mean this badly but you seem more straight arrow than her," offered Cory.

"Don't pay any attention to him. What would a man know? I thought she was cute. We had a nice talk in the kitchen the other night. I liked her."

I replayed the conversation while I was doing the dishes after they left. I decided that Jessie was more right than Cory. Maggie was cute and I liked her too.

***

There was no way I could blend in; my hair was still too short and my clothes too clean. In the last month my hair had grown positively shaggy compared to Capt. Lutz and most of the troops in the mountain. But when I stepped onto the Colorado College campus I was sure I stood out like Nixon at a Gloria Steinham rally.

I'd been on campus once before, my nighttime walk with Maggie. Things were different under the bright light of day. The buildings looked like a hundred other college buildings, surrounded by spacious plazas spotted with rows of leafless trees that offered the possibility of summer shade.

The plazas were populated with Len-like clones that seemed to be engaged in an indolent hygiene competition. The uniform of the day was dark colored torn fabric, in the shape of jackets, skirts and pants, draped over unwashed bodies. Shaggy, equally unwashed hair covered by dung colored knitted hats topped off many of the ensembles and the body language screamed "sloth."

This life form was not new to me; a variation of the species existed at the University of Washington. But we also had engineering and business schools and a Greek system that encouraged good fashion and Republican cleanliness. The counter culture, as we called it, centered on the liberal arts part of the campus, a part I passed through but rarely visited. Since

Colorado College was a liberal arts school perhaps what I was seeing was all there was.

In any case it was not a pretty sight. I felt very conspicuous. I'd worn jeans, but mine were clean and untorn. I'd worn sneakers but they were too white. My well used blue parka was my best hope of blending into the crowd but, while it looked ratty in my apartment, it somehow looked too stylish on campus. I topped off the ensemble with my favorite old Budweiser baseball cap which, though faded with age, was still too red.

A friend once told me, "You can put a dress on a pig but it's still a pig." I felt like a pig.

But no one seemed to care. However much I thought I stood out no one took notice and I was soon walking with renewed self confidence. Posters for the art show were nearly lost in the forest of signs for other campus groups like the Students Against the War, the Literary Society, the Sierra Club and Zero Population Growth. Most of the signs led to the Student Union Building fronting a large plaza that was bustling with sandal clad students, shuffling across the ruddy colored bricks. That seemed to be ground zero for campus activity.

I adjusted my cap, as if trying to conceal my identity, and strode up the wide stone steps.

***

"Hey man, did you lose your way or something?" said a vaguely familiar voice.

As my eyes adjusted, from the sunlight to the dimly lit lobby, I spotted a grubby looking Len sitting behind a poster wrapped old card table. The "SAW" logo identified it as a Students Against the War information center while a smaller sign urged visitors to "Send a Message; Sign the Petition."

My mind clicked into gear as I tried to come up with some knee capping response that would remove his sneer but the best I could do was, "Oh, hi Len. I didn't see you there." Weak, I thought. Very weak.

Doggie and a girl I remembered from the party were with Len at the table. Doggie actually looked friendly while the girl was concealed behind a frozen look of apathy. Standing further back against the wall, with his bulging arms folded in a most intimidating manner, was Luke, the guy from the party with the Ringo Starr haircut and droopy moustache.

"Hey flyboy, want to sign our petition?" Len asked when I hesitated near the table.

"What's it for, better food in the cafeteria?" That was better. A clever response that might throw him off.

Doggie smiled. Luke glared. Len sneered. "Foolish of me. You probably didn't know there was a war going on."

There was no reason for this conversation to be going on. Len appeared to be performing for his fans. I should have walked on but couldn't resist. I stopped in front of the table and gave him my best smirk. "This might surprise you Len, but I had heard that. And I suppose your petition is somehow going to stop it and make the world safer for mankind."

"It will do more than joining up and playing the suck up warrior role that you're playing. You gave in; we're speaking out," he retorted, raising the volume.

"And I'm sure the Viet Cong are listening," I replied, shaking my head in disbelief and turning to leave. I was pleased with that come back.

Several Len look-alikes, sensing the edge to the conversation, stopped to listen. Len, encouraged by the audience of kindred souls, rose from the old metal chair and leaned forward, placing his hairy knuckles on the petition. "The world will be safer when we knock some sense into you trigger happy military types who think the world will only be safer if we just drop bigger bombs on more villages. And maybe, just maybe, we can send a message to those assholes advisors to that shit-for-brains President of yours and he'll get his hand off the fucking trigger."

There was a murmur of agreement from the assembled unwashed followers. I was very aware that I was in enemy territory and badly outnumbered. But since I doubted the battle would turn from verbal to physical and my competitive instincts couldn't allow Len such a solid punch. I felt compelled to go another round.

I turned back slowly, assembling my words. "You must have me mistaken for someone else, Leonard." That was good. I'd been told he hated to be called Leonard. "My President is named Nixon. The trigger happy guys are in Moscow. But if you get that thing translated into Russian I'm sure they'd be pleased to read it," I said, waving at the petition beneath his now clenched fists.

There was no murmur of agreement this time. The crowd was hovering in eager silence. I glanced at Luke. He hadn't moved. Len leaned forward, skin turning red, and spouted, "You don't belong here. Your kind aren't welcome here. You should get the hell out …."

At that moment the card table groaned and collapsed with a resounding crack sending petitions, flyers and Len Hoffman sliding unceremoniously to the terrazzo floor. I jumped back to avoid both Len and the table while Doggie and the girl flailed wildly as they reached for a falling Len. The crash reverberated from the high ceilings of the lobby drawing the curious from surrounding rooms.

"Roger, what on earth is going on?" came the voice of Maggie, as she pushed her thin body through the stunned crowd of acolytes. Clad in a knee length loose fitting shift and leather sandals she blended into the crowd much better than ol'Lt. Munson.

Fearing I'd be blamed for the table collapse and would have to face a very angry Leonard, I decided a withdrawal from the field of battle would be prudent.

"Maggie, I'll tell you all about it but first, is there someplace we can grab a cup of coffee?" I mumbled, leaning close to her ear.

My insistence overcame her curiosity and we were soon drinking coffee in a darkened corner of the student union snack bar. "… so he leans forward, the table collapses, he ends up on the floor and I end up in here, with you."

"What a jerk. I can't believe he'd start an argument like that. You've done nothing to him," she said, playing with a package of sugar.

"I called him Leonard."

"You didn't?" she laughed. "I should never have told you that bothered him."

"I couldn't resist."

Happy to stay in the shadows of the snack bar we lingered with our coffee and I nudged the conversation from Len on to the art show. She was relaxed and effervescent as she recounted the morning activities. There had been few visitors but she was encouraged by their comments about her work.

"I'd love to see your stuff but maybe I should skip the tour," I said, when she finished her account. "After the Len incident it might be better for your reputation if you're not seen with me."

"Nonsense. Finish your coffee and then you'll see the work of Maggie Meyers. You'll be able to tell people you knew me before I was famous."

Chapter Seven

Dear Roger,

Thanks for the <u>short</u> note and photo of the apartment. It looks nice enough. What kinds of people live there? Have you met any of the neighbors?

Have you written your sister? Frankly, I'm worried about her. Lou's so young and that campus is just so radical. They always seem to be protesting something and I'm afraid she's going to get mixed up with the wrong crowd. I wish she'd gone the sorority route. Those girls are so much more refined. You can never tell who you'll meet in a dormitory. If you have a chance to give her advice, please do what you can.

Have you met anyone special? I hope you've put the Penny thing behind you. There are lots of fish in the sea. Nina, a friend at the club, heard that Penny is expecting. No details. Do you know her husband?

I'm co-chair of the club fashion show so will be busy the next few weeks. We want it to be perfect again this year.

That's all for now. Take care and don't scrimp on your food. You need a healthy diet.
Love Mom

***

I've never thought of photographs as art. Growing up we put photos in albums not on walls. Maggie's Cripple Creek photos changed all that. Playing with light, shadows and forms she'd turned black and white photos of mundane mine equipment into works of art. The effort garnered a blue ribbon in her category and a third place overall. She bubbled with enthusiasm while showing me the displays in the photography area. I was truly interested while truly distracted. I kept looking over my shoulder for Len and his gang. I didn't want to go another round with him and still felt I was operating in enemy territory.

At my suggestion we skipped the lobby area sculpture

display. Instead we slipped out a side door, avoided Leonard's lair, and began a slow walk across campus toward her house. We walked silently, each lost in our own thoughts until she said, "Would you like to do something this afternoon?"

Actually I very much wanted to spend the afternoon with her. I was enjoying our wandering conversations. "Sure," was my eloquent response.

"How about a drive?"

"A what?"

"A drive—you know—just hop in the car, head out and see what we see. I'll bring my camera. That is unless you had something else going on."

So we agreed. She ran to her house to get the camera and change clothes while I got the car and waited at the curb. I thought better of going inside. And then we went for a drive.

Heading east and then south across the golden plains that once inspired the writer of "America the Beautiful," we stayed on non-descript farm roads with no goal in mind. The stubbled winter fields were interrupted by farmhouses, rusty fence lines and little else. Occasionally she would see a photo-worthy object, I'd stop on the road and she'd take a picture.

The Maggie fragrance, I'd first noticed in her car, now filled mine. It was a nice addition. As we wandered, she ranged from silent to chatty. There were long stretches where nothing was said and then, inspired, she would take us off on a new topic. It was nice to be with someone where I didn't feel it was necessary to fill every moment with witty words. She didn't seem to object to the silence.

"Did your family ever take drives?" she asked after an extended period of quiet.

"Sundays. Not every Sunday but, if we went it was on Sunday, after church. How about you?"

"No. Manny was always too busy."

"Manny?"

"Oh, sorry. Manny is what I called my step dad. I could never bring myself to call him Dad. Anyway, when we lived in D.C. our neighbors often went on Sunday drives. But not us. He thought they were a waste of gas. It's too bad. I think it's nice to wander and look at the world with no schedule, no agenda."

I nodded in silent agreement concentrating on the road ahead. Maybe that's why I enjoyed family drives. It was one of the few times we could all be together, what with Dad's work schedule, Mom's meetings and other of life's interruptions. Yes, drives could be nice.

It was nearly 5:00 p.m. when Cheyenne Mountain loomed up west of the highway.

"Can you take me up there?" she asked. "I hear the view is wonderful."

Surprised at her interest I took the off ramp and wound my way to the top, showing her how the Camaro could corner as we ascended. In what I thought to be a clever manner I related the story about General Jackson, Colonel Hahn and the new landscape feature beside the road. She seemed to find the whole incident particularly funny.

Rounding the last turn I swung across the half empty lot and came to a stop where we had an unobstructed view of the prairie below.

"This is wonderful; what a sight," she said, leaping from the car, camera in hand. "Oh Roger, do you know what I'd love to do? Take a sunrise picture on a day where there are a few clouds to give the sky some color. Could we do that sometime?"

Leaning against the car, watching her standing on the curb, I was taken by the childlike enthusiasm she could show. "Of course we can. You just watch for the morning clouds and give me a call when they meet your standards."

Our viewing was interrupted by the arrival of a security police cruiser that came to an abrupt stop beside the Camaro. The driver leaped from the car with his hand resting on his revolver and ran toward us. "You there, this is a secure facility, no pictures. I'll have to take that film."

"Buck, wait. That's Lt. Munson from the engineers," came the voice of a second airman emerging from the passenger side of the official blue Impala.

I turned to the sound and was relieved to see the familiar face of Airman Emory. It appeared they'd intended to surround us in a very professional manner. Maggie, clutching her camera to her chest, moved to place me between her and a serious looking Buck.

"Oh hi Emory. Sorry if we caused any alarm. My friend here is a professional photographer and I was showing her the view from the edge of the lot. Nothing secret about that is there?"

Buck, who wore a single stripe, looked toward Emory who wore two. "The captain said no photos, no how."

"Take it easy Buck. The Lieutenant here isn't taking pictures of the complex. He's looking at the view." Emory shifted his eyes to Maggie who was emerging from behind me. "You ain't no spy are you ma'am?"

"Me? Heavens no."

"Didn't think so. Anyway sir, Captain Lutz is reading the regulations real close and is all over this photo thing right now. So if you ever want to do any picture taking around here I suggest you be real discreet with that thing and keep the lens pointing east, if you know what I mean."

As they turned to go Buck closed on Emory and grumbled. "That ain't right. At least we should take her film. We could really get our asses in a sling if...."

"Shit man, it's the Lieutenant for Christ's sake. The Lieutenant's OK," countered Airman Emory as he settled into the idling cruiser.

"Well, that was interesting," I offered as they drove away.

Maggie climbed back in the car and tucked the camera into the bag between her feet. "Well, I thought it was creepy. Let's get out of here. I don't want to lose my film and certainly don't want them to get into trouble with this Lutz person."

But on the way down the mountain she insisted on stopping one more time. She wanted to take a picture of the landscape feature beside the road.

***

We stumbled into the apartment lobby, burdened by two white paper bags of Chinese food, still laughing about a language problem at the take-out place. Pausing for my mail, I noticed widow Long's door open a crack and then noiselessly close again.

My apartment was not prepared for visitors. The bachelor slovenliness I relished when alone seemed inexplicable with a guest standing in the doorway. I swept through the living room collecting newspapers, the popcorn bowl and two beer cans. On the way to the kitchen I glanced into the cluttered bathroom, silently resolving to slip in and close the lid at the first opportunity. And my dirty dishes, clean dishes system displayed its shortcomings.

The dishwasher was empty which meant the sink was full and I was out of clean dishes. Since I wasn't a chop stick kind of guy I would need to wash dishes just to eat. Apologizing for the mess I explained my system to an amused Maggie.

"Roger," she laughed, catching her breath, "You sound like an engineer with a split personality. The engineer side gave you a system for managing your dirty dishes and the other side, whatever it's called, allows you to put up with a little mess. I think it's healthy."

"Maybe, but it's also a little embarrassing. Mother would never approve," I said running the hot water. "I may need to re-engineer the system now that I've seen its flaws."

Shaking her head she turned to leave the cluttered kitchen. "You do that while I use the little girl's room."

"Wait. I need to ... oh hell. OK."

She gave me a confused look and disappeared around the corner.

I washed what we needed for dinner, placed them on a freshly scrubbed table and tossed the rest of the dirties in the dishwasher. In three minutes I'd done a fair job of cleaning the kitchen and easing my embarrassment.

"I don't know why you're so concerned about maintaining your Emily Post rating," she said upon her return. "You've seen that place where I live. It's not exactly endorsed by the health department."

Actually I'd only been in her house one time. Lit by candlelight and hazed by smoke I hadn't taken a good look at the place. It had probably been cleaned up for the party. Or maybe not, considering the appearance of the party goers. I wondered what Maggie's room looked like. Was it an oasis in a sea of squalor or a cluttered girl's room like my sister Lou's?

"Some people think you can tell a lot about a person by how neat they are," I said, breaking open a little wax carton of beef with snow peas. "At one time I even thought you could tell a lot about a person by how tidy they kept their bedroom. But now that I'm living alone I may amend that rule since I don't think my cluttered room properly reflects my inherently tidy nature."

"I don't know about that," she replied, deftly serving herself with the chopsticks the restaurant provided. "People surprise me all the time. Take my roommates for example. Susan's put on gobs of weight and dresses like in the worst stuff but her room looks like a furniture store display and she keeps the bathroom surgically sterile. Val, on the other hand, gives the impression of being orderly but lives in a pig pen."

"How about old Len?"

"Haven't been up to his garret so can't say but he irks Susan by leaving things around the living room and kitchen."

"How about you? Tidy or sloppy?" I asked, offering her the rice.

"Oh, that's a mean question to ask a girl. Of course I think I'm neat enough but Susan might not agree. Let's see, how can I answer that? I guess I'm somewhere between Val and Susan."

"Well, I have no secrets," I said, sweeping my gaze to the living room. "You've seen the real Roger. Maybe a car is a better test; neat car—neat person, sloppy car—sloppy person …"

"Then I'm condemned. I sort of live out of my car and I guess it shows. Oh well, it's me; what can I say. How about your dad? Does his car reflect who he is?"

"Oh yes. He's a tidy man with a tidy house and car."

"Sounds like my stepfather. He's an orderly guy too," she said.

"Where do your folks live?"

"Here in Colorado now; but they've lived all over."

So that accounted for the Denver trips, I thought. It only makes sense that she would visit her folks.

"Do you mind if I put on some music? I see you have the new Simon and Garfunkel album."

"Better let me," I replied. "That little stereo has seen better days and has a personality of its own."

With the sounds of "Mrs. Robinson" filling the small

room I returned to the table to find Maggie dumping the last of our cardboard serving dishes in the trash and wiping down the table and counter.

"Gosh, it's nearly 8:30. Do you want to hang for a while or do you need to get back to your place?" I asked.

"I definitely don't want to go back to the house," she replied without turning from the sink. "Roger, you're going to think me an awful pest but could I stay here again tonight, just like before I mean. Len's having another one of his parties or meetings or I don't know what you call them but I don't like to be around those people. They remind me too much of...."

She paused with a white knuckle grip on the counter edge with both hands.

"Who do they remind you of?"

"People I knew at Boulder. Oh Roger, I shouldn't have asked. You can take me home."

"No, no, no problem. Of course you can stay," I stammered. "If you can put up with me and that crummy sofa you're more than welcome."

She relaxed her grip and turned, smiling, "You're a good friend. I'm really glad I ran into you. Are you sure you're OK with it?"

I thought her eyes looked moist but couldn't be sure. It was an awkward moment.

"No problem. What robust young officer wouldn't want a foxy lady to spend the night at his place?"

"You're both an officer and a gentleman are you not?"

"Right, a gentleman, that's me," I tossed over my shoulder as I walked into the living room. Actually I didn't know what I was. This girl, who I thought was just a friend, was looking very good to me in more than a friend sort of way. I felt a real need to put some distance between us. "Now how can I entertain you? Lawrence Welk and Green Acres look like the only choices," I said glancing at the TV section from the paper.

"You don't need to entertain me and neither of those choices sound too good. Do you play cards, gin?"

And that's how I learned to play gin that night in Colorado Springs. Separated by an old table, a deck of cards, a can of salted peanuts and two rum and cokes we began our second night together.

She taught me gin. She beat me. She slept on the sofa.

***

The guys in the frat house wouldn't believe it. Here I was alone in my apartment with a lovely lass and I hadn't "gotten any." That was always the question heard Sunday mornings after a party at the house. "Did you get any?" I heard wild tales of conquest told but took them all with a grain of salt. A conquest to one guy was a quick feel to another but the purported victor would often answer with a wink and a nod and let the listener draw their own conclusions. I believe if you tallied the number of guys that claimed they "got some" a particular weekend against a similar tally in the neighboring sorority house of the girls that "gave some" there would be a glaring disparity.

But I hadn't gotten any, nor had I tried. She'd given me a quick hug from behind while I was putting our glasses in the sink. "Thanks for putting up with me," she'd said with her head resting on my shoulder and her arms around my chest. Then she'd slipped away before I could make a move, which I wasn't going to do anyway.

Acting very much at home, she'd retrieved my sleeping bag from the closet and spread it on the sofa. Then I'd pulled my blue sweats out of the dryer, where they'd spent the last week, and tossed them on the back of a chair for her use. We were growing very familiar. She even had her own toothbrush sitting in her own cup in the bathroom. The toothbrush actually came from our family dentist. Each exam resulted in a free toothbrush and an admonition to floss more. That, plus my frugal unwillingness to toss out my current brush, meant I could supply Maggie and four other women with their own brushes should the need arise.

Now I was lying in bed with the morning sun bursting around the edges of my beige drapes not wanting to do anything that would disturb her. Had I been a cold fish last night? Had I missed some signs? Was she hoping I would come on to her? Was she pleased with the way things turned out?

I eased from the bed, opened the curtains for light, retrieved my "Newsweek" from a pile on the floor and returned to bed with pillows stuffed behind my back. The magazine failed to hold my attention. I found myself thinking less about her not being my type and more about how much I enjoyed her company. I could relax with Maggie, let my hair down so to speak, what little hair that I had. I didn't feel I needed to be "on." I could just be my unpretentious self.

But were we dating? How would I feel if I ran into her with some other guy? How would she feel if she ran into me with Nurse Lentz? If we were just friends then it wouldn't matter. It was all very confusing.

My musing was interrupted by the first flush of dawn. She was up and about.

***

"You are about to be treated to my breakfast specialty, Belgian waffles," I said as she emerged from the bathroom clad in yesterdays clothes with her still wet hair hanging in loose curls.

She seemed very much at ease but I felt self conscious about my appearance. I'd slipped on old Levis and a tee shirt but I was sure my slept-on hair and unshaven face looked scruffy.

She leaned against the counter as if surveying my work. "I'm impressed you have a waffle iron when you don't even have a toaster."

"Thank my sister. Lou knows I love waffles. This was my going away present from her. You're my first customer. You do eat waffles?"

"Absolutely. Can I pour you a cup?" she asked, reaching for the percolator which was perking its last perk.

The first waffle stuck and came out in small pieces but the rest were perfect; golden brown and crispy. After splitting the last one she took our empty plates to the sink, refilled the coffee cups and rejoined me at the table.

"What do you think of me?" she asked out of the blue.

"Think of you?"

"Yes. I live in a nut house, run around taking pictures of weird things and invite myself to stay in your apartment. You must wonder about me."

"Ahh, not really. I mean, I have girls sleeping on the sofa all the time."

She gave me a look that said she got the joke but wasn't amused. She had asked a serious question and I'd avoided answering. She turned her gaze to the parking lot and fell silent. I followed her eyes and watched Jessie and Cory drive off toward their church.

The pregnant silence lingered until she looked back and asked, "What was your college girlfriend like?"

"College girlfriend?"

"Jessie said you broke up with someone when you joined the Air Force."

"Oh, that college girlfriend," I replied, wondering what else Jessie had shared with her.

"I'm sorry, it's none of my business really ..." she began.

"No, it's all right," I replied before launching into a "Readers Digest Condensed" version of my life with Penny. "So we decided to end it before I left," I concluded. "It seemed like the right thing to do."

Maggie watched me over the rim of her cup while I spoke. I wasn't good at this kind of conversation and hoped it didn't show. After a pause she twisted to a new subject. "In college did you have any friends that were girls as opposed to a girlfriend. You know someone you didn't date but someone you could talk to as a friend?"

"Like you and me?" I blurted, immediately wishing I could retrieve the words.

She blushed and avoided eye contact. "I mean while you and, what was her name, Penny were going together."

I leaned into a thoughtful pose. A girl as a friend? Not bloody likely. Penny was the jealous type up until the day she decided we were no longer going together. She was very insecure about our relationship and was upset if I appeared to converse with any other girl, even her best and most trusted friend. "Not really," I responded, not sure if I sounded convincing. "Why?"

"Just wondering."

"Did you?"

"In high school I had what I'd call a guy friend. But not in college. I think it's hard to do, to have a male friend I mean.

When people see you with someone they just draw conclusions that there must be more than a friendship involved."

She was right. People who knew we spent time together would make the same assumption even if they didn't know she'd spent the night. That information would just be icing on the rumor cake.

Maggie slipped into one of her silent times, walked to the sofa and folded up the sleeping bag lost in thought. When she returned, I decided to satisfy my curiosity.

"Well, it seems you know all about my love life. How about yours? Other than Len how many broken hearts have you scattered between here and Boulder?"

"Oh you're awful," she said sitting back down and kicking me under the table. "You know there's nothing between Len and me. And as for the highway to Boulder I'm afraid there isn't much to report."

There was something in the way she said it that made me believe there was something on that highway. But she wasn't planning to share it with me.

Deftly she steered the conversation away from Maggie Meyers to safer ground, the weather, the best place to get an oil change and why the light is better for photography early and late in the day. Before I knew it 1:00 p.m. was upon us and she had to leave to begin her research for a paper on Italian art.

Slowly I drove her home, not looking forward to a long afternoon alone. She sat silently gazing toward the bare row of trees passing on her side of the car. As I pulled up to the curb she turned, clutching her coat tight as if she was freezing. "Thanks for putting up with me Roger. It's been a nice change from this place," she said nodding toward the house.

"Anytime, but you have to cook breakfast the next time."

She stared straight ahead without reply.

"Seriously, if you ever need a quiet place to study you're welcome to use my little table."

"I may take you up on that. Yes, I just might. Goodbye Roger and thanks."

She leaned over, kissed me on the cheek and was gone. God that woman could move fast. I had no idea what it meant but it aroused me more than a good night of necking with old Penny. Well, maybe that's an exaggeration but still, it was nice. And I wondered exactly what she was thanking me for.

Chapter Eight

3/20/69   In Hell's Half Acre
Rog,

 Colorado F'ing Springs! I don't believe it. You get a snow covered village in the Rockies and I get this stinking so-called "base camp" in the jungles of F'ing V.N. Careful you don't get frost bite walking into your office. Might not be able to hold your pen properly!!!

 Do I sound bitter? I'm not really. Count it as envy, old buddy. I wouldn't wish this place on anybody and I get some satisfaction knowing no one will be shooting your ass off any time soon.

 FAIR WARNING: The rest of this letter is going to sound like a bitch session. Read at your own risk!

 I wanted to be upbeat but I need to be honest with someone. I write Sally and the folks and keep a sugar coating on everything: good food, sunny skies, don't believe everything you see on the evening news...that sort of thing. They'd worry sick if they saw this place and what I do. Fact is, I'm convinced there are bad guys over here who want to kill me and they are very good at their jobs. Every time I go into the bush I feel like some gook has me in his sights. I think I mentioned my Purple Heart. I gave up a piece of my ear for that little medal. Now the ear was no great loss (you can hardly see the scar) but the fact the bullet was six inches from my forehead stays with me. I tell myself that lightning doesn't strike twice in the same place so maybe the gooks have blown their only chance but find little satisfaction in the thought.

 I share a hootch with five officers. Of the five here when I arrived, two rotated home, one left on a medivac and two in flag-covered coffins. I'm now the "old man." You do the math.

 You asked if drugs were a problem over here, as the evening news suggests. Short answer, yes, cheap and plentiful. We tend to tolerate the light stuff in base camp but not out in the bush. In fact my team self-polices itself pretty well. Nobody

wants some dope-head covering his six o'clock in the field.
We've had to toss out a couple of guys who just didn't "get it."
Not sure what happened to the in the rear.

    O.K. I feel better. I needed to spout off to someone.
Please do not repeat this to anyone. In case you fear, inside I'm
still the same old curmudgeon engineer you knew and loved. And
I hope I'm still the lunk that Sally loved. I have now seen photos
of my son. I do nice work if I do say so and his mother is still as
gorgeous as I left her. Motherhood seems to appeal to her but I
can tell that being close to her folks is trying for her...too many
suggestions, if you know what I mean.

    Don't break a leg on the ski slopes.
Hunk

FIGMO Countdown: 224

P.S. You asked about FIGMO. In polite company it means,
"Forget It, Got My Orders." Over here it starts with another,
more popular "F" word. The orders, of course, are orders home.
At the main camp there are guys who will print you what's called
a figmo chart listing all the days till the end of your tour. It gives
you something to check off. Not much use here, no wall to hang
it on and the humidity turns everything to shit.

***

    Doesn't it rain a lot in Seattle? That was often the first
question I'd hear when people learned where I was from. I was
raised there. I lacked a point of reference. I would say, "... not
really. The weather is quite nice." After a month in Colorado I'd
revised my answer to "yes." Seattle was green the year around.
After a burst of spring green, the dry Colorado plains turned
brown. Moss was a common four letter word in Seattle; it was a
word rarely heard in Colorado. Sunny days were celebrated in
Seattle; they were assumed in Colorado.

    This contrast was going through my mind as I cruised
with the Monday morning traffic to brown faced Cheyenne
Mountain. The snowy blanket that had concealed the mountain
since my first day was nearly gone, not so much melted as
evaporated into the dry high desert air. I missed the rolling hills

of Seattle but I didn't really miss the gray days and drizzle that maintained the city's emerald elegance. I could get used to this place, I thought: clear, cold and dry.

In a driving daze I mulled over the week ahead. No great challenges loomed. The Engineering group ran with remarkable efficiency. It struck me that I was assigned to the squadron more to take the blame or credit than to really provide direction. That was OK with me. I'd concluded that as long as I protected Capt. Kirkwood's backside he would be happy. He in turn covered Col. Hahn's and so on, up the line. It wasn't that they weren't dedicated to their jobs. But they were also dedicated to keeping their official records clean so they could advance their careers.

I eased onto the access road, delighted to see a clear stretch of pavement ahead. The first half mile offered three turns that called out to me as I shifted down and listened to the throaty V-8 respond to my urging. The Security Police were too busy to watch for speeding, much to my delight. The Camaro was made for this part of the drive. Coming out of the third turn I caught up with the traffic, trapped behind a slow-moving delivery truck, and coasted back to reality.

Another thoughtlet struck me; I wasn't the new kid in the Squadron anymore. I was the newest officer but, with the constant transfer of troops in and out of the unit, my rookie shine had quickly tarnished and I was blending in like a long time mountain fixture. Yet I still couldn't think like a true mountain veteran. They had an uncanny ability to adapt to situations I found absurd. Take my conversation with Sgt. Snell in the electrical shop last Friday.

Snell was a lanky Mississippi farm boy who moved through the halls with a camel's lazy gait. He always appeared to be busy, in a half speed sort of way, though I was never sure what he did.

"Good morning Sergeant," I said when I entered the shop looking for his NCO.

"Good morning sir. What's happening?" he replied, turning to me on his workbench stool and shifting a toothpick from left to right.

"Do you know where I can find Evans?"

"Don't rightly know sir. Ain't seen him this morning."

I approached the workbench, noticing electric drill parts spread in a neat pattern. "Doing a little drill repair?" I asked, to continue the conversation. I thought talking to the troops informally was a good way to build their allegiance and for them to see that I was really an OK 2nd lieutenant.

"Kind of. Actually I'm building a new one."

"A new drill?"

"Yes sir. You could say that. You see, sir, we needed a drill but our request was denied. No money for new stuff. But Sgt Evans says there's plenty of money in the repair budget so he ordered all the parts for the drill using that budget and I'm putting it together."

I tried to conceal my disbelief while I looked over the array of new parts laid out on the bench. "That sounds like an expensive way to buy a drill,"

"Expect so sir. But we'll get our drill."

"Do you do this sort of thing often?"

"Not really, sir. I know the plumbers built a pump last fall and the grounds guys put a compressor together. That's about it."

I was still reflecting on that Friday conversation when the slow moving line of cars reached the parking plateau and dispersed. I suspected the maintenance guys could probably build a pickup truck from "parts" if I asked them to. I pulled into a vacant space next to Kirkwood's coned-off Porsche and gave the Camaro a "good boy" pat on the dashboard as I turned off the ignition. She was no Porsche but she was plenty of car for me.

Then I strode across the sun drenched lot to face a new day in the mountain defending the continent against the red horde.

***

Scurrying down the hall I nearly ran into Gruber and Kirkwood as they emerged from the captain's office in a cloud of Gruber smoke.

"It's a nice car Andy. Don't get me wrong," said Capt. Kirkwood as they fell into step ahead of me. "But compared to mine that GTO is like driving a truck, you sit up so high."

"Fuck man, of course you sit up high. It's a car not a juiced up Volkswagen. And I've got a honkin' engine and a real back seat and trunk. If you and Gail take a trip in that Porsche you'll have to mail your luggage ahead," Gruber spat back.

"Good morning gentlemen."

"Oh, hi Rog," said Kirkwood, slowing so I could catch up. "Can you believe old Andy here? He goes out and buys a '65 Pontiac GTO from some Army guy and now is trying to convince me it's more car than mine."

"Well sir, he may have a point," I offered, just to stir the debate. "I suspect we could fit your car into that GTO trunk."

Andy guffawed a cloud of smoke and gave Kirkwood an "I told you so" knuckle to the shoulder.

"You bastards. Why do I waste my breath on you two disciples of Detroit metal? I ought to ship you both to Greenland and find some replacements who appreciate automobile craftsmanship and performance. Now get moving. I can't stand having George glare at us when we're late."

I couldn't help smiling to myself. Bob Kirkwood had a terrible sense of time and was already late. He always was and likely always would be. And Capt. George Lutz did glare at us when we arrived.

Though late, we still beat the colonel who soon arrived with Cory on his heels whispering last minute instructions.

The meeting fell into its familiar pattern of official reports interspersed with Hahn's now familiar sidetracks: the antics of his new dog, the new shipment of golf balls at the Base Exchange and the pending arrival of his son and daughter-in-law. The Lutz black rock was soon out of his pocket and gripped in his hand while he tried to massage the shine off.

Seated beside the colonel, I watched him tick off each agenda item as it was discussed. When we finished the agenda and chairs were beginning to scrape the tile floor in anticipation of our departure, Hahn surprised us with, "I've got a couple of other items to cover while you boys are here." I watched his pen come to rest on three hand-written margin notes on his agenda.

"First, Roger, why is that dirt pile, or landscape feature as you call it, still there? Major Wiser never misses an opportunity to ask, preferably when he's in front of the general."

"Sorry about that sir but we're having a little trouble getting the replacement valve. The plans showed a particular valve so we ordered that as a replacement. But when they exposed the pipe they found a different system had been used and ..."

"Right, right, right, I've heard all that but why so slow?" he asked in his slow drawl.

"The valve is due in ..." I began before Lutz interrupted.

George leaned forward, clunking his black rock on the table. "Begging the colonel's pardon but might I suggest you tell Wiser to shut his fucking eyes when he drives by and then ..."

"George, that kind of talk won't help the situation."

Lutz exhaled a Gruber size puff of smoke, recovered his rock and pushed his thumb deeper into the black stone.

"And that brings me to my next area of concern. I've been getting complaints about the morning lines at security. It seems we only have two or three turnstiles open when we used to have four during the busy times."

"Complaints, from whom?" growled Lutz.

"Well, of course, I've noticed it and the Major ..."

"Wiser again? Colonel, if that ass kisser spent as much time worrying about his own operation as he does yours that command post wouldn't be such a ..."

"Hold your tongue, George," interrupted the colonel.

"Wiser doesn't even go through the turnstile most mornings. Mr. General's Aide rides through the vehicle gate with the general," spat Lutz.

Capt. Kirkwood leaned forward in a clumsy effort to calm the tempest. "Now, George, you know I'm no Wiser fan but I was wondering about the morning backup myself. It never used to be this bad. Are you short some guys or something?"

"Some of the troops have been putting in long hours on special projects. We're stretched thin, even in normal times and these are not normal times. The colonel knows I've been asking for more personnel."

"Special projects? What special projects?" the colonel asked, glaring at Lutz over his reading glasses.

"And if I lose the security cameras I'll need even more manning," Lutz said, ignoring the question.

It was a good tactic to use with the colonel. I learned it my second week when I saw Cory bury a question with a counter question. Hahn had a short attention span. If you could distract him, an awkward subject might simply fall from the agenda.

"I have an update on that subject sir," I said receiving a nod from the colonel and a surprised look from Kirkwood. I hadn't had time to brief him on my plan.

"Well, sir, when we dug into the repair records it seemed the biggest issues were with the four cameras exposed to the high winds: the two at the security check points and the ones at the tunnel entrances. My guys suggested building metal boxes for each camera that will protect them from the wind and weather. I believe it's worth a try."

"What good's a camera in a box?" said the colonel giving me an official glare.

"Oh, we'll either put glass in the end or leave it open. We haven't finished the design but I think it's worth pursuing."

"What do you think?" he asked, looking towards Kirkwood.

"I agree with Roger, sir. I think we should give it a try. The boxes shouldn't be too expensive and…"

"OK, OK. Give it a try. But I don't want to see those electricians putting in a suggestion to leave the cameras after they received an award for suggesting we take them out. Why didn't they suggest boxes in the first place, those scoundrels?"

I listened to the conversation thinking I now knew how Alice felt after she fell into the rabbit hole.

***

"Got a minute Lieutenant?" asked George Lutz as we filed from the conference room.

I wasn't sure how to respond even to such a simple question. There was something mysterious about him. Since my first-day interrogation we'd crossed paths in meetings and lunched at the same table on occasion, but always with others present, never one on one. He was nice enough but his intensity was unnerving. I always felt a need to measure my words in his stern presence. With his steely glare it seemed as if he was mentally dissecting each remark, looking for hidden meanings or subversive intent.

"Sure, what's up," I said, as casually as I could muster.

"Let's hit the mess hall. I'll buy you a cup."

A step behind, I followed him up the cold steel stairway to the third floor mess hall. We filled our heavy crockery cups from the towering urn, left our money at the unmanned cash register and slid into seats at an isolated table.

The suspense and my curiosity built as Lutz ritualistically stirred in sugar and cream and then lit a Viceroy from his neat, crush proof pack. Leaning back and exhaling a narrow smoke stream he said, "You did well in there."

"Sir?"

He leaned forward and flicked filter fuzz from his tongue with his pinky finger. "The security camera matter. You did well with that. I appreciate that. You're a good man and I'm glad you're part of the Squadron. I need those cameras. I can't believe that dickhead ever approved scrapping them in the first place."

"Which dickhead?"

"Take your pick. Anyway, I've been watching your work and your performance at staff meetings. You're a good officer. We need more like you."

"Thank you sir. I appreciate that," I responded, still not sure where this conversation was headed.

He assumed a reflective pose, taking a long draw on his cigarette. Abhorring the silence, I decided to break the ice and satisfy my curiosity. "Sir, I was wondering, how did you get into security?"

"Always interested in it for some reason. Came out of Oklahoma with a degree in criminology and an ROTC commission. This was a natural fit. I'd planned to go to law school. Still might. May even stay in and let the Air Force pay for my degree."

George Lutz was the short-answer man which made conversation stilted at best. While I considered other topics to explore, he surprised me with a dramatic change of demeanor.

"Roger, I'd like a chance to get to know you better, you know, socially and away from all this. How about we get together for dinner Saturday night? You can meet the wife. What do you say to that?"

"Sure, fine I guess. Yes, that would be fine. Where and when?"

"Seven at the 'O' Club. This is seafood weekend. That

should suit a guy from Seattle. I'll have Larson make reservations. Why don't you bring your lady friend?"

"Lady friend?"

"Mills says you're seeing someone, some local girl."

Thanks Cory for keeping everyone current on my social life, I thought. I guessed there were no secrets in either the city or the Squadron. "Oh, I met this girl but she is hardly my lady friend, at least not as I think of the term."

"Well, whatever. I'll get reservations for four. Bring someone if you want. It's up to you. Got to run now. We'll see you. And good job on that camera project. Keep it up."

He snuffed out his half smoked cigarette, took a last swig of coffee and strode out of the dining hall.

***

I refilled my cup and wandered back to the table. Dinner with Lutz. Now that should be an interesting evening, I thought. Perhaps the presence of his wife would moderate things a bit. Maybe she'd be easier to talk to and maybe, just maybe, he would relax when he took his uniform off. But he called his wife Victoria, not Vic or Vicki—nothing casual or endearing but just very formal Victoria. That was not an encouraging sign.

The second question concerned my "lady friend." I could go alone. That would be the easiest thing to do. Or it might be a good excuse to track down nurse Lentz. I'd seen her once since the "O" club. She was in the produce department at the commissary. It was a brief "… how are you doing? We should get together sometime …" conversation and I hadn't had the inclination to place the call. But taking a stranger to a dinner with people I didn't really know could be awkward.

Maggie, the girl Lutz had heard about, was clearly the third option. She had a disarming way of moving a conversation and might even get Lutz to loosen up. We'd never been to anyplace nice for dinner. Just fast food, take out and dinner with the Mills.

I was leaning toward inviting her when the image of her in sandals, beads and a long flowing dress flashed across my mind. She would stand out at the club like I stood out at her party. People didn't dress that casual at the club, not even in the bar. Coats and ties were required for men in the restaurant which is why I'd never moved from the informal bar.

Now I was torn. It would be interesting to include her but not at the expense of putting her where she didn't fit. I recalled my discomfort at Val's party. I didn't want to subject her to the same. But it was mostly the clothes. She could acquit herself nicely in a conversation. Maybe she had an outfit that would blend in. But how would I ask that question without knocking her normal wardrobe?

Cory Mills approached the table interrupting my contemplation. "Hey man, I've been looking for you. I saw Lutz leave the mountain and I was dying to know what he had up his sleeve. The only time he invites me to have coffee is when he wants me to lobby the colonel about something." He sat down, leaning forward with anticipation.

"Relax, Perry Mason. It was purely a social call."

"Did he try to recruit you as an intelligence operative for his undercover operation?"

"Are you bullshitting me? Does Lutz really run an undercover operation?"

"Oh, I don't know," Cory responded with a laugh. "He's kind of a security fanatic. No one's talking but I suspect he's doing something off the mountain, background checks, watching people, that sort of thing. I just don't want to know too much about his extracurricular programs. He doesn't have the authority to spy on people and, if the doggy doo hits the fan, I want to be as surprised as everyone else and not get any on me."

"But wouldn't the colonel be aware of it?"

"As you may have noticed, our colonel isn't aware of too much. He fashions himself as a 'high level' manager. Or as he says, 'I focus on the big picture and let my staff handle the details.'"

The conversation was interrupted by a group of boisterous airmen who jostled their way into the room, purchased Cokes and then took a table as far as possible from us, the only two officers in the area. With their chatter in the background I leaned forward and said, "How did you learn about Lutz's extra activities?"

"Oh, he gives me tidbits from time to time. I think he trusts me and knows I'm not going to screw him. He even invited Jessie and me to dinner once so we could meet on a more informal basis. Of course, informal to him is tight ass to most people."

"He's invited me to the O' Club Saturday night," I said, giving him the details of our pending dinner.

"Well, there you have it then. Maybe he trusts you."

"And, by the way, thanks for telling him about Maggie. Man, a guy's private life is an open book around here."

"Read your officer commission," he said with a laugh. "The Air Force has your soul 24 hours a day, seven days a week. They know everything. How did her name come up?"

"He said to bring her along if I wanted."

"Hmmm," was his reaction as he pursed his lips and stared into space in thoughtful contemplation.

"What do you mean by that?" I said.

"Are you going to invite her?"

"I haven't decided. What do you think?"

"Whoa, now that's an interesting question. Would Maggie and his wife have anything in common? Other than gender, no. Victoria is a hat and glove society type from Georgia, not a Maggie free spirit. Would you have a better time with Maggie there? Yes, it might be a long night otherwise. The most pressing question is, would Maggie be comfortable at the club? She might find the atmosphere a bit stuffy, if you know what I mean," he concluded.

"That's the question that bothers me. And I wonder if she has anything—oh, you know—anything fancier to wear. I've only seen her in jeans or, how shall I say it, campus attire."

"The flower child look. I know what you mean. But surely she owns some big girl clothes."

"Hell, I don't know. When you get down to it, I don't know all that much about her."

"Ah, well, you'll figure something out."

"Yes, thanks, you're a big help," I replied. "By the way, is Lutz always a man of few words? I learned where he went to college and that he was in 'Nam for a tour. That's about it."

"Congratulations. Most people don't do that well. He doesn't talk about 'Nam much. He didn't have a good tour."

"Nasty action?"

Cory laughed and shook his head. "You could say that. He mostly fought higher authority. You see, he was assigned to perimeter security at Da Nang. He inspects the set up, concludes it's a lax outfit and cracks down. Where they'd been sloppy before they now go by-the-book. He bugged the heck out of the brass who didn't see the threat the way Lutz did. So one night his entry guards intercept some reporters, newspaper types I think, trying to smuggle girls onto the base. The reporters get a little mouthy so the guards call Lutz. He comes to the post and the reporters really rip him. He takes that for about a nanosecond and orders them and the girls locked up."

"Did he tell you all this?"

"No, Airman Lewis was on duty that night. He's assigned here now, one of our security guys. Anyway the phone gets hot the next day. One of the reporters was a poker buddy of the base commander. One of the girls was the daughter of a Vietnamese general. The commander was most embarrassed."

"Was Lutz out of line?"

"Who knows? With him it's often not what he does but how he does it. Officially he was probably doing the right thing for the right reasons. But it's my-way-or-the-highway with George. As you've seen, there are times he could be more diplomatic. Anyway, to make a long story short, George gets reassigned to an admin post, the reporters don't write any bad stories and the general's daughter goes to boarding school in France."

"Well, I won't bring Vietnam up at dinner. The way you describe his wife, maybe I should invite Maggie just to have someone to talk to."

"I would, good buddy. I would. I'm sure she cleans up real well," he said, rising from the table.

"Thanks. I'll let her know you think so highly of her," I replied, following him into the corridor.

Chapter Nine

April 7
My Dear Big Brother,

Thanks for the note. Colorado sounds very cool (get the pun?)

Well, your little sister stepped in it this time and I may need your help w/Mom. See, I went to a rally at the Army recruiting station near campus. Things were good until some shithead broke a window and then the pigs descended, grabbed those that didn't run (like me!!) and loaded us in an old school bus for a trip downtown. No big deal. They took ID, scolded us and sent us home, no charges that I know of.

Problem: My cute little face made the news. If Mom ever sees that news clip the fit will hit the shan. She has an amazing way of finding out about stuff. So bro, you are on standby to defend me. She's been looking for a reason to pull me out of here and I don't want to go sooo.....

News from Home: I hear Penny's husband got/is getting drafted. A friend knows his family. Guess he is known as the "deferment king." He's pulled every string, short of moving to Canada, to avoid the draft but they got him. Even Penny's pregnancy couldn't save his sorry ass. I have mixed emotions. I hate to see anyone drafted but the way she dumped on you a little payback sounds good. Aren't I the evil one?

Take care. Next letter I want to hear about your love life. I'm sure you're "wowing" the snow bunnies of Colorado.
Love ya,
Sis

***

I eased the Camaro to a stop and shut down the throaty V8.

"See, what did I tell you?" cooed 1st Lt. Rachel Lentz from the seat beside me. "Isn't this view the absolute most?"

I looked at the moon, just ascending from the distant

prairie edge, and then fixed my gaze on Rachel. It was times like this that I regretted selecting bucket seats. She looked delicious in her snug wool sweater topped off by a string of pearls lying loosely beneath her throat.

When I reached across and took her hand she snuggled down and rested her head on my shoulder. The smell of her shampoo or perfume or whatever reminded me of old girlfriend Penny. But Penny was then and this was now and this promised to be a wonderful evening.

She mumbled a few things and I mumbled back. Maybe we spoke about the moon or the dinner or the movie. What was said didn't matter as the words were just there to fill the gap between what was and what was going to be.

After a quiet interlude, I tilted her chin back and pressed my lips to hers. The single kiss exploded into a passionate embrace as our arms drew our bodies closer and the gear shift lever jammed against my thigh. Our tongues touched, gently at first, and then with a thrusting zeal that suggested two souls, too long apart. My hands began to explore and ….

The phone rang.

I snapped upright in bed with my little soldier at attention beneath my boxers. Where was I? What was that ringing?

Gradually the night fog lifted. I stumbled from my bed and made my way to the kitchen intent on silencing the infernal bell.

"Hello dear," came Mother's cheery voice. "I hope I didn't disturb you but wanted to catch you before we left for church and…."

***

The rest of Sunday passed in a blur. After mom's call I wandered to Dunkin's and turned two cinnamon twists and a cup of coffee into a breakfast. Nurse Lentz, Maggie, Lutz and other random reflections keep pinballing about the recesses of my mind. But last nights dream seemed to land in the brightest spotlight.

I didn't normally recall my dreams. Last night was an exception. It was vivid. I'd been tempted to crawl back into bed to see if I could finish the scene but the lure of Dunkin's won out. My sister, Lou, found dreams full of meaning and would have had a field day with this one. But then she was into all sorts of ethereal stuff that made no sense to my engineering mind. No, a dream was a dream and nothing more. But still, why was she in the dream instead of Maggie or Penny or anyone else? It didn't make any sense.

Then, as I contemplated the second twist, Lutz bumped nurse Lentz from the spotlight in my mind. As much as I tried to repress him he had a way of slipping into the front row of my thoughts.

I shouldn't have let the Lutz dinner invitation bother me but it did. It wasn't the prospect of spending an evening with him that occupied my mind; it was the question of who to invite, if I invited anyone at all. The Lentz dream only added to the confusion.

Attending the dinner alone had a certain appeal. I'd only have to be concerned with my own conduct and not worry if my "date" fit into the party. But somehow it seemed going alone would brand me as a social loser and, besides, it would be nice to have a fourth at the dinner if Victoria turned out to be the prig Cory described.

The dilemma was not resolved at Dunkin's but persisted as the work week moved on.

By Tuesday morning I'd decided to invite someone but was still unsure who that someone should be. Maggie was first choice by a narrow margin but questions of social compatibility kept me from dialing her number. Nurse Lentz was a strong second both because I felt she would pass the social compatibility test and she was the only other reasonably attractive girl I'd met in town. The crazy dream even inspired me with the possibility I could score with her. I went so far as to look up her number in the base directory but, rather than call her, I saved it for later addition to my little black book at home.

It wasn't until that evening, as I stood at my stove stirring Rice-A-Roni into a pan of boiling water, that I resolved the matter. I would meet with Maggie, see what she thought of the idea and invite her if she had an interest. Nurse Lentz would be the backup. If all else failed I would go alone. That was an orderly solution I could live with.

I turned down the heat, put a lid on the pan and dialed Maggie. As usual she was out; I left a message with Val.

***

"Hey Lieutenant, there's a Maggie for you on line two," hailed Airman Lopez, across the crowded office.

It was Wednesday morning and everyone was at their desks when the call came in. Before I reached for the black phone on the corner of my desk, I considered telling Lopez to take a number. That would give me time to find a more private phone for the return call. Instead I picked up the receiver, sure the seven others in the quiet office had their antennas at full extension.

"Lt. Munson," I answered in an officious manner.

"Roger, it's Maggie. Val said you called."

"Yes, I did. I was wondering if we could get together this evening to go over some things."

"Are you OK? You sound sort of....oh is this a bad time? Are you in the middle of something?"

"That's correct," I answered, clicking my black U. S. Government ballpoint pen.

"Got it," she replied. "I'd love to see you but it needs to be early. I have a study group at 7:30. How about dinner?"

"That would work."

"OK, you can just answer yes or no. How does 6:00 o'clock work?"

"Fine."

"There's a little Mexican place, El Casa, just west of the campus. Do you do Mexican?"

"Absolutely. I'll see you then."

"Now I do feel like a spy, talking in code. And I'm very curious what 'things' the Lieutenant would like to 'go over,'" she said with a laugh. "OK, El Casa at six. See you then."

As I hung up Andy Gruber spun his chair toward me exhaling a circular trail of Viceroy smoke. "Let's hear it. Who's this Maggie?"

Across the aisle Sgt. Lawson turned to take in my reply, a cigar planted solidly between his smiling lips.

"Oh her, just a friend. We share an interest in photography."

"Come on stud. You don't expect us to believe that 'just a friend' crap," scoffed Gruber. "What's the real story?"

"I don't know, fellows; there may be no story," chimed in Sgt. Wade, from his desk in front of Lawson's. "The hoity toity way he was talking to her it sounded like she might be his stock broker. 'I'd like to go over a few things with you tonight' he says. Sounded pretty formal to me."

"Formal, my ass. That was for our benefit. He knew you bastards were listening to the call. Now who is she?" Gruber pressed.

"All right you guys. You're too tough for me. She's an exotic dancer at the Blue Moon Club downtown. She spotted me in the crowd, took me home and now she can't get enough of me. That's the truth and no, she doesn't have any sisters for you leering asses. Besides, you're all happily married if I'm not mistaken. Now, if you'll excuse me," I said, heading for the door, "I need to sketch out some new moves for this evening."

***

El Casa was a crowded little place with six booths on one side and five tables on the other. An order counter and kitchen closed off the rear area. Background noise was provided by an out-of-balance kitchen fan that struggled to drag the cigarette smoke from the seating area and expel it through some roof-mounted orifice. The glaring light from the fluorescent strips reflected off the worn plastic table tops and the yellowed expanse of nicotine stained walls. Ethnic atmosphere was provided by rich, spicy aromas, faded Mexican travel posters and bright sombreros painted on the plywood menu board hanging over the order counter.

My blue uniform seemed out of place in this student hangout so I slipped into a booth near the door and tried to appear inconspicuous. I didn't want to start another student riot.

I was early. Maggie was late. Dinner was quick and filling.

"Sorry I couldn't talk this morning. You correctly assumed that eight pairs of ears were tuned into our conversation. I finally got them off my case by telling them you were an exotic dancer. They're dying to meet you."

"Roger, you didn't."

I gave her my innocent smile. "Well, I don't know that much about you. Maybe that's what you do when you go to Denver."

"You're awful," she said, slapping my forearm and nearly spilling my iced tea. "Well, if I take up dancing, I won't tell you. I don't want to have a bunch of ill-mannered Air Force types leering at me. Now, tell me why we're having this meeting. You sounded so mysterious on the phone."

"You're going to be disappointed then. Here's the deal," I began, explaining the Lutz meeting and subsequent dinner invitation. "So if you'd be interested in coming it could be fun or it could be very boring."

"Don't be silly. It would be fun to meet this Lutz guy and besides, I've never seen you dressed up as a civilian. I'm not sure I'd recognize you."

"I'm glad you mentioned that, dressing up I mean. You see they have this dress code at the club and …."

"And you're afraid all Maggie has in her wardrobe are baggy shifts, beads and sandals. Am I right?" she asked, fixing me with a smirk and steady gaze.

"Well, not exactly it's just …"

She sensed my misery and seemed to relish it. "Lt. Munson, it may surprise you to know I've been to an officer's club before and know they are picky about attire. And yes, most of my wardrobe consists of baggy shifts and jeans but I do know how to dress up."

I tried to hide behind my tea glass, wishing I could change the subject, but she kept going.

"You remind me of my mother. She's sure all I have are 'commune clothes,' as she calls them, so from time to time she sends me something 'nice.' It's actually a wonderful way to get new things and she has great taste in clothes. Like, she gave me a nice conservative gray pant suit for Christmas. It's really quite nice though I haven't had occasion to wear it yet. To put your mind at ease I think I'll wear that to dinner. I'm sure you'll be impressed with the 'dress up' Maggie."

"I never doubted for a moment," I stammered.

"Oh yes you did," she laughed. "It was written all over your face. You're so funny. I look forward to an elegant dinner with you on Saturday. Now I need to run. And I promise I won't get a garish tattoo between now and then"

She eased from the booth, put on her coat, kissed me lightly on the forehead and was gone.

I was looking forward to meeting the "dress up" Maggie.

***

The rest of the week spun by and Saturday evening found me on Maggie's porch. "I'll tell her you're here," said Val, greeting me at the door.

I wandered into the living room while she called for Maggie from the foot of the stairs. The place looked different without the candles, the smoke and Leonard and his friends. It was an old house with old furniture and a musty charm that suggested grandparents, not students, made their home there.

The squeaky wooden stairs announced Maggie's entry. I turned and was awed by the sight that greeted me. Val stood with her hand on the balustrade, beaming as if showing off a work of art she'd created. Maggie, for her part, stood there looking incredible.

She was wearing a tailored gray pant suit, presumably the Christmas gift from her mother. The tunic reached to mid-thigh where trim cut pants took over the descent to her ankles, now concealed in black leather. The look made her appear even taller and trimmer than normal, in a very good way. A tasteful beaded necklace, which was all Maggie, matched a pair of dangly beaded earrings that swung carelessly when she moved her head. And her pinker than normal lips suggested she'd applied just a light touch of makeup, not part of her normal routine.

"Wow," was the best I could come up with, trying not to gawk.

"Cleans up good, doesn't she," quipped Val as she seemed to present Maggie to me at the bottom step.

"I, well I ...," was the best I could utter.

"Will you two take it easy? You're making me feel self-conscious. If you don't back off I swear I'll go back upstairs and put on my baggiest shift and then we'll see what your officer's club buddies have to say."

"You two have a nice evening. I'll just stay home alone

116

in this big house and catch up on my reading," said Val as she swept a heavy book off the coffee table and plopped into a well-worn easy chair.

"It seems so quiet here," I said in an effort to utter a complete sentence. "Where is the rest of your gang?"

"It is quiet and it's been wonderful today. Susan, Len and his rock-climbing buddies went to Boulder for the weekend so Val and I are basking in the serenity of the place," said Maggie, throwing a wool shawl over her shoulders. "Don't feel sorry for Val. She's loving it. Now let's go to that dinner."

Once in the car any discomfort I'd felt upon seeing dress-up Maggie descend the stairs vanished as the old Maggie chattered away beside me. I dropped her at the club entrance and then found a cramped parking space in the far corner of the crowded lot. Clearly seafood night was a popular event.

Maggie had checked her shawl and was studying a display of base sports trophies when I returned. "We'd better check in. It's after seven and George is very punctual."

The hostess studied us as we approached the dining room. "We're meeting the Lutz party," I said while scanning the room beyond.

"The Lutz party? Oh yes, it will be just a moment." The hostess looked us over carefully and made a note in her book before retreating toward the kitchen. She soon returned with the tuxedo-clad maitre'd close behind.

"Good evening sir and welcome to our club. Would you mind stepping to the side so we can discuss a small issue," he said as he steered us away from the hostess desk. "My name is Alex and I fear we may have a bit of a problem."

"We do?" I replied, annoyed that the hostess was now seating a party of four that arrived after us.

"Well you see sir, club rules require skirts or dresses for the ladies. No pants are allowed at any time. So I am not able to seat you and your ...ah, friend."

"You've got to be kidding. Her outfit is classier than ..."

Maggie touched my arm as if restraining me. "I know pants used to be a club 'no-no,' but I assumed the rules would have evolved to deal with fashion changes and dressy outfits like this," she said, applying a touch of feminine charm.

"It's a very nice-looking suit, ma'am, to be sure. But I'm afraid pants are pants no matter how fine the fabric."

"This is a very important dinner engagement," I blustered. "Where is the manager? Maybe he can …"

Maggie politely placed herself between me and the maitre'd. "Oh Roger, I'm sorry. It's been so long since I've been to an officer's club I didn't even think about this being an issue."

At that moment a young woman exited the rest room and pranced into the dining area wearing a mini-skirt not much longer than the black leather belt that was responsible for keeping it up. "What about that? That's permitted and this is not?" I exclaimed, gesturing toward the wiggling ass and then to Maggie's pants. "I've got handkerchiefs bigger than that skirt."

"I'm sorry sir, but those are the rules."

We slipped into a silent stalemate. Maggie had her arm wrapped in mine while I stared at a confident Alex and tried to think of my next move. The standoff continued until Maggie whispered "I'll just be a minute," released my arm and disappeared into the ladies room.

Alex excused himself leaving me to pace and seethe. Now what? Lutz was probably waiting in the dining room and we were already late. We could zip home so she could change clothes but that could take a half an hour and would start the evening off on a sour note, as if it hadn't already turned sour. Pacing the lobby I looked up and locked eyes with George Lutz, sitting four tables back in the bustling dining room. Shit! I was discovered. He waved and gestured for me to come over.

I took a final look at the motionless lady's room door and headed for George's table.

"Good evening Roger. I saw you out there and wondered what the holdup was."

I was just about to launch into an explanation when Maggie's voice intervened as she came up beside me. "Roger, you didn't even wait for me. Oh well, hi," she said thrusting her hand toward George's seated wife, "You must be Victoria. I'm Maggie, Maggie Meyers. And you must be the captain. I've heard so much about you. It's a pleasure to meet you at last. I'm sorry we're a bit late. It was all my fault; I had to make a few last minute adjustments."

Time seemed compressed by her arrival. Victoria nearly dropped a cigarette into her drink trying to shake hands with Maggie. George jolted the table leaping to his feet when she approached and reached to shake his hand. And I was simply awestruck both by the way she took over and the way she looked. The pants were gone. Her long tunic was now serving as a mini skirt that revealed her lovely legs and black leather knee high boots. The legs that looked long in the pants now seemed to go on forever.

"Not a problem, not a problem at all," said George as he helped Maggie with her chair. "Victoria and I are a drink up on you so you'll need to play catch-up."

We tried to catch them but never did. Victoria liked her martinis and was on her third before we ordered dinner. George was more restrained with his vodka tonics but still uncatchable. Maggie stuck with a house Chardonnay and I kept the Coors tap limber.

Victoria wasn't quite the shrew Cory suggested but could hardly be described as warm. She appeared very prim in a snug fitting navy blue dress with a neat row of white buttons marching to her throat to meet the tidy white collar that enclosed her neck. Like George she was short and solid; my mother would describe her as big boned.

Maggie seemed at ease with the surroundings and company. In keeping with her curious nature she kept the conversation moving with questions to George and Victoria which revealed where they met, how long they'd been married, their opinion of married officer housing on the base and a range of other topics. Maintaining the verbal initiative, she avoided politics and religion and, in true Maggie fashion, revealed little about herself.

When we first joined them at the table I was very conscious of the fact that Maggie was sitting there without her pants. But the evening progressed so well the pants incident slipped in importance, though I was reminded by her post-dinner trip to the ladies room that turned more than one head as she glided by.

It wasn't until the coffee was served and George was engaged lighting dessert cigarettes for Victoria and himself that he was able to fit a question into the flow. "So, what's it like on campus these days? Is everybody out protesting something or are some of the kids still studying?"

"Oh, I don't think you'd find things too much different from when you went to school," Maggie replied, watching the swirl of creamer melt into her steaming coffee. "Some study and some protest. I suspect the press kind of blows up the whole thing."

Victoria set her cigarette down and leaned in. "Well, we didn't have all this marching stuff when we were on campus. People were there to get an education or their daddies would cut off the tuition payments. Isn't that right George?"

"Damn right. You may not notice it Mag but I believe some of the student movements have grown more sinister in the last year or so. And their actions put our fighting men's lives in danger. You're naive if you don't see it."

I thought that remark was a bit over the top. Maggie's change of expression suggested either that she didn't like to be called "Mag" or felt the same way so I jumped in to steer the conversation in a new direction.

"So, what are your summer plans?"

Victoria took the bait and outlined their planned trip to Ohio to visit college friends. Vacation talk carried us through two cups of coffee and into the club foyer.

Alex, the maitre'd, visited us as we waited at the coat check room. "I trust everything was satisfactory," he said directing his attention primarily to Maggie.

"Fine, thank you," clipped Victoria as if annoyed at having to speak to a staff member.

"Salmon was delicious Alex. Please tell the chef how much we enjoyed it. And I hope we didn't cause too much of a disturbance when we arrived," said Maggie, reaching to shake his hand.

"Not at all, and I do hope you'll come again," answered an appreciative Alex.

Victoria glanced from one to another with a quizzical expression.

"Here you are sir," interrupted the coat check girl, handing me the wool shawl and a pair of gray pants.

So that's what Maggie did with them, I thought. What a smooth move. Simply remove your pants and check them like a coat—quite ingenious. I felt a little odd carrying her pants so I folded them over and tucked them under my arm in an unsuccessful effort to conceal them.

"Are those what I think they are?" mumbled George as we approached the two women.

"These? Oh yes," I replied.

George raised his eyebrows and tried to catch my eye as he helped Victoria with her coat. I avoided eye contact and laid the shawl over Maggie's shoulders while both of the ladies did the "I had a delightful time, we'll have to do it again sometime" platitude exchange. We bid farewell and went our separate ways.

***

"… so she takes off the pants, checks them and then appears at the table as if nothing happened," I recounted in response to Val's persistent questions about our evening at the club. "She's so smooth about it that Lutz had no idea there was ever an issue with the pants. I'm not sure what he thinks now. He saw me carrying them as we departed, but still has no idea how they made it to the coat room."

Val turned to Maggie who was standing with her back to the gas-fueled fireplace radiating next to Val's reading chair. "Sounds like you had an interesting evening."

"Interesting is the right word, but don't believe everything Roger tells you. He's embellishing the story a bit. Right now I just need to warm up my tush. Those vinyl seats in Roger's car were like sitting on a block of ice."

"It's no wonder; you have more thigh exposed than covered," said Val.

"And the officers at the club appreciated the design," I offered, earning a smiling glower from Maggie.

"Anyway, how was your evening?" asked Maggie. "Did you read all night?"

"Heavens no. I'd fry my eyes. No, I watched an old Hepburn flick on Saturday Night at the Movies and then tried to read. Actually I may have dozed off before you got here."

"You know what?" Maggie asked, stepping from the fire. "I'm going to put on some water for tea and then run up stairs and change. I'm still cold. Make yourself at home, Roger. I won't be a minute." Shoeless she glided to the kitchen on nylon covered feet leaving me with Val.

I loosened my tie, flopped onto the sofa and placed my feet on the well-worn coffee table listening to Maggie clattering pans and cups in the kitchen. Val locked me in a steely gaze as I settled in.

"How are you and Maggie doing?" she said finally.

"Doing?"

"I mean how serious are you about her?"

I was taken aback by the question. I hardly knew Val and the question came with an accusatory edge. There was no smile in her voice or manner. At that moment Maggie came out of the kitchen and took the stairs two at a time calling back, "I'll just be a minute." When it seemed she was out of earshot I responded.

"Maggie is a good friend. We have done some fun things together."

"Do you always sleep with your friends?"

"Excuse me?"

"I'm sorry," said Val, showing the first sign of softening her approach. "I shouldn't have said that."

"Well, what did you mean by it?"

"It's just that she's not some fast and easy girl; she's vulnerable right now. But you've only been in town for a month and she's already stayed at your place several times."

This was getting personal and I was beginning to get pissed. Val was acting like some sort of moral guardian. "I didn't know anyone was keeping score. What has she told you about those visits?"

"Nothing."

"Well, that's all I'm going to tell you. If you want the passionate details you can ask Maggie. But I will say you're not giving either of us much credit for good sense."

Val twisted the ends of her long hair and stared into the fire. The house was silent except for the hum of boiling water in the kitchen and the floor squeaks that traced Maggie's movements upstairs.

Like Val, I studied the fire while I poured over her

comments. "What do you mean 'vulnerable'?" I said, finally.

"Forget it. I've said too much and it's none of my business. It's just that ..."

"It's just what?"

"It's just that I don't want to see her hurt again." She took a deep breath and continued. "Did she tell you why she left Boulder?"

"She mentioned a change of majors, smaller school, that sort of thing," I said. "Was there more?"

Val nodded and paused again, as if she didn't intend to go on. As I prepared to probe further she continued. "She went with a guy, Brian Evans, for a couple of years. They were like tight, real tight. Then she finds he's doing both drugs and her roommate. I wasn't there but I understand it wasn't pretty. So now Brian and roommate are in Canada, so he can avoid the draft, and Maggie is here. That's the story and you didn't hear it from me. And that's why I don't want to see another guy dump on her, that's all."

"Who wants tea?" asked Maggie, as she bounded down the stairs in fluffy pink slippers, gray sweat pants and green hooded sweat shirt.

"I'll have one," I said smiling at the rapid transformation from foxy lady in mini skirt to frumpy lady in sweats. Even the frumpy lady looked good to me as she slipped into the kitchen.

"None for me," said Val. "I'm about ready to call it a night."

With Maggie busy in the kitchen I rose and took a seat on the hassock at Val's feet. "Listen, I think you're way out of line with your questions. I barely know you. Hell, I barely know Maggie. But we have a good time together and I don't intend to screw that up. So I'm going to assume your intentions are good. I have no intention of 'dumping' on anyone so you can rest easy."

Val stared at me as if gauging my sincerity by the look of my eyes.

"Well, here you are. I hope ...say, you two look like you're up to something," said Maggie, entering with two steaming mugs. "Who's telling secrets to whom?"

I jumped to my feet and retook my place on the sofa as Val placed a magazine on the coffee table to protect it from the hot mugs. "Val was telling me how she found this house to rent. It sounds she really had to maneuver to ace out the competition."

"Really?" said Maggie, with a suspicious twinge in her voice. "You'll have to share the story with me sometime. I've never heard it."

Val pushed herself upright and moved toward the stairs. "Well, it shows what a boring life I lead. I'm trying to entertain your company while you change and that's the best story I could come up with. I'm out of here. See you in the morning, Maggie. G'night Roger."

Maggie curled up on the other end of the sofa and pulled a blanket off of the back to cover her legs. We sat there watching the fire until she said, "OK, that was a good story. Now what were you really talking about? You looked very engaged."

"Nothing really."

She studied me without comment, as if confident I would break down and confess. She was right. I sipped my tea and nearly singed my lips in the process. That evoked a smile but no words.

I would have been smart to let the silence linger. I wasn't smart. "OK, I'll tell you only because you may be able to help me answer the question." I should have stopped there but didn't. "In a very motherly way, Val wanted to know my intentions."

"Your intentions?"

"With you. I mean, like what's up with us."

"With us?" she laughed. "You've got to be kidding. You mean she was afraid you're taking advantage of me or something?"

"I guess, something like that."

"That Val is such a dear, always looking out for others. Well, what did you tell her?"

"What should I have told her? I mean, am I ... am I taking advantage of you?"

A look of concern replaced the smile as she leaned forward and took my hand. "Roger, I'm very glad you like donuts and, no, you're not taking advantage of me."

For a moment she held my hand in a warm, almost electric way, before bolting upright as if recovering from a trance. Snapping back to the chatty Maggie role she said, "I'll have to talk to Val about questioning my friends when I'm not around. Now, tell me what you thought of little Victoria?"

With that question the tone grew lighter and we returned to our normal banter. I wasn't sure if I was disappointed with the change or not. On one hand the banter allowed us to avoid any serious conversation. On the other hand it kept us from asking any questions about the nature of our relationship which still had me confused. The "let's avoid entanglements" me thought that was just fine. The "I really enjoy being with Maggie" me wasn't so sure. It wasn't until I was about to leave that the atmosphere took a turn.

I'm not sure what happened. We put the mugs in the kitchen and walked toward the front door. Halfway across the living room I found we were holding hands. Yes, it's true, holding hands like high school sweethearts. When we reached the front door I turned and the next thing I recall is looking down at the most beautiful pair of eyes gazing at me from a radiant face. I kissed her or she kissed me or we kissed each other …it doesn't matter. But we fit in each other's arms and the warmth of the moment flowed from my lips to my soles. It wasn't a frantic kiss. It was a practiced, paced and passionate kiss. Did it last five seconds, ten, twenty or 120? I couldn't tell. It lasted long enough; it was far too short. And then it was over.

"Good night. I really did have a wonderful evening," she said, looking slightly up at me.

"Maybe we could do something tomorrow," I said, lamely. She squeezed my hand, let it go and pushed me gently out the door.

***

I was hoping to see "Sunny" in the Dunkin' lot when I walked up to buy coffee and a Sunday paper. I was destined to be disappointed. There was a crowd of cars in the sun-bathed lot but no yellow bug. So I returned to my empty apartment and began poring over the bulky Denver Post.

As I finished the comics the silence of the apartment was broken by the clattering phone. A glance at the clock convinced me it was my weekly "how are you doing, are you making any new friends, are you eating well" call from home. Mom had quickly fallen into the habit of calling before she left for church and could be fairly sure I would be home. She still had trouble determining whether I was an hour ahead or an hour behind Seattle time. I'd given up trying to explain that complex concept.

"Good morning, Mom," I said thinking myself very clever.

"Mom? You've got the wrong girl, sailor."

"Maggie?"

"Yes, it's just me. Disappointed?"

"Huh? No, not at all. It's just ..."

"I'd like to see you today. Interested?" she asked in a subdued voice.

"Sure. Absolutely, but are you OK? You sound a little ..."

"No, no, I'm fine. I need my morning coffee, that's all," she replied, with elevated enthusiasm. "I was thinking maybe a hike?"

We settled on an 11:00 o'clock pick-up for a short hike on the lower slopes near Pikes Peak. She would pack a lunch and I would furnish pop and water.

I finished the comics and sports section and then crawled into the shower to complete the wake-up job the cold air and coffee hadn't accomplished. The cool water jarred me as I reflected on last evening and the morning call. As for the call, there was something restrained about her tone. I couldn't quite get a handle on it. Maybe she was having her period. Penny was always an unpredictable shrew when her "granny" made its monthly visit. That could be the culprit.

Or maybe it was last night. I woke up thinking about last night and that wonderful goodbye lingered in my consciousness. I prided myself in being rational in my approach to girls. I planned my moves. I set up romantic situations to maximize success and minimize the risk of interruption. I wasn't into spontaneous. Last night had been spontaneous. Was I losing my touch, my control? If so, losing both at the same time was not good.

But she didn't complain last night. She seemed the willing participant. Oh well. Perhaps a Sunday hike would answer a few questions.

The shower reflections were far from my mind an hour later as we trudged up a steep portion of the trail at over 8000 feet of elevation. Maggie plowed ahead while my sea-level lungs struggled to extract oxygen from the thin air so I could match her pace.

While she'd been a bit down on the chattiness scale during the ride to the trailhead, hitting the trail seemed to energize her. With a camera slung around her neck and a small backpack for her gear she provided a running account of the plants and birds we encountered. The hills were beautiful in a Colorado winter sort of way. The bare and dry sunny slopes were showing the first hints of spring green life. The shady spots were still covered with a build-up of winter snow slowing the pace. As we climbed, the view of Colorado Springs and the distant prairie opened up below us. After a 90 minute march we arrived at a sunny ledge that would serve as our dining area for the luncheon feast she'd prepared.

"You've been here before, haven't you?" I asked, as I fished the lunch from the dark recesses of the pack.

She looked up with her face shaded by a well-used straw hat. "Once, last fall. Great view, isn't it?"

"Wonderful," I replied, finding a flat spot with a semblance of a backrest. I enjoyed simply watching her lay out our luncheon fare. It wasn't fancy: cheeses, crackers, apples and a large bag of M & M's for dessert. But she received high marks for presentation. She produced a small red tablecloth, a cutting board, paper plates and cloth napkins from her pack. When she was done with her magic, the simple foods were laid out between us in a fashion that would suit a picky gourmet. If I'd known her plan, I would have brought a bottle of wine. It would have fit the atmosphere better than the Coke and a canteen of water.

Preparations completed she plopped onto the rock ledge, sharing my granite backrest. Separated by the red tablecloth we sat silently listening to the sounds of scattered birds on the windless hillside while sipping our Cokes and sampling her cheeses.

Still staring into the distance she finally broke the silence. "Roger, we need to talk."

"Talk?"

"Yes, talk seriously. I'm confused."

"Confused?"

"About us. I'm confused about us."

This was not good. Her voice had an unfamiliar serious edge about it. I was never good at serious conversations with girls. Penny said I was never serious. Her common complaint was that I tried to make a joke about everything. Yet, somehow, a joke didn't seem right for Maggie.

"Oh ...," was the pathetic best response I could utter.

"Remember that Bergman-Bogart movie set in Morocco ...?"

"Casablanca?"

"Yes, that's it, 'Casablanca.' Well, there's that great scene at the end when Bogart walks off with the policeman and says 'this could be the start of a beautiful friendship.' Do you remember that?"

"Oh yes, I think the cop's name was Louie," I said, warming to the subject and hoping the movie talk would save me from a serious conversation.

She nodded, returning her gaze to the distant slope. "A week ago I thought that's what we had, a beautiful friendship. And that was good: good fun, good company, good conversation and no pressure to ... oh I don't know, boy-girl pressure."

Oh man, I thought, looking at a very serious Maggie. There might be no way to avoid a serious conversation if I was reading her signs correctly.

"At least that's what I thought until last night," she continued. "Now I'm not so sure about us. I feel our friendship might be turning into something else, something more. Something I'm not sure I'm ready for." She fixed me with a questioning gaze. "Am I making any sense?"

Absolutely. I'd had some of the same thoughts. Had we gone over some line last night? Was it possible to be great friends and not have the feelings I had when we kissed?

"I don't know," was my weak response. "Was there something wrong with last night?"

"God, no, Roger, everything was wonderful. The dinner, the evening, the us, the ... I don't know. It's just I'm confused about ... I'm confused about what it all means, means for you and me. Means for our beautiful friendship." In apparent frustration she began tearing a napkin into long, uneven strips.

"Oh," was my feeble reply.

"Oh?" she said leaping to her feet and spinning toward me. "Oh? My God what a fool I am," she continued with a forced laugh. "Here I am spilling out my feelings thinking you might be feeling the same way and all you can say is 'oh.' Doesn't our friendship, or whatever it is, mean anything to you?"

I felt helpless. Should I tell her how wonderful she tasted when we kissed at the door or how much I enjoyed just sitting by the fire with our tea? We could talk about how great she looked coming down the stairs in the gray suit. It was a wonderful, confusing evening. There was much to talk about. But I wasn't sure I wanted to go there. Then the dam burst and I began babbling on in a most unfamiliar fashion.

"Maggie, Maggie, Maggie. It's just that I have trouble talking about this sort of thing. But I think I feel the same way. We're good together. I really enjoy being with you and last night was incredible. I didn't plan anything like what happened when I left. It just happened and I'm not sorry it happened. Maybe I feel the same as you; I just don't want it to screw up what we had before."

Maggie studied me as if gauging my bullshit coefficient. "Can I believe this guy," her eyes seemed to be asking.

I gave her my best look of confusion, which was easy. I was confused. But we'd been together as friends. Now my feelings were going somewhere else. Persuaded she was not my type, I'd let my guard down. I'd convinced myself there would never be any serious feelings for a girl like her. But last night the beautiful truth came out. Wherever she fell on my feminine rating scale there was a delightful chemistry between us. I wanted to be with her, talk with her, hold her, feel her warmth. My heart wanted to move well beyond the "coffee and donut" stage to the "I want to spend every minute with you" stage. But, even in my babbling condition, I couldn't tell her all of that.

"I enjoy being with you too, doing things with you. But I find myself having feelings that I don't want to have for anyone right now. I'm not ready" she said, still standing down slope, some distance away.

"I hope they're good feelings."

"Oh, they're wonderful feelings. God, you must think I'm crazy, trying to avoid wonderful feelings. But they're feelings I'm not ready for. It's like I've spent months building this emotional wall that was protecting me very well until you came along. And then you sort of snuck under the radar and here I am, caring for you in a way that ..."

"So what do you want? Do you want me or us to back off a bit?"

"Roger, I don't know what I want. I want to be with you. I don't want to be with you too much. I want to talk to you. I don't want to talk to you too much. Besides, we are so different. You're so organized and I'm so scattered."

"In a good way."

"I'm serious."

I feared I'd laid another egg, trying to be light. She sat back down, pulling up her legs and wrapping her arms around them in an upright fetal position.

"What do you want?" I asked.

"Maybe we need to slow down, see less of each other, I mean. Take things slower, that sort of thing."

I stood and walked a short way down slope before responding. "Can I ask you something?"

"It's not you, if that's what you're wondering. I think you're a great guy. No, it's not you."

"Is it someone else? I mean have you had a bad time with some guy? Is that why you're so, I don't know, so cautious."

She winced, like pricked with a pin, and laid her head back on the stone backrest. "That's a fair question but I'd rather not answer it, not now anyway. Just know it's not you. You've been a breath of fresh air."

"OK then. Let's throttle back and see what happens," I offered, half relieved and half disappointed. She was offering me a way out of an entanglement I wasn't sure I wanted and I was torn by the prospect.

Silently she gathered the picnic leftovers, folding them into the table cloth which was slipped into my backpack. I stood nearby as if fearful of a close encounter. Dark clouds to the south suggested it was time to head off the mountain. As she turned toward me I thought I noticed tear streaks glistening on her cheeks.

"Are you OK?"

"Yes, yes I'm fine," she said as she buried her head in my chest.

I lifted her chin and kissed her, gently at first and then, in response to the moment, with the passion of lovers, possibly parting forever.

As suddenly as we'd kissed she regained control and pushed me away, wiping her eyes with her sleeve. "Damn you Roger. You're making this very hard for me. Very, very hard. But please stay in my life."

***

It was a long trip home. Maggie walked ahead of me most of the way down, saying little. Once we got into the car, the chatty Maggie returned, talking about everything but us. I let it go. If she wanted to avoid the "us" topic that was fine with me. I wasn't sure what to do with it.

It had been quite a weekend. It would be quite a week. We were going to throttle down. I didn't see much of her before. I wasn't sure what that would mean now. But for now I was feeling like the country singer who said something like, "here comes that lonely feeling again."

Chapter Ten

April 14, 69
Dear Son,

Missed you when we called yesterday. Were you doing something fun?

Busy Monday here. Cleaning lady comes at 11 so I had to pick up the house to get it ready. Pot luck for the mission guild at church tonight. I'm doing that chicken casserole you like so well. I'll make a little extra and leave it here for your father. No way I could drag him to this program.

I'm sure you're tired of me harping about your sister but I'm so worried about her. I just don't know how I failed her so.

We stopped in Eugene and took her out to dinner on the way back from Ashland. It was a short visit but it seems like every time I try to make a suggestion we end up arguing. And my gracious, you wouldn't believe how she lives. I don't think she (or her roommate!!) has picked up that room since the day they moved in. I can only imagine the germs that thrive in that mess.

Maybe you can get through to her. She always looks up to you.

Write again soon.
Love, Mom

***

Monday turned out to be a normal day, at least normal by Cheyenne Mountain standards. Parts were overdue for an important water pump. Airman Jefferson, from the electrical shop, was in jail on an assault charge, the result of a fight over a girl. A new man in the supply section claimed he was claustrophobic and couldn't work in a granite cave. A glitch in the power plant had shut down the sensitive Philco radar tracking computer in the middle of an exercise. Fortunately Kirkwood had been in the office to handle that angry general. So, all in all, it had been a pretty normal day.

The distraction of work had been a welcome relief from

thinking about Maggie. Sunday afternoon, after I returned from the hike, she lingered on my mind. She'd turned down a dinner invitation, claiming homework beckoned, so I dropped her at home at about four o'clock. If she wanted to try the 'less is more' approach for a while I could live with it. Maybe she was right. Neither of us really wanted to get into a serious relationship. A cooling-off period might save the friendship if we could successfully walk the friendship tightrope. Now reflecting back on what had been a long, boring Sunday evening, I wasn't too sure.

Maybe I needed to visit the officer's club and take another run at the nursing pool.

As I passed the exit turnstile, I was jarred back to reality by a hail from Airman Borkowski, seated on a stool behind the security console. "Hey Lieutenant, Captain Lutz would like to see you. He's in his office."

Lutz had been most cordial at the staff meeting. It was as if I'd passed some social test and could now be viewed as something more than a suspect. He called me Roger, rather than Lieutenant. He told me how much Victoria enjoyed meeting Maggie. He said we'd have to come to his place and sample Victoria's barbequed ribs sometime. Watching Cory's reaction to the conversation I could see that even he'd been surprised by the Lutz warmth.

When I walked into his office it appeared the love fest was to continue. He rose when I entered. His uniform jacket was off—a rarity—and his sleeves were rolled up. "Roger, come on in and sit down. Need a cup of coffee or anything?"

I'd learned not to accept afternoon coffee from any of the unauthorized coffee makers in the mountain complex. The only consistently drinkable coffee was in the mess hall. For fire reasons, private pots weren't even allowed in the mountain, a rule observed more in the breach than in fact. In any case, after perking all day, most of the contraband coffee was the consistency of diesel oil.

"No sir. I've had my daily ration," I said as I took a seat in front of his desk. "Say, I meant to ask you at Hahn's meeting; is there anything you can do to spring Airman Jefferson? I can't believe he's still in jail. He's my best man on motor controls."

"Jefferson? Sure, I'll have Larson make some calls tomorrow. Damn foolish to get into a fight, any fight. But I'll see what I can do."

"Bork said you wanted to see me."

"Oh yes, so I did," he said as if he'd forgotten the request. He hadn't. "I wanted to talk to you about Maggie, great girl, Maggie. Not like most of the girls you see on campus these days. Of course she may be a bit older than most coeds but, in any case, nice kid."

Calling her a "kid" struck me as a bit odd since she was only a year or two younger than me and not far from his age.

He picked up his black rock and massaged it between his thumb and forefinger. "How much do you know about her? I mean, where she's from, friends, that sort of thing."

As he spoke, he walked slowly to the door, closing it before returning to his desk.

"Not much really. She's lived a number of places from what I gather. Seems her father, or stepfather to be correct, was in some sort of government work that meant he moved around some. She started school in Boulder and moved here last summer. That's about it."

It was true. I didn't know much about Maggie. She had a disarming way of deflecting personal questions. It wasn't as if she was hiding something; it just didn't seem like she felt her background was as important as whatever question was on her mind at the moment. I knew about her real father, though there wasn't much to know. I knew nothing about the step dad. I was learning about her mother in bits and pieces. I knew they were cordial but not too close. But most of the childhood Maggie was still hidden behind a gossamer curtain which she kept closed, allowing only measured glimpses.

"How about friends?"

My visit was beginning to feel less like a conversation and more like an interrogation. "She's pretty new in town. She has roommates that are sort of friends. And I suppose she knows kids in class. Say, why all the interest in Maggie? It seems more than just casual. I mean, after all, we're just friends."

Now I wasn't even sure if that was true but that was not a subject to share with Lutz.

"Ever hear of a Leonard Hoffman?" he continued, ignoring my question.

"He lives in the same house."

"Have you met him?"

"He's a prick. What about him?

Lutz smiled at my description and then returned to his interrogator countenance. "What I'm about to tell you is for your ears only. It is not to be repeated, is that clear?"

"Like a government secret or something?" I replied, feeling as if we were about to move beyond the preliminaries.

"Precisely." He rose and walked slowly to the office TV, which had been silently displaying the evening news, and turned it off. He moved to the small window overlooking the parking lot as if assembling his thoughts. Finally he turned, sat on the window sill and began.

"Remember how I've said it's easier to catch a wasp before it leaves its nest? Well, I believe Maggie lives in a wasp nest and Leonard Hoffman is the head wasp. I believe he and his acid-head buddies are planning to pull something here at the mountain. Not try to destroy it or anything but use this complex to further their anti-war bullshit agenda and embarrass the U. S. of A. I don't know the details but I'm sure he's involved up to his unwashed armpits."

"George, you've got to be kidding. Hoffman is an idiot but I don't see him as the ringleader for some grand scheme. He doesn't even know how to wash a pair of socks."

"Trust me on this, Roger. My information is from good sources. But I'm lacking details. I need to fill in details."

"Now wait a minute. If you think Maggie is mixed up in this, you're way off base. She's a good ...."

He raised his hands to silence me and returned to his desk. "Calm down Roger. I'm not accusing Maggie of anything. She seems like a great gal. No, Hoffman's the ringleader. But her two other roommates," he paused and glanced at his file, "a Susan and a Valerie, could be a part of whatever it is. We're still putting the puzzle together."

Forgetting that he was a captain, and I a lowly lieutenant, I stood and leaned on the edge of his desk. "Now wait a minute. Did you invite me to dinner Saturday just so you could get a look at one of the suspected wasps? If you did, I think that's lousy. I thought it was just social. But if you used it to further some campus witch hunt then I think that's crap. Christ, George, next you'll be accusing me of being a spy or something."

My ranting didn't appear to faze him. He leaned forward placing us nose to nose. "Sit back down, Lieutenant. And don't forget who you are and where you are. This is serious shit. I don't play games or make accusations lightly. I'm not accusing you or Maggie of anything and I didn't invite her to dinner to 'check her out.' I didn't even make the connection until I was going over a list of people who have visited that house recently. I had no idea she lived there until today."

"How the hell do you know who's visiting the house?"

"Don't ask. Now sit back down."

"This whole thing stinks." I followed his order or suggestion or whatever it was and sat back down, avoiding his searing gaze by staring out the window at nothing. "OK, so why are you telling me all this."

"I want your help, Lieutenant."

"Help? I'm an engineer not a sleuth."

"You're fully qualified for this assignment. You're at the house occasionally, right? You get inside and see people besides Maggie."

I nodded.

He paused, picked up his black rock and clenched it in his left fist. "Right. Well all I want you to do is to keep your eyes open. Pick up anything you can that might help us figure out what Hoffman is up to. Ask Maggie. Don't tell her what you're doing but pick her brain and learn all you can about what goes on in that place."

"No, no, no. I'm more than willing to keep my antenna up when I'm there, which isn't very often, but I'll not use Maggie as an uninformed informer. That's not fair to her and it's not fair to us. I can hardly build an honest relationship with the girl by being dishonest with her, now can I? George, this is too much. I need some air."

I was back on my feet headed for the door when he said, "Lieutenant, you haven't been dismissed. Sit your ass back down." The charming Lutz had left the room. The Lutz that remained was all business. I turned and stood behind the chair. I liked looking down at him.

"I'm not asking for a favor. Consider this an assignment if you must. I'm not just dreaming this up. Here are the facts. You put the pieces together. Maggie lives with Leonard Hoffman."

I interrupted. "He rents a room in the house."

"Look at it anyway you wish. So she lives with Hoffman. Hoffman uses the house for both open and not-so-open meetings with his dirt bag buddies, some of which have clear connections to the anti-war movement.

"But let's go back to Maggie. Her Boulder boyfriend is a kid named Evans. He's a big guy in several radical campus organizations at CU. I've got a list and photos if you want to see them. The Feds turn up the heat and he bugs out for Canada. Maggie moves here, conveniently ends up in a house with Hoffman and then conveniently runs into you the day you arrive in town. Coincidence? Maybe, but a convenient one."

"Oh shit, George. Are you telling me Maggie ran into me in a snowstorm as part of some grand plot? Do you think she's a spy or something? Is she going to drug me next? You've been watching too many spy shows."

"Watch your tongue. Don't forget you're still a lieutenant and I'm still a captain. I can see you're a bit emotional. Sleep on it. Think about it, that's all. We can talk again tomorrow. But don't rule anything out. You could be a big help and I'm not asking you to do anything dishonest or seedy. Just listen, that's all."

I turned to face him before opening the door. "Captain, how do you know this isn't just a bunch of rumors? What makes you think there's some sinister plan out there?"

He studied me for a moment before responding. "Last weekend the largest gathering of anti-war types ever held in Colorado took place near the University of Colorado campus in Boulder. By the way, did you happen to run into Hoffman when you picked up Maggie last Saturday?"

"No he and Susan were in …were in Boulder."

He smiled. I left the office and wandered to my car.

***

It was a miracle I wasn't pulled over on the way home; I drove like a madman. My Maggie confusion combined with my new Lutz confusion created a tension brew that had me shifting gears and changing lanes with careless abandon. As my tires screamed on a downhill turn my mind flashed to the famous Steve McQueen chase in Bullitt. The only thing missing were the San Francisco hills. I finally careened into the apartment lot, startling Cory as he pulled groceries from his trunk.

He stopped and watched me maneuver into a parking spot before wandering my way.

"Well, if it isn't our own Mario Andretti? What, are you late for your favorite game show or something?"

I locked the car and walked with him toward the entry door. "Man, I had a shitty day."

"Really? The way you and George were chumming at the staff meeting I thought you were having a pretty good day," said Cory.

"Yes, well there's been a change in that department too. Do you have a minute? I'd like to get your advice on something, something official I think."

"My place or yours."

"Mine."

"OK. Let me drop off the groceries and I'll be up. If Jessie doesn't get what's in this bag I don't get any dinner."

I was working on a beer when Cory walked in without knocking.

"Well, what's on your mind? You look a little confused," he said, flopping onto the broken down sofa.

"Don't stand too close to me while I talk," I began. "Lutz said not to repeat this to anyone so lightening may strike me down at any moment. But I figure you have the same security clearance as me and I need to talk with someone, so here goes."

As I told Cory of my meeting with Lutz, I began to wonder if I'd read too much into his orders or suggestions or whatever they were. Somehow, the Lutz request to spy on Maggie and her room mates didn't seem so out of line when I described it in my own words. His motives seemed sound enough. He'd only asked me to listen and report, not burglarize the place looking for clues. Cory didn't see it that way.

"I can't believe it. It sounds like George is running a one man spy operation. It's ridiculous!"

"But maybe he's right; maybe Hoffman or his buddies are planning something. Shouldn't George be concerned?" I couldn't believe my own words. I was actually defending the actions that had pissed me off just hours before.

"Roger, his motives aren't at issue here. The question is, what's he responsible for in his current position? What's his assigned mission? He's responsible for Cheyenne Mountain security, period. That means, in simple terms, guarding the mountain. It doesn't mean snooping all over town."

"He would argue that he's stamping out the trouble at its source rather than waiting for it to come to him. So, in a way, he's working on mountain security."

Cory studied me for a moment and then rose, joining me at the kitchen table. "Did you ever play hockey?"

"No, but I've watched the local team."

"Good, then this might make sense. What's the goalie's job?"

"To guard the goal."

"Right. And all the other guys have their assignments as well. So how would it work if the goalie decided the other guys weren't doing a good job, left the goal and skated down ice to straighten things out?"

"It would leave the goal wide open." I could clearly see where this was going.

"Captain George Lutz is our goalie. His job is to guard our goal and our goal is Cheyenne Mountain. So, no matter how he feels about the rest of the team, he needs to focus on his mission. He can leave the spy stuff to the investigative branch, the local police or even the F.B.I. It's simply not his job. I don't know what he's up to, but it sounds like his little operation has wandered way too far from the mountain."

"So what are you going to do; tell the colonel? It would sure put me in a pickle with George since he told me not to tell anyone."

Cory doodled large swirls on a napkin with his black government pen while pondering his strategy. "Let me think

about it. There are no lives at risk here so it's not like I have to
jump in to save them. I'm not even sure I can tell the colonel. He
gets flustered too easily. There is no telling how he'd react or
what he'd do. Actually, at this point I'm not sure what George
has really done."

His ramblings were interrupted by the phone. "Tell Cory
if he doesn't like dry pork chops he'd better get his little self
down here pronto," said Jessie, on the other end of the line.

I turned to Cory. "It's Jessie. She wants me to take her
away from all this to a small Caribbean island. Says she's had it
with husbands who don't show up for dinner on time."

"I'm on my way," he replied with a laugh.

"Cory says if you run off with me you will have to take
all of your shoes. He doesn't want to store them if you're gone,"
I reported back to Jessie.

"Roger Munson, how you talk; you're awful. Do you
want to join us? I've got plenty."

"No, I'm good, but thanks. Cory's on his way."

Cory turned as he was leaving the apartment and offered
a final comment. "Don't worry about George. I'll think of
something. Whatever you do don't screw up your Maggie
relationship for some George conspiracy. See you in the
morning."

I wandered to the kitchen partially regretting that I'd
turned down Jessie's invitation. My dinner choices were limited.
I finally selected a Swanson's TV Dinner from the fridge—
turkey with mashed potatoes and mixed vegetables—and put it
in the oven to bake. Then I was back to the phone. I needed a
Maggie fix.

Val answered. Maggie was out. She would have her call.
***

It was after 11:00 when the phone rang. I was propped
up in bed working on my pile of unread Newsweeks. I slipped on
my terry cloth robe and scurried to the kitchen grabbing it on the
third ring.

"It's me. I hope it's not too late," came the sound of
Maggie's voice.

"Late. No, it's not too late. I was just catching up on my
reading." And waiting anxiously for your call, I could have

140

added but didn't.

"I wanted to call earlier but Len and a buddy were holding court here in the kitchen and I decided I didn't need an audience. Anyway, I was glad to see you called. What's up?"

Now I wanted to be cool. We were supposed to be amping down a bit so I didn't want to sound like I was reneging on our informal ill-defined agreement to try the friend thing again. "I just wanted to see if we could get together sometime soon—nothing big. I haven't forgotten yesterday's discussion." Now why did I add that postscript? Dumb, dumb, dumb.

"Oh Roger, you putz. Of course we can get together. What did you have in mind?"

"Maybe dinner or a movie or something."

"Dinner would be great. How about tomorrow?"

So we made a date for dinner at the El Casa again. And she didn't sound anything like a spy.

***

I was hoping to avoid Lutz the next morning. It was not to be.

"Lieutenant, would you step into my office for a minute?"

It was Lutz addressing me from his office door. He looked ethereal silhouetted by the morning sun streaming in the office window behind. Without a word I stepped from the security line and approached his office. He waved me in and closed the door before speaking again.

"Sorry about yesterday Roger," he said leaning against the door. "I fear I may not have been as convincing as I should have been, but I didn't want to burden you with too much information. Come here and sit down. There's something I want to show you."

The nice Lutz had returned.

While he fumbled in a secure file cabinet I spoke to his back. "Captain, I do have a question about yesterday's conversation."

"Shoot."

"Isn't this sort of thing—this spy thing—beyond the scope of your mission?"

Without answering he pulled a file from the cabinet and

turned, pushing the drawer closed with his back. "Roger, I'm not running a spy operation here. I am doing some surveillance that I feel is directly related to the security of this complex. I may be pushing the mission envelope a bit but what we're doing is important to this place." he concluded sweeping his hand toward the mountain. "Now why don't you take this file to the table over there and look through it. I think you'll find it of interest. I'm sorry but I can't let you take it from this office."

The simple manila folder was labeled "Leonard Arnold Hoffman." It was filled with notes, some typed and some handwritten. There were dates and times and descriptions of his movements to and from various places, most of them in the Colorado Springs area. Other people were mentioned as contacts or friends: Val, Susan, Doggie and a few others I recognized made the list. Maggie's name didn't jump out but I could have overlooked it. The center piece of the file was a ten-page, double-spaced report that seemed to be a grand summary of the life of Len.

Len, born and raised in Cleveland, was suspended from high school for drug use but regained admission and graduated with his class. He was a mediocre student but fair SAT scores and his parent's substantial donation to the college capital campaign gained him admission to Colorado College. He wasn't suspected of dealing in drugs but was reputed to be a good customer. He was heavily involved in two local anti-war groups and had been seen at events sponsored by an alphabet soup of organizations with names like SDS, SAW and NMW. In 1968 he'd been charged with vandalizing a Denver Army recruiting office but the charges were later dropped with no reason given. The report simply reinforced my original assessment of the guy.

There was way more information than I wanted to know about Len. But, as a courtesy, I shuffled through papers for a respectable time before closing the file and returning it to George, who was at his desk reading, chain smoking and working the black rock.

"What do you think?" he said, looking up as I sat across from him.

"He's a prick."

He smiled after sending a string of even smoke rings

coursing across the room. "That's not an official term for describing bad guys but I agree and I don't trust him. But about yesterday, I didn't mean to set you off so. I can see how what I asked might seem a little out of order ...."

"Don't worry about it. I'll get over it," I replied trying to maintain my glower.

"...but I still want to know what goes on in the house. I still want you to keep your antenna up, look around, pick Maggie's brain, that sort of thing."

"I can't spy on Maggie, George. No can do."

Without a word he picked up Leonard's file and returned it to the secure cabinet. Then he slammed the file drawer, spun the combination lock and turned to me with eyes on fire. The mood had shifted.

"Colorado Springs is a cushy assignment, Munson. Nice home, nice place to work, plenty of women and other diversions. But with a couple of phone calls I could see that your ass is either weaving baskets in 'Nam or shoveling snow in Greenland and you'll look back on my simple request and say to yourself 'what a dumb shit was I.'"

"You can't do that. That's bullshit."

"Oh bullshit is it?" he spat, coming toward me and leaning both fists on the desk. "Well if you think it's bullshit then you try to stiff me on this simple little assignment. Now I want some information. It's that simple. Help me out or pack your bags."

Fists clenched I stood and glared, thankful that an official air force desk separated us. "Will that be all, sir?"

"You're dismissed, Lieutenant."

I spun and reached for the door.

"Oh, one more thing. We did not have this conversation. If you decide to run to Mills or Hahn, I won't have any idea what you're talking about. Do I make myself clear?"

Our eyes locked for a moment and then I was gone.

The day was not starting out well.

Chapter Eleven

April 5
Rog,

I should be writing Sally but I'm in a pissy mood so think it's better to bitch to you and get it out of my system.

First, thanks for the letter. That NORAD place sounds great. Just the thought of being in a cool place, underground, is appealing. God, this heat and humidity is oppressive. One of my hootch mates did trade a Seabee some captured pistols for a small generator so we now have more reliable power to run a couple of fans which, I suspect, he stole. He is quite the business man! But we benefit.

The longer I'm here the more I wonder why we're in this fucking place. Thinking is not a good activity for a grunt. What's the purpose? We take a place and then leave. Since I've arrived we appear to have accomplished nothing and screwed up a lot of good kids. It's like sticking your finger in a glass of water. While it's there is makes a big impression but, when you remove it, you can't tell it was there. We go in, root around and tear the ground up for a few days or weeks but, in the end, we leave and the gooks and jungle take over. The next week we do it again. Different place, same result.

What's it all for? What did the troopers die for? Will it all come out in the history books; noble effort, good cause, saved SE Asia? I don't know. But, from a six foot elevation, things look like shit to me. I just want to go home. I want to see my family

I can't imagine what this place is doing to the young grunts. Some of them are barely out of high school. I hope all of us can bury what we've been through in the deep recesses of our minds or we're going to be mega screwed up when we get back to the world. For now I just plod on and avoid looking in a mirror. The heat and shitty food really take the weight off. I've lost 15 pounds and can actually see my ribs for the first time in ten years. Sally keeps asking for a photo of me "in my camp." No can do until I put some flesh back on my gaunt face.

There, the whining is over. Now I will try to think of you sitting with your view of Pikes Peak. It may put me in a better mood to write Sally. Ciao
Hunk

FIGMO Countdown 209

***

The morning Lutz encounter was the low point of the day. Nearly everything else looked good by comparison. Airman Jefferson was back on the job, sprung from jail by a call from Sgt. Larson. Captain Kirkwood was on duty saving me from an ass chewing by an angry colonel in the communication section who thought our power supply was too irregular for his sensitive computers. Lt. Gruber was on leave which lowered the office pollution index to tolerable levels and Sgt. Baker served tacos for lunch, one of his best offerings.

And I was having dinner with Maggie.

I still hadn't decided how to deal with the Lutz spy assignment. I wasn't sure if I should take his Greenland threats seriously but was not eager to test them. I wanted to get Cory's read on Lutz but feared how that might play out. I would make an accusation, Lutz would deny it, I would look like an ass and still end up in some hell hole assignment.

Now, as I drove home, Maggie became foremost in my mind, replacing Lutz. That was a pleasant change. I needed to swing by the apartment to change out of my uniform. Maggie said she wanted to have dinner with a "civilian." Speed was essential if I was to get to dinner on time. In the fading light I made the final turn into the lot and swung toward my spot almost running into a yellow VW pulled forward in the space. Maggie had pirated my spot!

By the time I'd found a vacant space, she was standing beside her car with a smile on her face and two large bags in her hand. It was the campus Maggie with a wool sweater, baggy knee-length shift, floppy red hat and leather sandals, a far cry from Saturday at the O Club but appealing none-the-less.

"What a coincidence," I said, helping her with one of the big paper bags. "I'm on my way to have dinner with a girl who looks just like you."

She gave me a courtesy smile. "Well, there was a slight change of plans. Hope you don't mind. Mexican's been changed to Chinese and restaurant's been changed to your place."

"I can deal with change. Anyway, this way I won't get to dinner late."

She took my arm and clung to me in a warm but carefree way as we walked to the entrance. "I apologize in advance for the mess," I said as I opened the apartment door. "I wasn't expecting company."

Maggie entered the kitchen and surveyed the carnage. Table and counters were clean enough but the sink was heaped with dishes as it was nearly time to load the dishwasher on my "sink to dishwasher" rotation. She put her hands on her hips and shook her head in mock disgust, much like Mother would.

"OK. I'll tell you what. I'll put dinner in the oven to warm and take a stab at the dishes while you change. You look too formal in that thing and besides, you smell like a cigar. Now get out and let me do my thing."

"It's a deal. See you in a flash. There's beer in the fridge if you feel the urge."

"Sorry, no beer tonight. It's Chinese night. I'll put on water for tea," she called after me as I disappeared into the bedroom.

She was right about my uniform. It did reek of cigar smoke. I'd taken to hanging my uniforms in the hall closet so they didn't stink up my other clothes and that move proved modestly effective. I slipped into a clean pair of jeans and a polo shirt with the logo of some resort my folks had visited for a convention. I ran across to the bathroom to rinse as much of the cigar taint from my skin and hair as possible and then returned to give the bedroom a once over.

While organizing my shoes under the foot of the bed I had a weird discussion with myself. At some level I knew I was straightening up the bedroom with the hope that I would be entertaining there later that night.

But my other self said, "What the hell are you doing? You've agreed to hold at the 'friend' level for a while and friends don't seduce friends. Besides, this is a special girl. Do you want to risk a long-term relationship on a one-night stand?"

"Yes, but she is so appealing and so loveable."

"Exactly," my other self responded. "She's all those things. And she's also intelligent and seems to like you. So why do you want to risk it by making a move that might scare her off? And if she did agree or succumb, what would you think of her then?"

"But …."

"But nothing. Behave yourself Lieutenant. Now get in there and enjoy the presence of this lovely girl."

I stood for a moment assessing the room and my conversation with self. I did straighten up the comforter but I left the magazine and dirty clothes piles where they were. As I returned to the kitchen I wasn't sure which self I'd given in to.

"I found a sink in there," she exclaimed, pointing to the shiny white depression that had so recently been a pile of pans and dishes. "And I think I've disinfected enough dishes for dinner. Are you ready to eat?"

Without any internal discussion, I found myself embracing her as she stood with her outstretched still dripping wet hands. When released she grabbed a towel from the refrigerator door and said, "I'll take that as a yes. Now sit down and get ready for a fabulous Chinese dinner."

She'd brought enough food for three meals and it was all good. We began with barbecued pork before moving to the beef with snow peas, sautéed chicken, some sort of vegetable thing and white rice. Maggie was deft with the chopstick but I struggled, as I had all my life, with the slippery little utensils. Finally, after providing her with considerable amusement, I reverted to my conventional silverware with greater success.

"This was a good idea," I said, pushing the last of the rice onto my fork with a knife. Finished I leaned back, tea cup in hand, to watch Maggie manipulate the awkward wooden sticks.

After a brief silence and mindful of the Lutz threat I asked, "So what's new at your place."

Her mouth full, she gave a non-committal shrug.

"What's my buddy Len do to keep out of trouble? I mean he's not going to school, is he?"

Taking a sip of tea she paused before responding. "How

did Leonard make it to our dinner conversation?"

Good question, I thought. Why did I ask such a dumb question? I'd resolved to ignore the Lutz request and yet here I was asking about what he would call his "prime suspect." "Gosh, I don't know. Isn't it funny how ideas pop into your head and you don't know why? Who cares about Len, anyway?"

She gave me a dubious look. "He does work, you know, at that record shop."

"And he has some weird friends. Now, is that Doggie guy a student or does he just hang like Len?"

Why don't you let it go, stupid? Quit asking dumb questions. Why are my mind and lips not able to operate in sync? Could it be the image of winters in Greenland driving my stupidity?

"Doggie? He creeps me out. I think he works but I avoid him." While she spoke she used a fork to push the remaining food into a pile that she could handle with the chopsticks.

"I still remember that first time I met Len at Dunkin's and he was trying to get you to commit to some meeting. He seemed disappointed that you wouldn't attend." Let the subject die, you clumsy oaf, I thought. Let the Leonard thing rest.

She shrugged but didn't pick up the bait. "How about a little music?"

"Music, you got it," I said, heading to the bookshelf-mounted stereo, thinking that her indifference to the topic was letting me off of the Leonard hook. I fumbled with the albums, finally deciding to simply restart the three records that were already on the turntable. As I fumbled, my mind tumbled.

What a clumsy spy I was. Why did I even bring Len up in the first place? We were having a wonderful dinner and I had to send the conversation into a black hole. Dumb, dumb, dumb. At least it was black for me. Perhaps she hadn't noticed. Resolved to shut down my spy operation I pressed the reject button and watched the first LP drop to the turntable.

"Stay in there" she said when I turned for the kitchen. "I'll join you in a minute."

I plopped down on the sofa where I could see Maggie. It was a treat watching her move about the kitchen, my kitchen. The loose-fitting shift gave the impression she was floating from place to place. In a few moves the table was clear, the leftovers stowed and she was headed my way with two steaming cups of tea.

"I hope you like John Denver. I'm not sure what's going to come up next. It could be anything from Barbra Streisand to Johnny Mathis," I said.

"I love John Denver. Some people say he's country and some say folk. I vote for his folk music side," she said, balancing a cup of tea as she sat on the other end of the sofa.

I reached back and grabbed the album cover. "I'd always thought 'Leaving on a Jet Plane' was a Peter, Paul and Mary song but it says here that he wrote it."

"Really? I think I like his version best."

We sat through two songs with me looking at Maggie and her looking at her tea cup. Finally she broke the silence.

"Roger, could we talk…talk about our Sunday conversation?"

I didn't really like how that conversation turned out and wasn't sure if renewing it was a wise choice. But I had a feeling the subject was unavoidable.

"Love to, what's up?" I responded, trying to look enthused.

"Well, I'd like to change or, err … propose an amendment to the agreement we made."

I squirmed a little, trying to get comfortable and wishing I had a beer in my hand.

"You may have noticed that, in many ways, I'm not the most organized person in the world. I've been described as will-of-the-wisp or something like that. And that's OK with me. Super-organized people annoy me. But, since I moved here, I've tried to be something else, particularly where guys are involved. I've tried to be measured and controlled. I've tried to keep emotions in check. Maybe I've tried to be something I'm not. In the past I've let my heart run wild and paid a price for that carelessness. I didn't want to do that again."

"Kiss some frogs?"

She gave me a pained smile. "Yes, I suppose you could say that. Well, anyway, last Sunday you heard the organized Maggie calling for help. You see, when I first met you, I thought

you'd be easy to handle, easy to keep as a friend. You were so …
so unlikable. I don't mean that in a bad way. It's just that you're
so different from me. You're so organized. You're an engineer.
You're in the military. It's like you seem perfect in so many
ways that we could never hit it off. I've always been more
comfortable with flawed guys, guys that are not quite
mainstream, if you know what I mean. Of course, I usually end
up in flawed relationships as a result but …"

I wasn't sure where this was going. Being described as
"unlikable" didn't portend well. I felt the need for something to
fondle and settled for a #2 yellow pencil from the coffee table. I
was soon chewing on the eraser end in a contemplative manner.

"You probably think I'm wacky but if I don't go on I'll
never get this out," she continued after a brief pause. "The
trouble is, I find myself attracted by all those traits I thought I'd
find repelling. You are organized, but in a good way. You are an
engineer but one with a personality and sense of humor. And
seeing how you live I know you're not perfect. You have real
loveable flaws."

"Maggie Meyers, you're a bundle of surprises," I offered
as she turned toward me and pulled her legs under her, Indian
style.

"I hope they're good surprises."

"Mostly, now tell me more about this amendment you're
proposing."

"My amendment, you silly goose, is to do away with any
agreement and just do what we feel like doing. All I ask for is
honesty. I want to know that you're a genuine article. That's all.
No games. No deception. I've been there and done that. No
more. I don't know where we're going but I want to enjoy our
time together and look back on it, whatever the outcome, with no
regrets."

I was delighted by what I was hearing and feeling very
badly about our dinner conversation. I'd tried to use our
relationship for the benefit of government security as defined by
Lutz. I wasn't sure she would consider that very honest of me.
But since her new honesty requirement hadn't been mentioned
until now perhaps it hadn't applied during dinner. I wasn't sure
how she would look at such a technical violation but I wasn't

going to ask.

"Well, what do you think?" she said, rocking forward and taking my hand. "I hope it doesn't sound like I'm being too weird or anything."

"You're just a bundle of surprises. Why don't you come here where we can discuss this more thoroughly?" As I pulled her hands she rocked forward, ending up across my lap, looking up inches from my lips. I crossed those inches without hesitation.

Some would call it "necking," others would say "petting" or "making out." I'd call it great. And it ended too soon. Our restraint meters seemed to be in sync and, as the temperature rose, we seemed to pull back in unison until she'd returned to her end of the sofa in her cross-legged pose, just holding my hand.

"I need to go. I'm still a student you know," she said with a coy look.

She grabbed her coat, floppy hat and macramé shoulder bag and we were soon walking to her waiting car, holding hands like freshmen.

"How about dinner tomorrow? I've got lots of leftovers. Do you like Chinese?"

"You're a crazy, dear boy, but no. I can't."

"This weekend then? We could do something maybe?"

"Maybe. Yes, that might be good. Good night. And thanks for renewing my faith in your gender."

After one more long and wonderful kiss she slipped into the car and lurched from the lot.

***

The rest of the week ground on at a glacial pace. Maggie and I traded a few phone calls but never connected.

To confuse things further, a surprise training exercise was launched at the mountain Wednesday evening. Under the watchful eye of observers from the Pentagon, key personnel were called back to the mountain to track and destroy a simulated enemy force. While the generals watched radar screens and moved game-like pieces across their wall-sized plotting boards the engineers went through back-up procedures and tested critical support systems.

For me it was both exciting and tiring. As junior officer

in the group, I was assigned the worst shifts and didn't get out of the mountain from Wednesday morning until the exercise ended at 0400 Saturday.

It seemed like I'd just crawled into my bed when I was hammered back to consciousness by the persistent ringing of the phone. I ignored it the first time, hoping the caller would get the hint. But, whoever it was redialed and the clatter began again. Giving in I staggered from the darkened bedroom into the bright light of day and pulled the receiver from the hook.

"Roger, it's me, Maggie."

"Well, good morning, or is it afternoon?" I asked squinting at the clock on the stove.

"Morning, a little after 9:00. Can we talk? Can we get together and talk?"

My mind wasn't in complete focus but, even in my bleary state, I couldn't miss the tension in her voice. It was urgent and edgy and it wasn't like Maggie.

"Sure, love to. My place or yours?"

There was a pause before she responded. "Ah, neither. Do you know the Holly Sugar Building?"

"The tall white one downtown?"

"That's it. It sits on a big plaza with a fountain in the middle. We could meet at the fountain."

"Shall I pick you up?"

"No, no, I can walk. I prefer to walk. I'll leave in ten minutes and see you when you get there."

"Maggie, is something wrong? I mean you don't sound like …"

"No, I'm fine, really. I'll see you there," she said, hanging up without a "goodbye."

I stood for a moment staring at the silent phone. There was something odd about the call but I would have to go to the Holly Sugar Plaza to find out what. I cradled the receiver and opened the refrigerator hoping to find a quick pick-me-up. Apple juice was the best I could do. The cold shock helped but a cold shower would clearly be required.

In a muddle I managed a quick shower, grabbed the nearest clothes from a pile on the floor and was soon weaving down East Platte with the Holly Sugar Building silhouetted against the towering Pikes Peak. Saturday morning quiet lingered and I found a parking space on the street near the sprawling plaza.

There was a spring warmth in the air, magnified by the reflection of the sun off of the light-colored stones. I spotted a fountain-like structure looming at the rear of the plaza and what appeared to be a person sitting on the surrounding ledge. As I approached, the sculpture took the form of a woman pouring water from a jar into the pool below and the person took the form of Maggie sitting as still as a marble statue.

She spotted me as I approached but made no sign of welcome—no wave, no gesture. Instead she stared at or through me in a trance like manner. I sat on the narrow ledge beside her, close but not touching. "Good morning," I offered.

As if repelled she scooted a few inches away and turned, fixing me with a soulless gaze. "Are you spying on me?"

Shocked by the question I scooted even further away, turned and swung a foot over the low wall, facing her. "Am I what?"

"Len says you are. He says you're spying on me and on him and on all of his friends. He says you're just using me."

Her voice was both firm and quivering while her tear-filled eyes fixed on mine, as if reading my soul. Why the hell would she ask a question like that? What could possibly give her that idea? It made no sense.

"Since when has Leonard become an expert on anything? The guy's a ..."

"Well, what's the answer?"

"No. Of course not. Maggie, what do you think I am? I mean really ..."

"So you can sit here and look me in the eye, in all honesty, and tell me you're not snooping around for your Captain Lutz or anyone else?"

I locked onto her eyes but didn't answer. We just sat staring.

Finally a hint of warmth melted the steely gaze. "Roger, I want to believe you. I want Len to be wrong. But you have to give me something. I hear your answer but I don't feel; I don't feel I'm hearing all I need to hear. I don't know why; it's just a feeling."

I swung my leg back to the plaza, stood and walked to a nearby bench studying a collection of flags that hung limp from their aluminum poles. What could I say? I didn't want to destroy our bond of trust. I didn't want to breach mountain security. I didn't want to have this conversation.

Turning back I said, "I can't talk about it. I don't want to talk about it."

The warmth melted from her eyes. "Then Len is right. There is an 'it.'"

I was distracted by two small boys wheeling their bicycles across the plaza closely followed by their parents walking hand-in-hand. When I turned back to the fountain Maggie was gone, making her way toward the street at an angry pace. I caught up with her at the top of the stairs and jumped forward to block her path. She tried to step around.

"Please get out of my way."

"But Maggie, we need to talk. It's not what you think. It's really not."

She stepped back and stopped. "Well, what is it then? Are you spying on me? A yes or no will do."

"I'm not supposed to talk about it."

"Well, call me when you can," she retorted and tried to escape.

"No wait," I said, gripping her arm to slow her flight. "You've got to promise me you won't tell anyone. Can you do that? Particularly you can't tell Leonard anything."

She pulled her arm free and stared at me as if weighing my words. "Talk," she said finally.

"Can we go back to the fountain?"

"This will do," she replied, sitting on the top step and leaning against a concrete planter as if getting as far from me as space allowed.

I joined her on the step and sat staring at my hands while I tried to put my thoughts in some order. I could sense her steely gaze but I avoided turning her direction. "You've got to believe me; it has nothing to do with you. It's Len. Lutz isn't sure what he's up to but he apparently hangs around with some pretty radical types and, well, he suspects Len and his buddies are planning something."

I paused hoping for a response but was met with more silence.

"So somehow he found out Len is your housemate and he asked me to keep my ears open, that's all. I think he just wants to insure Len doesn't do anything stupid. I mean some of these radicals have even threatened to blow up government buildings. It's serious shit…"

"So you think Leonard Hoffman is going to blow up a building?"

"No, no, it's not that at all. We, or Lutz, doesn't know what he's up to. That's why he wanted to get more info on the guy. That's all. But I couldn't do it. And I told Lutz I couldn't do it; it wouldn't be fair to you. He's pissed and I'm likely on his shit list. That's it, end of story. I'm not a spy."

As I turned to face her she rose and walked down two steps before turning to face me.

"That's it? Lutz asks you, you say no and that's the end of the story?"

"Pretty much…"

"Roger, how could you? How could you look me in the eye and say 'that's it.' What about those questions you were asking at dinner the other night? What about the people that are watching our house? What about the people that are following Len and, no doubt, me? You expect me to believe that you, the good soldier, would turn down an order from Lutz? I'm not stupid you know."

"I don't know anything about people watching your house. That's crazy. What do you want from me? I've told you the truth. You've got to trust me."

"You're a bad liar. And it's too bad because against my better judgment I was beginning to care for you, care for you very much." She began to walk away, paused and turned back. "You know, Len is a disgusting person but at least I feel I can trust him. And that means something. Goodbye, and please don't call."

"Maggie," I called as I rose in pursuit. But her walk turned to a run; she crossed the street against the signal and disappeared. I thought of running after her but my legs seemed frozen as I stood on the sidewalk, replaying the mental tape of our conversation. Nothing about it made sense. Nothing.

***

I knocked on the front door and rang the bell. There had to be someone in the house, I could hear music.

Leonard finally appeared at the door, greeting me with a knowing smirk. I should have wiped it off his face.

I pushed past him and nearly ran into Susan, who was coming down the stairs. "Where's Maggie?"

"Hey asshole, who do you think you are barging in here? Get the hell out," growled Len, coming up from behind.

He grabbed my elbow which really pissed me off. I rammed the elbow back, catching him square in the chest and knocking his stinking body backwards, over the back of the sofa and onto the floor against the coffee table.

I turned to meet his next move as Susan placed herself between me and the sofa. "Roger, stop it. Don't be such a shit."

Luke, my Ringo man, appeared in the kitchen door, attracted by the commotion. He moved toward the action, stopping in response to a gesture from Susan. God, he looked like he could take me apart.

"Where's Maggie?" I pressed as Len rubbed his chest and glared at me from his knees.

"She's gone."

"What do you mean 'gone'?"

"I mean she flew in here, grabbed some stuff in her room, stormed out the back and drove off," snapped Susan looking from me to Len and back again in an effort to keep between us. "Now get the hell out of here. We don't need any trouble."

Bolstered by his cohorts presence, Len's bravado returned. "Looks like the stud can't handle our Maggie. Is she too much for you?"

Susan was right. None of us needed any trouble. I glared at a sneering Len, considered my options and then walked to the door without another word. My John Wayne instincts wanted to kick his ass but my better judgment walked me to my car. I sat for a moment, with the engine throbbing beneath the sun-baked hood, before ramming the gear shift into first, popping the clutch and, tires screaming, lunging down the narrow street. I needed some air and space. I needed to get away from that place.

***

I'd done a stupid thing. With little more than a candy bar and half a canteen of water I'd returned to the mountains and retraced the hike Maggie and I had completed last Sunday. It wasn't that it was an arduous hike. It's just that I prided myself in always being prepared in the back country and I would have been screwed if the weather had turned. But it favored me and I savored the chance to be alone and try to get my head back on straight.

Now, as I drove into the apartment lot, I was lusting for the leftover Chinese food that no doubt was stinking up my refrigerator in its little cardboard boxes. I stormed into the building lobby and nearly ran into Jessie, coming down the apartment stairs to check her mailbox.

"Hey, don't you look like a mountain man today."

She was probably right. In my morning haste I'd skipped my shave and now, with my dusty jeans and wind-tangled hair, I must have looked a bit rough. "Yeah, I was checking my trap line. How're you doing?"

"I'm feeling a little lumpy," she replied, patting her protruding tummy. "The baby's been kicking up a storm. What are you up to tonight? Big date with little Maggie?"

"I'm afraid the Maggie star has burned itself out. She's decided I'm a rogue." I continued, giving Jessie a condensed version of my day, skipping anything that might be viewed as sensitive by Lutz or the U. S. Air Force.

"Well, I want to hear more. Why don't you join me for dinner? Soup's on and I could use the company. Cory's playing chaperone for the youth group at church. I'm not sure when he'll get home."

That sounded like a good choice so, after collecting the best of the Chinese leftovers as a menu contribution, I joined Jessie for a "tell-all" dinner at her place.

"Sounds like you have a problem with little Miss Maggie," she concluded as she gathered the last of the dirty dishes from the table. During our dinner of leftovers I'd given her a more detailed version of my past week's romantic saga.

Jessie was a good listener. She seemed to absorb everything, ask the right questions and be genuinely interested in my dating foibles.

"So how do you feel about this girl? I had the impression, from you or Cory, that she was just a friend. Is, or was she, something more? Frankly you seem a bit smitten by her."

"Just between you and me?"

"Top secret," she replied as she rejoined me at the table.

"Call it smitten, call it anything you like but I was really enjoying her. I can't recall feeling that way about anyone before. We had a great time together. Now she thinks I'm CIA or something. It really sucks, if you'll pardon the expression."

She had a determined glint in her eye as she studied me over a cup of tea. I could almost hear the wheels turning in her feminine mind. The room was silent except for the sounds of Barbra Streisand who was assuring us that people who need people are the luckiest people in the world.

"Do you love Maggie?"

I was taken aback by the questions. Clearly she was not one to mince words. "Cripe, you go for gut, don't you? I've never thought of it in those terms. I enjoy her. I miss her. I think about her all the time. But do I love her? Jeeze ..."

"Hmmm. You've got all the symptoms. Yes, Roger Munson, you've got all the symptoms. Well, this calls for a little of my famous Jessie magic. Leave it to me."

" Leave it to you for what?"

"Trust me, just trust me."

As I watched TV later that night those final words kept tumbling over in my mind.

Chapter Twelve

Tuesday
Brother dear,

Had a close call last week. Folks were on campus and, when I saw the car, I thought I was screwed. I was sure they were coming to move me home. But nothing was said about my TV cameo at the recruiting station. (Whew!) I guess what's news in Eugene isn't necessarily news in Seattle. Turns out they were just passing through.

She said they just stopped to say "hi" but it kind of felt like an inspection. I'm sure she'll tell you about my "living conditions," as she puts it. I'm not tidy enough for her taste. Gail (my roomy) and I are happy with our setup and our room is spotless compared to some others I could show her. Oh well....

Did get a good meal out of it, at least, and it was fun to see dad. They took Gail and me out to Jake's Seafood Buffett; not the best place in town but a welcome break from dorm food.

By the way, I think you'd like Gail. She may be a bit granola but she's only three years younger than you, loads of fun, smart as a whip and likes to ski. If you come out maybe I'll play cupid! It's time you gave up on the social climbing sorority types. They are too hard to maintain!

Take care, thanks for the advice and your efforts on my behalf with mom.
Love ya,
Sis

***

I'd hoped my new morning exercise regimen would be a good distraction from my morose Maggie memories. It wasn't. It only gave me more time to think. But morning runs over the weekend had given me an excuse to get up and, except for my aching quads and calves, I was feeling pretty good. Today, Monday, I was determined to run my entire three-mile course through the neighborhood, no walking.

It had been nine days since the Maggie blow off; nine long and miserable days. My calls had gone unanswered, assuming she'd even received the messages. And hopeful trips to Dunkin's had been fruitless. My Maggie relationship was no more.

I turned onto Hudson Street, startling the local milkman as he stepped from his truck with an early morning delivery. I gave him a silent wave and continued east into the glare of the rising sun.

Like a good engineer I'd tried to approach Maggie's departure in an analytical way. The approach had worked for me in the past. Tuesday evening, following a solitary dinner in the mess hall, I'd even sketched a simple table that outlined my social choices in her absence. I had listed my options across the top and positive or negative factors down the side. As options I listed, in no particular order, Maggie, Nurse Lentz, Unknown New Girl and Sport/Hobby. I found it a useful way to organize my thoughts on such a weighty matter. All the female alternatives had their downsides; with women involved there were simply too many variables I couldn't seem to control. The "Sport/Hobby" option actually held the most promise in a lonely sort of way. It involved no one but me, making it by far the most uncomplicated.

I glanced at my stopwatch as I passed the half-way point; good, I was ahead of my best pace.

My thinking had gone like this. If I started running, joined a baseball team or got serious about skiing and hiking, I would fill my spare time, be less lonely and could escape Colorado Springs at the end of my tour without any serious romantic entanglements. That, after all, had been my goal when I first arrived in town. Even under this alternative I could still date on occasion but my focus would be on sport and fitness. I wouldn't have to deal with "that time of the month" emotions and all of the other ups and downs of even a casual relationship. At the end of my tour I could return to Seattle, find a country club spouse and settle into a productive engineering career. It made absolute sense to me in a methodical sort of way.

I reached the corner and turned south startling a giant German Shepherd that, thankfully, was tied up in a dusty front yard. Its excited bark scared the hell out of me and likely woke the entire neighborhood. Overcoming my surprise I slogged along, hoping to clear the area before anyone looked out. Maybe I'd carry a dog treat with me tomorrow.

So far my sport/hobby option was showing promise. In addition to the morning runs I'd purchased a book, "Hiking Colorado's Front Range," and was investigating a local mountaineering club. Organized sports could come later.

Work, on the other hand, had lost what little luster it had previously displayed. Bureaucratic mumbo jumbo that was a novelty before was an annoyance now. My tolerance for sloppy performance had been replaced with a by-the-book approach to business that surprised me as much as those that shared the office. I was confident my popularity rating, if I'd had one, would be in the low single digits. In short, my personal troubles had turned me into a blue-suited bastard and I seemed unable to reverse the slide. Perhaps it was a temporary condition. I hoped so, for my Air Force tour had three years and nine months to run.

I'd successfully avoided being cornered by Lutz, though he'd been cordial enough at the staff meeting. I had taken to working late and eating dinner in the dining hall. That allowed me to visit the night shift in the power plant, to just sit around and bullshit with them. I thought of it as a morale builder for the men but, in fact, it was more of a morale builder for me and kept me away from an empty apartment a few hours longer.

I made the last turn toward home, checked my stopwatch and slipped into my cool down walk for the last quarter mile. It was time to start another week at the mountain, another week without Maggie in my life.

Damn, there she was again. When was I going to get her out of my mind?

***

"OK George, what all do you have on your agenda?" asked Col. Hahn gazing at Lutz over his reading glasses.

To this point the Monday staff meeting had been routine. As George cleared his throat and shuffled through his papers, I had a feeling that was about to change.

"Actually sir, I'd like to skip the normal reports—you have copies—and place a new security initiative on the table for discussion."

"OK, but make it snappy." Hahn fidgeted, casting a glance at the wall clock. "I've got a…an appointment coming up. So what's this initiative?"

Lutz pushed back from the table and walked to the blackboard, picking up a stubby piece of chalk from the tray. After scrawling "Security Upgrade" across the top of the board he turned to his audience.

"As you know I've been concerned with the level of our security here at the mountain, particularly with all the…the anti-war activity that is fomenting around these days. So I, or we, have come up with a three-part initiative that will result in a significant security upgrade at minimal expense."

Hahn glanced at the clock again.

Lutz turned, wrote and underlined: 1. Gate Relocation.

"I propose we establish a new check point below the final hill up to the entrance and restrict all non-essential traffic from the upper lot and parking area." Walking to an old aerial photo on the side wall, he pointed to a wide spot on the access road before its final climb to the parking lot. "A security gate here keeps the bad guys away from our entry and gives us a warning if anyone tries to breach our perimeter. I've even found an old gatehouse out at the airfield that we can have for the hauling. Needs paint and I'd need the engineers to move it but I think it would work."

There was some shuffling and head-nodding around the table but no one spoke.

He returned to the board, picked up his chalk stub again and wrote: 2. Perimeter Enhancement.

"In addition to the gatehouse for traffic control, I need more perimeter security. So I want to install a new fence both directions from the new gatehouse to the ridge on the south and the gully on the north." Using a pencil as a pointer he traced his proposed new fence on the aerial photo.

"We've no money for a fence like that," said Kirkwood. "And have you ever tried to install a fence on a rock slope. I don't even have the equipment for that sort of thing."

Lutz held up his hand to silence Kirkwood while shaking his head in agreement.

"10-4 on that. I read you loud and clear. That's why I've convinced my Army buddies down the hill at Fort Carson to help out. They have enough concertina wire down there to wrap the globe. That stuff is nasty, doesn't need posts, can be installed quickly and they've agreed to do it as a training exercise."

Without a word Kirkwood studied the wall photo, nodding his head approvingly.

"I don't know about that, George," offered Colonel Hahn, leaning back with his arms behind his head. "Having a bunch of grunts running around here makes it look like we can't do our job. You know how the Army likes to point out they're the 'senior service' and all that rot."

"I thought that might be an issue with you sir. But the major I'm dealing with assures me he can do the work in four days, tops. And, after all sir, the Army is on our side."

"Don't get smart with me George. It's just that … Oh what the hell. So, is that your plan, a new gatehouse and a new fence?"

"Just one more thing, sir."

Lutz returned to the board and wrote: 3. Supplemental Personnel.

He sat the chalk in the tray and stood behind his chair, gazing down the length of the table at the colonel.

We seemed to be seeing the "nice" side of George Lutz and he was, in my opinion, putting on an impressive show.

"Now, you are all aware that I've been concerned about my staffing levels for some time. Adding this gatehouse and more perimeter will increase the challenge. So I have developed an augmentation plan I believe will reduce the risks to this complex with minimal full-time staffing increases.

"I propose we develop what I call a Special Action Response Team or SAR Team. The 40-man team will act like a reserve force that can be called out for security emergencies. My troops will train them and we will supply any needed equipment, weapons, that sort of thing."

"More Army guys?" asked Hahn.

"No sir, engineers. I would ask for volunteers from the ranks of our engineering force."

I could almost feel the air being sucked from the room.

Gruber exhaled his customary plume of cigarette smoke engulfing Baker, who was sitting across the table. Baker smirked. Cory looked at Hahn as if gauging his response. Hahn let his reading glasses drop from his nose to dangle from the chain around his neck.

Kirkwood slammed his fists on the table. "Too much. George. Too God-dammed much. Like my guys are sitting around with their thumbs up their butts?"

Lutz stepped away from the table with a look of surprise.

Kirkwood turned to the colonel and continued. "Sir, this is bullshit. I've got a mountain to operate and I can't do that if my men are all joining some posse and running around the hills playing cowboy."

"Oh take it easy, Bob. George said it was an idea. No one's taking your troops and making them into policemen. I trust your guys with tools but I'm not sure I'd feel the same way if they were packing M-16s." Turning to Lutz he continued. "I don't see any trouble with items one and two if you can pull them off on the cheap but three is a non-starter. You'll have to come up with a better idea on staffing. But if you can deal with that, I don't see any harm that can come from the new gatehouse idea."

Kirkwood looked relieved.

Lutz looked exasperated. "But sir, the plan is like a three-legged stool. You've just removed one of the legs. I don't see how ...."

Colonel Hahn stood and gathered his papers. "It's your stool. If you need a third leg it's up to you to find it as long as it doesn't involve the engineers. Bob is right. They have a full dance card and don't need any extracurricular activities. Now, if you'll excuse me, gentlemen."

Lutz glared after him.

If looks could have killed, the colonel would not have made it from the room.

***

The staff meeting proved to be Monday's high point. The balance of the day devolved into a morass of meaningless reports and paperwork that left me with a need to take a break and get out of the mountain. Rather than stay for dinner I joined

164

the 5:00 flow bouncing down the tunnel on the chugging little bus which deposited us on the pavement outside the security building. My mindless passage through the turnstiles was interrupted by the sound of a familiar voice.

"Roger, got a minute?"

I turned to see Lutz standing in the doorway to his admin office dressed in full uniform with his coat neatly buttoned up. I marveled at how the guy could look so put together at the end of a long day. Without responding I changed course and followed him through the now-empty outer office into his inner sanctum. He closed the door behind me and gestured to a chair opposite his desk. I dropped my briefcase beside the chair, took a seat and loosened the buttons on my uniform jacket, trying to appear more relaxed than I was.

He took his place behind the desk, folded his hands on his desk blotter and fixed me with his gaze. "Roger, I'm sorry you don't approve of my methods but I had hoped that...."

"Forget it, Captain. It's not my job to approve your methods. I just don't want to be a part of them, that's all," I interrupted.

"I understand and I'm not asking you to do anything that, well, that you're not comfortable with. It's just that my sense is that something is coming down real soon and I need all the help I can get. So, a simple question, have you seen or heard anything of this Leonard Hoffman that would be useful for me? You're in there and see those people. What's he up to? Who else is he seeing?"

"Look George, I'm an engineer. I'm a good engineer. I'm not a spy or intelligence operative or whatever you call them. I agree, Hoffman's a scum bag. But we're not on speaking terms so I have nothing to tell you. Now if you'll excuse me?" I reached for my briefcase and started to rise.

"Hold on a minute. Don't forget your rank. You've not been dismissed." He reached for a file under a stack of papers on the edge of his desk. He opened it and turned over the top two pages before pausing on the third. "Do you recall me mentioning Maggie's Boulder boyfriend—or perhaps ex-boyfriend—a guy named Brian Evans?"

"Vaguely," I replied, nodding.

"Bear with me on this. Here's a summary. Evans was involved in or a leader of several anti-war groups on the Boulder campus of the U of C. His actions were noted by the F.B.I. He got a draft notice and then disappeared, may be in Canada or just may have gone underground. Any of this sound familiar?"

I shook my head again. "Nope. Are you finished?"

"According to my sources Evans and your Maggie Meyers dated or were together or whatever for over a year."

He paused for effect. The silence was broken only by the sound of the bus pulling away for another load of uniformed bodies.

"I know Maggie Meyers. I don't know this Evans guy. Are you finished?"

He let out a sigh, placed his elbows on the desk and chin on his fists as he contemplated his response. After a pregnant moment he fixed me in his gaze and began. "I didn't want to have this conversation but you leave me no choice. Connect the dots. Brian Evans is a creep. Meyers is with him for nearly a year. He disappears and she moves to the Springs with this Hoffman guy. He's a creep. She lives in a house frequented by a string of creeps. I've got a list of names here. I won't bore you with them. One of the people going in and out of that house is you, Lt. Roger Munson."

"Now wait a damned minute. Are you accusing...?"

He picked up his black stone and glared across his open file and tidy desk. "Draw your own damned inferences. I'm just telling you what's been observed. And there's just one more piece of information for you to mull over. Someone's been leaking info about this complex to the creeps. info you'd have to be in the mountain to know. I don't know who or why but I intend to find out. If you're not going to help me then I suggest you at least help yourself by staying away from that bunch. Whatever happens, your reputation is at risk."

That really pissed me off. Now he was accusing me of being a spy. It seemed like everyone wanted to accuse me of being a spy. It was too much but I knew if I responded in a fit of angry passion I might regret the outcome. Instead I tried to out-glare him for a moment before grabbing my briefcase, rising and heading for the door. Pausing, with my hand on the knob, I turned back to an immobile Lutz. "Just for the record, I haven't seen or heard from Maggie for over a week and don't expect I will be hearing from her anytime soon. So if you want to know what's happening in that house you'll need to get yourself another spy. This one's out of business."

***

"You've got to be kidding. George thinks you're a spy?" said Cory Mills in a loud whisper. "So when did you have this conversation?"

"Last evening, as I was heading for home. He called me in, real friendly like, and lays the big guilt trip on me." I lowered my voice as two officers took the table next to ours in the crowded mess hall.

"Grab your cup and let's get out of here. I've got to hear the gory details and this is no place to talk. The colonel's out this morning; we can use his office."

I welcomed the chance to talk to Cory about my Lutz meeting. I had a need to talk to someone I could trust and I trusted Cory. Without a word I followed him down the stairs, trying not to spill coffee on the way. We greeted Airman Rigby, Cory's clerk, and then settled into Hahn's spartan office behind a closed door. I eased into a side chair where I had a nice view out of Hahn's poster window beside his desk.

Cory plopped into the colonel's squeaky desk chair. "This will give Rigby something to think about."

"What?"

"My clerk. He's the number one rumor monger in the squadron. The two of us in here with the door closed will give him lots to think about. He probably suspects we're planning a coup or something. Anyway, tell me why this Lutz thing has you so wrapped around the axle."

"Think about it. First he implies that Maggie is or was a spy. Then he suggests that I may be in on it, leaking information to the 'creeps,' as he calls them. He either thinks I am, in fact, one of them or that Maggie is a Mata Hari or something, extracting secrets from me under her magic spell. However you read Lutz the whole thing stinks."

Cory leaned back, put his feet on the gray desk and gazed at Hahn's faux window. "I guess that would be unnerving."

I stood and leaned toward him with both hands on the cluttered desk. "Unnerving? It's more than unnerving. Look, I don't plan to make the Air Force a career or anything but I did intend to complete my tour without embarrassment or a court marshal. But the way Lutz lays out his circumstantial evidence, I'm not so sure he couldn't convince a panel of officers that I was a serious security risk. Now, I've never been to Kansas but I suspect that Leavenworth is not that great a place to spend time."

Cory smiled at my discomfort. "Relax Roger. Everyone knows Lutz overreacts to stuff. Besides, I doubt they'd send you to Leavenworth. Greenland maybe but not Leavenworth."

"Oh, that makes me feel better." I slumped back in my chair. Maybe I was making too big a deal out of the Lutz threats. Cory didn't seem to be taking the Lutz gambit too seriously.

"Look, good buddy. I wouldn't sweat about this Lutz thing too much. He's known to cry wolf. But if I were you I think I would start a journal or log or whatever you want to call it. Keep a record of your activities with Maggie, visits to the house, conversations with Lutz and anything else that may jog your memory. You have a good story to tell and, if this ever did blow up, having your own record could only help cover your ass. Then just sit tight."

"You think I'm overreacting, don't you," I offered, feeling a little embarrassed.

"Heck no, not at all. Lutz does that to people. Just try not to let him get to you."

"Sure, easy enough for you to say. You're not in his sights. He sounded damn serious about this Greenland thing."

I rose and began pacing the narrow room while Cory leaned forward and studied his pencil, twisting it in a nervous fashion.

"I need to change the subject. There...there's something I need to ask you," he began, in a halting manner.

I looked at him, surprised by his change of demeanor. "Whoa, that sounds like the voice of someone about to ask for money."

He smiled or, perhaps, winced. "Very perceptive. Actually, asking for money might be easier. OK, this is painful for me but do you remember Jessie saying she had a friend coming to town?"

I couldn't help but smile at his apparent discomfort. "A Patti something?"

"Right-a-roo, Patti O'Neal. I'm not trying to play cupid or anything but Jessie hoped you'd still be willing to join us for dinner. Patti's not shopping for a husband or anything and we thought it could be an OK evening if you'd consider it. She's really a fun gal."

"Cory, you and Jessie have been so good to me since I arrived in town that I'd dine with the Wicked Witch from the West if you asked me to. Just tell me where and when and I'll be there with a smile on my face, oozing charm as best I can."

Cory perked up as if a load had been lifted from his shoulders and turned my direction. "You've made my day. I wasn't sure how you'd react, what with the Maggie breakup and all. And I wasn't looking forward to passing on a 'no' answer to my dear wife. So, here's the deal. Jessie doesn't feel like cooking so we're thinking the officer's club, this Friday. I'll give you the time after Jessie makes the reservations. Trust me. I think you'll be pleasantly surprised."

"Don't worry, I trust you. I just wish Lutz trusted me."

Chapter Thirteen

Thursday, April 24
Dear Folks,

Hope all is well there. First, let me answer Mom's questions from her last ltr.

Yes, I'm eating well.

Yes, I'm getting enough sleep.

Yes, I've made a few "new friends," mostly work related.

No, I didn't send Grandma a birthday card. I'll find a late one.

As for the rest of my life, things are pretty quiet. Having dinner with friends on Friday evening and then the rest of the weekend is open. May go hiking or something. (Yes mother, I'll watch for snakes though I don't think there are any at this altitude.)

Actually, you need not worry about your little boy. The work is interesting, weather fantastic, if not a bit nippy, and no one is shooting at me.

I'm sure Lou enjoyed your campus visit. Mom, you worry too much about her. She's a bright girl with good judgment. By the time she's a sophomore she will probably hook up with a nice conservative engineer type like me or Dad, settle down and give you a boatload of squirming grandkids. So don't worry so much!

Dad, when you guys come to visit, I think I can pull a few strings and get you a tour of the mountain. I know you'd find it interesting. I still discover new stuff every day. Why don't you think about coming out this spring some time?

All for now.
Love, Roger

***

"For Christ's sake Lopez, have you been typing with your gloves on? This report looks like it's written in some secret

170

code," I barked, tossing the bundle of papers on his desk.

"Begging the lieutenant's pardon, but you know I banged it out quick. No one ever reads it anyway." He seemed to cower as if expecting a blow to follow.

"You miss the point. The point is…. Oh hell, I don't know what the point is. At least clean up the first page so it looks decent. Now, hold down the fort while I try to find a cup of coffee." I stormed from the office leaving Lopez alone so he could call his girlfriend and commiserate about his irritable boss.

I'd been riding him hard. He was not the only victim of my unwarranted abuse. Lately, lacking a dog to kick, I'd taken to issuing sharp and inconsistent orders to Lopez and the senior NCOs who were now avoiding me when possible. Cory had even commented on my sour disposition. Of course, it wasn't them; it was Maggie or, rather, my reaction to no Maggie. And it was really pissing me off.

The Friday morning coffee break bustle was underway in the dining hall. I weaved among the tables nodding silently to those I knew, picked up a heavy crockery cup and filled it with fresh coffee from the steaming cauldron at the end of the cafeteria line. I paid the cashier, offering a forced smile, salvaged a copy of the Air Force Times from a vacant table and retreated to a spot hidden behind an artificial ficus tree.

I spread the paper and tried to appear engrossed, hoping no one would stop by to chat. I didn't feel chatty. I didn't feel like reading. I felt confused. I even caught myself nervously tearing a napkin into little strips, forming them into a pile. Now where had I acquired that habit?

I needed an attitude adjustment. I knew that nothing would be accomplished by sulking about Maggie and bitching at the troops. It certainly hadn't worked so far. I was not even clear why I was so irritated. Was it because I'd lost her or because I was still feeling bad about how I lost her?

My engineer mind said get over the girl. That was the sound, rational and logical thing to do. We hadn't even really been going together. Hell, I'd been with Penny for two years and the getting-over-it time had been two weeks, max. Oh, I still thought of her from time to time but more with a sense of relief than a sense of loss. But I wasn't getting over the Maggie thing and her memory gnawed on my consciousness in a most persistent manner.

Maybe the Patti O'Neal dinner would be a good thing. It would fill the evening and, unless she was a real loser, I could suggest a hike or something tomorrow. Jessie would appreciate my interest in her friend and it would give me a chance to show off my limited knowledge of the local mountains. Of course, after a shitty dinner experience she might not be interested in seeing me again for any reason. That just might serve my sulking ego right.

Armed with that cheerful thought I brushed the napkin strips into my empty cup, dropped it on the dish conveyer and headed back to the office.

***

It was nearly 6:30 when I walked into the smoke filled lobby of the officer's club. I'd considered asking Cory and Jessie for a ride but their car was not in the apartment lot so I'd driven alone. Perhaps they'd gone somewhere to pick up this Patti person which was just fine. This way I wouldn't be stuck in the back seat of their two door Plymouth with some stranger and I could make a polite after-dinner escape if need be. In spite of my low expectations for the evening I'd dressed well, blue blazer, gray slacks and well polished penny loafers. The ensemble was topped off with a new necktie emblazoned with tiny vintage airplanes, a gift from my sister upon my commissioning.

Groping my way to the smoky dining room entrance, I was greeted by the same pompous young hostess who had rejected Maggie's pantsuit that Saturday night which now seemed a long time ago. Standing imperiously behind her heavy-looking wooden podium with its leather bound reservation book she scanned her list for the Mills' name, made a note in the margin and then wordlessly nodded for me to follow. She led me deep into the bustling dining room. Great, I thought, she'd saved us the table in the back by the dumpster. Then we passed into a small anteroom off the main dining area and approached a single woman at a table for two. From the rear she looked remarkably like....

"Maggie," I exclaimed.

Maggie turned, rose from her chair and looked first to

me and then to the hostess. "There must be some mistake. I'm supposed to meet a friend…a girl friend for dinner. I'm supposed to meet Jessie Mills."

"That's right ma'am. She reserved the table but she's not attending. She said it was for two other people, a Maggie and a Roger. You said your name was Maggie and he said his was Roger so I guess this is your table. Enjoy your meal." The hostess turned and strode from the room.

Maggie looked wonderful. She was wearing a frilly white blouse of some sort and a cool looking plaid skirt that seemed to wrap around and tie on the side. I wanted to hug her.

The clink of dishes and chatter from the dining room were the only sounds creeping into the little room. I stared at Maggie while she gripped the back of her chair and stared at the menu on the table. My mind was racing to put the scene in some order. Jessie invites me to dinner. Jessie invites Maggie to dinner. Jessie reserves a table for two. Jessie doesn't show up.

"This is awkward," I offered after a moment that seemed like an eternity.

"Yes it is, isn't it? I was expecting Jessie."

"So was I. I was expecting Jessie, Cory and, her friend, Patti. And I'm beginning to suspect that we aren't going to see any of them this evening."

"Patti?" she asked, looking toward me for the first time.

"Some friend of Jessie's. I'm supposed to show her a good time. Look, why don't you sit down. Sit down and let me buy you a drink."

"No, I shouldn't. I should really go." She bent down to retrieve her purse from the floor and seemed to be ready to bolt. "I never expected to see you here."

"I know you think I'm a putz but…."

"Oh Roger, that's not fair. I…"

"Whatever. Then stay, just for a quick drink?"

She hesitated and gave me a hint of a pained smile. "OK, just one, if you're sure you don't mind."

I moved to help her with her chair but she was down before my chivalry was displayed. Taking a place opposite her I found myself gazing across a sea of glassware and a crystal bud vase holding a single red rose. A glance into the dining room confirmed that ours was the only table adorned with a rose. Jessie had thought of everything. But I was sure it would take more than a rose to rekindle Maggie's interest.

June, our proper waitress, arrived to take drink orders. Maggie first ordered a glass of Chardonnay and then changed her mind to match my Coors order. "Our specials for this evening are…." June began.

"That's OK," said Maggie. "We're just going to have a drink, no dinner."

"Suit yourself but this is the dining room. The bar is off the lobby."

I gave her my best "get the hell out of here" glare without uttering a word. It seemed to work for she gathered up the wine list, unused menus and wine glasses and beat a hasty retreat.

Maggie gave me her beautiful smile which seemed to say "nice job." She really looked good.

We then began a verbal ballet. How've you been? What've you been doing? How's work? How's school? How are you enjoying the spring weather? We were talking about everything. We were talking about nothing at all.

We finished one beer and ordered a second. We emptied the bread basket. We finished an appetizer, an artichoke spread, and ordered a second, potato skins.

The old Maggie seemed to be there across the table but just out of reach. I was hearing about what she was doing but not about how she was doing. And I began to fear we would run out of things to talk about and then, like Cinderella, she would race from the club, without leaving a glass slipper behind. At least our little room stayed empty and June left us alone between servings.

I don't know how long we talked. It seemed like a few minutes but must have been more than an hour. After I finished up what I thought to be an amusing story about my mother's new car, we lapsed into a deafening period of silence. It looked like the evening might be near an end. I had nothing more to say and the tension around what was unsaid had become overwhelming. I'd hoped the conversation would thaw our relationship but she was still tense and appeared uncomfortable. Perhaps nothing had changed. I'd lied to her. Apparently in her view nothing could change that. I might not get a second chance to show her how worthy I was.

As if in a daze she carefully arranged and then rearranged the sugar packets in their small chrome container never quite satisfied with the final arrangement. Then, pushing the container aside, she folded her hands as if praying and stared at me.

"Roger, there is something I want to say. I don't know quite how to begin. I don't know quite how to end either but here goes. First of all, Jessie thinks the world of you. And she's probably right. She's been really concerned about you since, well, over the past few weeks. Anyway she called me and we met for lunch."

I thought I should say something but nothing came out. Jessie had been meeting with Maggie? What was that all about?

Maggie dumped the sugars on the table and began sorting them again as she talked. "Jessie told me about the pressure you were under from Lutz. She told me you'd nearly been insubordinate. I think that was the word she used. She told me how you'd been since, since I last saw you. And she told me she thought there was something between us that was worth saving. Can you imagine? She hardly knows me."

"What do you think?"

"About...?"

"About us. Do you think there's something worth saving?" I watched her squirm while I nursed the last of my beer.

"I, I just don't know. And I have thought about it. I just didn't know we'd be here, together, having this conversation. Maybe sometime but not here, not now. Oh Roger," she said, leaning across the table and touching my hands, "I've been miserable these past few weeks. First because I thought you'd lied to me and I'd fallen for your line and then Jessie convinces me that I was wrong about you and us and the whole Lutz thing. You see, I hadn't wanted to fall for you or anyone else in the first place. Breakups are just too much to deal with. Now we're here, having this conversation and I'm feeling miserable and...and I just don't know...."

A blanket of silence covered us again. Reaching around

the rose I tried to take both her hands in mine but she pulled back, just out of reach.

"I think I should go," she said finally, placing her twisted napkin on the table. "I'm really sorry. It's not you this time, it's me. I need some space." She pushed back from the table, gave my arm a squeeze and disappeared toward the main dining room.

I tossed a couple of bills on the table, leaving a bigger tip than was warranted, and rushed after her. When I caught up she was standing beside Sunny fumbling with her keys. Without really thinking I made a Clark Gable move, turning and embracing her. After a moment of hesitation she returned my embrace with her head on my shoulder and hair smushed fragrantly into my face. That was it. No kiss, just a wonderful moment together before she seemed to recharge her defenses and squirm away.

With me standing empty handed she found her keys, slid into Sunny and started the growling little engine. "Can I call?" I asked as she pulled the door shut. There was no answer but I thought I saw tears in her eyes as she backed from the space and jerked forward toward the exit drive.

***

At that moment I wished I was a smoker. The closing scene from "Casablanca" flashed through my mind. But instead of Humphrey Bogart, standing at the airfield with a cigarette in hand as Ingrid Bergman's plane lifted off, it was me standing empty handed as a yellow VW disappeared from view.

I shuffled back into the club. I didn't want to be alone just yet. Entering the lobby I was nearly run down by Nurse Lentz as she emerged from the ladies' room. "Oh, hi," I offered.

Without breaking pace she turned smiling, "Hi Larry, nice to see you again."

She continued across the lobby where she took the arm of a tall captain with flier's wings on his uniform jacket and disappeared into the bar.

I was deflated. She didn't even remember my name. Of course, not counting the encounter in the commissary produce department, I'd only met her the one time. But for weeks she'd served as my backup fantasy date and now she didn't remember my name. Maybe being alone wasn't such a bad option.

I retreated to the Camaro, my one trusty companion, and began a meandering drive home. Maggie, Maggie, Maggie, what was I going to do about Maggie? I'd started the evening without her in my life and it looked like I was going to end it the same way. What happened in between simply added to my confusion.

Jessie was another story, bless her heart. I couldn't decide whether I should be mad or grateful for her intervention. Her meddling had brought us together one more time but toward what end?

That thought was still coursing through my mind two hours later when the urgent sound of the phone interrupted my TV viewing and dragged me back to reality.

"Roger, it's me, Jessie. Are you alone?"

"Yes, my dear friend. Despite your matchmaking endeavors I'm home alone."

"Can I come up? I'm just dying to hear about your dinner."

"Yes, I'll bet you are. Sure, come if you dare." I glanced at the clock, surprised that it was already after 10:00.

"You're not mad at me are you? I was only trying to....?

"I haven't decided yet. Maybe I am and maybe I'm not. But come on up."

I was at the door to greet her when she arrived clad in Cory's loose fitting sweat suit and blue fluffy bedroom slippers. "Where's Cory? You may need his protection if I decide I'm mad about your little charade."

"He got called to the mountain for something. It's just as well. He wasn't too happy about the dinner setup with you and Maggie. He thinks I'm meddling. You didn't really mind, did you? You didn't mind seeing her again?"

I sat her in my most comfortable chair, made her a cup of herbal tea from a package that Maggie had left after one of our dinners and then told her the tale of the officer's club encounter. As I gave her the highlights I was struck by how unreal it all seemed. Had I really met Maggie at the club? Had we really had the conversation I thought we had? Was she really gone? Or was the whole thing a sketchy dream?

"So now it's your turn," I said at the conclusion of my

story. "What did you two talk about when you got together? I suppose she told you I was a terrific guy?"

"Oh Roger, you're making me feel awful. I was only trying to help. I'm sure she wants to be back together. We mostly talked girl talk but, when I explained the Lutz pressure, she seemed almost relieved to think you weren't the cad she thought you were. Maybe tonight was too big a shock for her. Be patient. I'm sure she'll want to see you again."

Under her concerned gaze I pulled a tablet and pencil off of the coffee table and drew a series of meaningless circles before responding. "Tell me one thing. Is this Patti person real or was she fabricated too?"

"Oh yes, she's real enough. Remember my sister you met last weekend?"

"I suppose that was Patti and you don't even have a sister."

"Good guess Sherlock. I do have a sister but that girl was actually my friend, Patti. But I couldn't introduce you to her then because I needed to preserve the thought of Patti for tonight's dinner. What did you think of her, cute huh?"

"You're incorrigible."

Jessie left shortly after that, smothering me with encouraging words and trying her best to cheer me up. I hoped her optimism was well placed but I had doubts about my odds with Miss Maggie. All I knew for sure was that my weekend was looking bleak; no Maggie, no Patti and not even the fantasy of Nurse Lentz.

***

The stress and confusion of the past week bled off when I crawled into bed after Jessie departed. The sleep I feared would elude me instead consumed me until nearly 9:00 o'clock in the morning. I was shocked to see the time since I rarely slept that late. I climbed from bed and wandered around the apartment in a stupor with no meaningful goal in mind for the morning or the day. After a shower and shave, a dry toast breakfast and cup of coffee supplied the start-up fuel for the morning. Then, somewhat disgusted by the look of the place, I took a stab at tidying up. The laundry went into the washer, the uniform shirts into a bag for the dry cleaner, old newspapers and magazines into a pile near the front door. I performed cleaning magic in the kitchen that would have made Mother proud. After hearing the TV weatherman predict a period of sunny dry weather I decided the next major task would be to find a gentle carwash for the Camaro.

I'd just tossed on old jeans, a faded sweatshirt and my most comfortable sneakers when I heard a knock at the apartment door. I clicked off the TV, answered the door and was greeted by a most welcome sight; hiker Maggie in a bluish flannel shirt and rolled up jeans.

Without a word or thought I took her in my arms and exchanged the most delectable kiss I had ever experienced. Actually it was a string of kisses of varying lengths applied to her lips, forehead, ears, neck and any other part of her lovely face and head I could reach. Weeks of confusion and longing exploded through that embrace. I can't describe it but it was fabulous.

Pausing, she laid her head on my chest. "Are you going to invite me in?"

I wanted to laugh for joy. I wasn't yet sure what her presence meant but the early signs were promising. I took her hand, led her across the threshold, shut the door and repeated the hallway greeting. After a regrettably brief interlude she gently pushed me away with a "Roger we have to talk."

"Oh, man," was all I could say. "Every time you say 'we have to talk' things go sideways and I get all confused. Do we really have to talk now?" I made a move toward her and was again restrained with a warm smile and firm hand.

"Please, just talk for now. And maybe a cup of the coffee I smell if there's any left."

I obediently backed away and gestured for her to sit on the sofa while I recharged the percolator. I wasn't sure where the conversation might go but didn't want to run out of coffee at an inopportune moment.

She ignored the sofa and took a seat at the table. I started to drag my chair closer to hers but she sat me down with her eyes, across from rather than beside her. It was my apartment but I had willingly ceded control of the space to Maggie Meyers.

"Roger, you may have heard some of this before so bear

with me. I've been so confused these past few weeks I can't recall what conversations I've had with you and what I've had with myself."

She gripped her empty cup and paused, as if sorting words for delivery. "Anyway, first I run into you at Dunkin's in a snow storm. That was no big deal. I don't mean hitting your car was no big deal and I'm sorry about that. I mean we were no big deal.

"Then I see you again and you seem like a nice guy and I invite you to Val's party. Maybe I felt sorry for you, alone in a new town and all that. I wasn't thinking of you as a boyfriend. I wasn't trolling or anything. Anyway, we seemed too different and I wasn't interested in playing the boyfriend game again. I'd been there and it wasn't that good in the end.

"Then this 'friend-thing' comes along," she continued making little air quotation marks with her fingers around the words "friend-thing."

"I enjoyed being with you and you seemed to enjoy being with me and pretty soon I found myself thinking about you and wanting to be with you in a different way. Then, just when I'd convinced myself that it would be OK to feel that way, that you were a different kind of guy and that it was OK to feel vulnerable, the whole Leonard spy thing blows up and, bam, it's like I'm back in Boulder, back in the loser's column."

Her voice quivered and she paused, wiping her eyes with the sleeve of the shirt.

I wanted to gather her in my arms and let the tears soak my sweatshirt but instead I eased my way to the stove, filled our cups and returned to my seat with the coffee and a handful of whitish napkins. She retrieved a napkin and dabbed at her eyes.

"I'm sorry. I didn't intend to get sappy."

I smiled, reaching across to grip her free hand. She didn't pull away.

"So, at that point, you're out of my life and I feel absolutely awful, which only meant I'd fallen for you much more than I ever wanted. It seemed I'd made the same stupid mistake I'd made in Boulder. I'd let myself care for someone far more than I should have and, or so I thought, much more than you deserved. Roger, I was mad as hell, both at you for screwing me over like that and at myself for being such a sucker."

This was excruciating for me. I wanted to jump in and defend myself. I wanted to tell my side of the story, but her intensity counseled silence.

She tested the too-hot-to-drink coffee and then continued. "Then, just as I think I'm getting back in control of my life, Jessie calls."

"Exactly what did she say?"

"It doesn't matter. What matters is that suddenly I felt worse than before. I'd been pushing you away when I should have been pulling you close. I felt like that stupid nurse in 'South Pacific.' She didn't realize what she had until she nearly lost it."

I had to smile at that. I loved that movie and, much to Penny's annoyance, could sing most of the songs from memory.

"But last night, I wasn't ready for you. It was too much of a surprise. I just didn't know how I felt about you. I didn't know if I was ready to be…to be vulnerable again. I just had to get away, get away to think."

"But you're here now."

That evoked the first warm smile since she'd arrived. "Yes, I am aren't I? Well, you can thank Val for that."

"Val?"

"I guess she just got tired of seeing me mope around the place. She finally marched into my room, shut the door and said…. Actually it doesn't matter what she said. But in the end she says, 'would you be happier with him or without him?' And now you find me standing on your doorstep. Now how's that for being vulnerable?"

She rose from her chair without releasing my hand, eased around the table and settled on my lap. "Can I stay awhile?"

***

There are some days you never forget: the day Kennedy was shot, the 1965 Seattle earthquake, your first kiss, your first car…. Everyone's got a different list. I'll never forget that Saturday.

We sat and talked the morning away without interruption. Since Dunkin's was where we met we made a noontime pilgrimage to our regular booth and paid homage to our first encounter. I bought a dozen cinnamon twists. We didn't finish them. We played Frisbee in the park. We acted like kids again.

Returning from the park we stopped at the grocery and purchased a do-it-yourself pizza mix. The dough came in a little cylinder that popped open when you smacked it on the kitchen counter. Stretching it into a rough circle on a cookie sheet was a chore but we did it between kisses and ended up with dough on Maggie's forehead and my chin. She then spread the sauce with her hand and I helped with the clean-up, one finger at a time. It was a most delicious sauce.

With the addition of mozzarella cheese and pepperoni we had a pizza that, while looking a bit ragged, tasted delectable. Not that we cared. Our minds were far away.

***

We didn't really "do" the dishes. We did try. After she placed some dirty dishes in the sink, we embraced and I lifted her feather light body up and seated her on the counter. The kisses, playful at first, grew more passionate. She locked her heels behind my thighs, pulling me closer, while we pressed tight from hips to lips. Her short nails caressed the back of my neck as we clung together, nibbling and kissing.

Twisting from my embrace she pushed back, putting space between us, and deftly whisked my shirt over my head. She studied my chest for a moment and then began kissing it as her nails made feather light tracks across my back.

"Would you think me awful if I suggested making love?" she cooed, eyes cast down.

I lifter her chin and gazed into her delightful eyes. "I…yes, yes…I mean no, no of course not. But are you sure? I don't want to do anything that you or we might regret. I don't want to lose you again."

She shushed me with a finger to my lips. "Talk later. Love now. Do you have protection?"

Now that was a tough question. Recalling the post-sex, weeks of hell, waiting for Penny's period I knew I didn't want to go through that again. But what would it say to Maggie if I said yes? I screw women all the time? I'd planned on scoring with her so I laid in a supply just for tonight? So I hedged.

"Ah, yes, I think so. I might...."

"Well, why don't you find out then, Lieutenant?"

I kissed her hard. Relief, joy and anticipation carried me as I carried her into my room and laid her on the rumpled, partly-made bed.

I turned and fumbled in the back of my sock drawer unearthing a well worn but unopened box of Trojans that had traveled with me since my freshman year. I recall wondering if condoms had a "use by" date. No matter. It was too late to shop.

"I love your scent, Roger," she purred.

I turned to see her stretched out on her back, clinging to my pillow like a down-filled lover.

Without a word my clothes and inhibitions flew off and I slipped my naked body onto the bed beside hers. Her body seemed to melt into mine as my hands and lips traveled places I'd only dreamed of. As I explored I removed her clothing, piece by piece, revealing a body even more beautiful than I'd imagined. There was nothing Rubenesque about her thin limbs, flat tummy and tight, compact breasts. To my eyes she was sheer perfection. My lips caressed her breasts, toying with her excited nipples while my fingers explored her warmth. We were both on fire.

"Oh, Roger, I want you in me so much."

She rolled to the little box on the nightstand, ripped the top off and spilled the contents onto the bed. Grabbing a single foil wrapped condom she pressed it into my hand. "Here, do something with this," she urged.

All the locker room discussions of the little latex guardians paid off for I had it out of its wrapper and unrolled with the speed of a veteran Don Juan.

She rolled to me, presenting her breasts for renewed attention, as my little guy slipped into her warmth. Our groans intermingled as our bodies came alive and moved with a perfect rhythm as if we'd done this a thousand times before.

Even if, as I hope, we do it a thousand times more, I will never forget that first explosive, giving, loving time.

***

As I moved into my senior college year I feared I would graduate a virgin. Where sex was concerned everyone in the frat house talked about it, bragged about it but, I suspect, didn't really know that much about it. My classmates all seemed to have scored the big one at least once and some claimed multiple conquests. In hindsight, I don't know who was telling the truth but I suspect there was considerably less screwing going on than was being reported.

At times I wondered what was wrong with me. Was it the fear of Lutheran retribution? Was I afraid of getting someone pregnant or of catching one of those diseases they discussed in health ed class? It was likely a bit of all those concerns.

Penny and I had finally crossed the line our senior year. That was a little out of character for both of us. We had always talked about saving ourselves for the honeymoon night and of how wonderful it would be. Maybe it was for her. I just wasn't invited on her honeymoon.

My night with Maggie was incredible. We were wonderful together. Perhaps we were a bit awkward at first but the results were more than I could have imagined. And thank God for those old sock drawer condoms.

Later, as I lay in bed with her snuggled warm against me and the morning sun sneaking around the edge of the curtains, my engineer's mind tried to unravel what had made the night so exceptional.

The Penny poke had been my first and I thought it was pretty good. If I had nothing to compare it with I would have given it a high rating. But we'd been drunk first timers and I couldn't even recall the whole evening.

My experience with Maggie trumped my Penny time. Maggie set both my mind and body on fire. If there was a ten point scale then Maggie and I were a solid ten and the Penny encounter would have rated a mere five, tops. The difference finally hit me and, to my practical side, seemed sappy. Penny and I had sex. We had a physical encounter. Maggie and I made love, both a body and soul coupling. Maybe it was the difference between being in love and being in heat. Or, maybe I was simply over analyzing things.

Soon the analysis morphed into concern. Despite the high score I'd given our relationship I faced pangs of doubt about what we'd done. It seemed that every time I felt close to

Maggie in the past she would react in a surprising way and I would find myself alone trying to figure out what had happened. Now we had shared something very special and I didn't relish the thought of spending even a moment without her again.

When she rolled away, I slipped quietly out of bed, found my boxers on the floor and ambled off to the kitchen to start the coffee. I still couldn't quite believe what we'd done. It was like a dream but her warm presence in my bed suggested it was much more than a dream. The memory filled me with indescribable warmth.

As I put the last of the evening dishes into the dishwasher, the noise of a latch and running water alerted me that she was up. But still I was surprised when she came up behind and wrapped her arms around my bare chest.

"Do you think I'm awful?" she whispered. "I mean do you think I'm too easy?"

I tried to twist and face her but she clung to me, head against my back. "I think you're wonderful and we're incredible together. But are you sorry…?"

I could feel her head nodding "no" against my skin. "No, I wanted to be with you. I just…."

Squirming to face her, I lifted her chin toward me and was rewarded with a passionate morning kiss. She looked fetching in my terrycloth bathrobe which soon fell open to reveal her lovely breasts that were as exciting to touch in the daylight as they had been in the dark. I fell to my knees so I could kiss their fullness while my hands explored the small of her back and the firm ass. I don't recall how we made it back to the bed but our second time together was even more explosive than the first.

I was in love.

***

"This is truly amazing," I whispered in an ear that was resting near my lips. "Truly amazing."

She continued twisting the hair on my chest for a moment before responding. "Are we doing the right thing? I mean does this change the way you feel about me, for the worse I mean?"

"Dear Maggie, of course it changes the way I feel." She stopped twisting hair and set her nails firmly on my skin. "It makes me feel closer than ever to you. It makes me never want to let go."

She eased the fingernail pressure and snuggled closer.

Again we lay in silence as I relished the feel of her pressing against the entire length of my body. It was a feeling I'd never experienced before, like a spell I had no desire to break. Finally, and too soon, she eased herself to the edge of the bed, retrieved my robe from the floor and, modestly covered, turned on the bed to face me.

"There's someone I want you to meet. Do you feel up for a little drive?"

I sat up and tried to hug her but she pushed me down leaving her restraining hand on my chest. "Control yourself you lusty little man. Now answer my question."

"Right now I'd walk on hot coals if you asked. I think I can handle a drive. Where to and to see who?"

"I feel funny talking about it here. Could we go in the other room? And maybe you should put something on." She leaned forward, kissed me and bounded from the bed to avoid the hug she correctly assumed I would try for.

I pulled on boxers, jeans and an old tee shirt and found her in the kitchen setting two cups of coffee on the table. She resisted another playful advance, sat me in a chair and took a seat across the table.

"I want you to meet my grandfather, Grandpa Meyers. He lives up near Denver in the little town of Conifer. He's a dear man, very special to me and I want you to meet him."

"Meyers, so he's you dad's father?"

She nodded. "He's really all I have of my dad's family; I'm his only grandchild."

She paused for a moment, testing her coffee and gathering her thoughts. "He and Grandma Ruth have always been special to me. She died five years ago. He's alone now but still my special guy. They were my refuge when I needed a place to go, a shoulder to lean on or just a quiet space. They helped me pay for school, they helped with the car and they've always been my link to my father. I don't know what I'd have done without them at times."

"I'm envious. He's known you longer than I have."

"Oh stop that sappy talk. Do you mind if I use your phone to give him a call?"

***

I followed Maggie as she drove Sunny back to her house. Parking behind her on the narrow street I was relieved that Len's van was nowhere in sight. When everything seemed to be going so well the last thing I wanted was a Len encounter. Maggie waited by her car as I maneuvered into a space and then, taking my hand, led me up the stairs and into the house and living room.

"That you Maggie?" came Val's voice just before she emerged from the kitchen. "Oh, it's you too, Roger. Well, did you take in a late movie or something?"

I'm sure I blushed. I knew what we'd been doing. I knew what she suspected we'd been doing. Maggie never blinked.

"Now Val, you're not my mother. You can think anything you like but I assure you Roger here is both an officer and a gentleman. In fact, I'm afraid he may also think I'm a pest since I hang around his place so much." She squeezed my hand before letting go and heading for the stairs. "Now, if you can behave yourself, why don't you entertain him while I run up and change clothes. I'll just be a minute."

With Maggie gone I stood for moment in awkward silence while Val curled up on the sofa. "I guess I should say thanks," I offered at last.

"Thanks?"

"Thanks for being a good listener. Maggie said she had a long conversation with you yesterday and ...."

"Oh that. Well, I mainly just listened. She did all the talking. But I must say she looks happier now than she did when she left here. Seems you've cast a spell on our little Maggie." She adjusted the throw pillow against her back and then fixed me in her gaze. "May I be blunt?"

I nodded, taking a seat on the arm of the overstuffed chair.

"You two seem as well matched as oil and water but if she's fallen for you, and all indications are that she has fallen hopelessly for you, then I wish you the best. Like I told you once before, take good care of her."

There was a nasty tone in her voice that set me off. "Why do you have such a pissy attitude toward me and toward Maggie and me? Has your buddy Leonard been whispering evil things about me into your ear?"

She smirked and paused, fiddling with the lace doily on the sofa arm. "Do you really think you're right for Maggie, Mr. Straightarrow? I mean, really?"

I studied Val, not sure how to respond. Maggie's return rescued me.

"God, it's quiet as a morgue around here," she said bounding down the stairs in fresh jeans, a crisp cotton blouse and slightly soiled tennis shoes. "Where's everyone?"

"Susan's on campus and Len's off with his rock climbing buddies somewhere. Looks like you're heading out too," said Val.

"Denver. It's a wonderful day for a drive and Grandpa's invited us to dinner."

"Oh, this must be serious Roger; she's introducing you to the family."

"Yes, right," said Maggie, taking my hand and pulling me toward the door. "Let's get out of here so Val can let her imagination run wild. And don't wait up."

***

We turned off the interstate south of Denver and wound west, into the front range, toward Conifer. It had been a delightful Sunday drive and she'd been effervescent as she described Grandpa Meyers, the man we were about to meet.

"You see, Grandpa Meyers is a retired Army general," she prattled. "He fought in both world wars and didn't retire until 1947, after 30 years of service."

"So he's been retired over 20 years?"

"Heavens no. He'd never sit still that long. No, he went to work for a Denver Insurance company. He became a vice-president or something and retired a second time a few years ago when he hit 65."

The scenery continued to change as we wound ever further up the narrow road into the mountains. Maggie seemed to draw energy from the place as we covered, what was clearly, familiar ground for her. As I followed her directions, I tried to sort out how her grandfather fit into her life.

"OK, so your grandfather was Army and your father Air Force. How about aunts, uncles and grandmothers."

"Some each on mom's side but none on my father's; he was an only child. And Grandma Meyers was killed in a traffic accident shortly after Grandpa left the insurance company, so now it's just him and me. It was a horrible accident. All their plans for retirement, travel—his world was shattered. I'm all Grandpa has now," she concluded with her voice trailing off.

It was clear he was very special to Maggie.

As we neared the house her energy and enthusiasm returned. "You'll just love his house," she began. "It's nothing fancy, an old ranch house really, but it sits on ten of the most beautiful Colorado acres you've ever seen. He used to have a horse for me to ride and there were always cats and dogs around. Until I was a senior in high school, no matter where my family was stationed, I would spend the summer in Conifer and have a wonderful time. I think my half-sister was jealous and my step dad resentful but mom loved my grandparents and seemed to realize how important it was for them to stay connected with me. Maybe I was the last link to their son. I don't know, but it was sure special for me.

"Actually, when I turned 14 I got my first official kiss from the Scalia boy who lived just across the road from Grandpa's. Now there was a cutie. I wonder whatever happened to him." She leaned over and kissed me behind the ear.

"So all your trips to Denver you've just been visiting your grandpa? I guess I've been jealous for nothing."

"You've been jealous. Oh you dear, that's wonderful," she said with a laugh. "Sorry to disappoint you but he's the only other man in my life."

"What about your folks, your mom and step dad. You never say much about them. Where are they? What do they do?"

She turned forward, studying the road ahead, before responding. "They're OK, fine really. But could we just not talk about them today? I can't say why but let's make this day about Grandpa. Are you OK with that?"

Of course I was OK with anything she said or did at that

point. It was odd she didn't want talk about them but I could live with that. She was beside me and that was all that mattered.

She continued directing me on the small country roads until finally pointing to a gravel drive that led through an open wooden gate and on up to a compact rambler set back from the road in a cluster of pines. A tall, distinguished looking gentleman was on the covered porch, rising to greet us as I came to a stop. Maggie was out of the car embracing him before I could release my seatbelt.

"Gramps, this is the wild officer I've been telling you about. Roger, this is my Grandpa Meyers."

"Pleased to meet you sir," I said as his iron grip closed on my hand.

Without releasing his grip he turned to Maggie. "Isn't this the same guy you were telling me about? The guy who..."

"One and the same. But don't hold that against him. I'm afraid there were a few misunderstandings but that's all behind us now," she concluded, stepping forward to kiss him on the cheek.

He released my hand while eyeing me suspiciously. I could only imagine what he'd heard about my "spying" activities.

"Well, if Maggie's happy with you then you're most welcome here. Come on into my little home, son. And cut the 'sir' stuff. It just makes me sound older than I feel and I don't need that. You call me Norm, do you hear."

"Yes sir, I mean Norm. It's a pleasure to be here."

With that he turned with his arm still around Maggie and entered the house with me trailing behind.

The afternoon, which turned into evening, flew by. It was fascinating for me to see another side of Maggie and to hear of her past. Norm was full of Maggie stories and the house was like a Maggie shrine with photos of her childhood summer visits lining the hallway to the bedrooms and dominating the fireplace mantel.

As the sun began to set behind the mountains, Maggie volunteered to make us a spaghetti dinner and tossed Grandpa and me out of the kitchen so we could engage in "man talk" as she put it. It may have been a deliberate attempt to get us alone so he could look me over but it seemed natural and we were soon touring his woodshop, housed in a shed attachment to his nearby open carport. It appeared he could make just about anything out of wood but his specialty was wooden game boards for checkers, cribbage and backgammon. He was justifiably proud of his work, some of which was for sale in a nearby art gallery and a local gift shop; I was suitably impressed. As we toured he asked about my family, my work, my schooling and a range of other topics. It bordered on an interrogation but he was so charming that the questions came across as natural, questions any father would ask of a boy dating his daughter.

I could see why Maggie loved this man; I could see why she valued his opinion. I just hoped I'd given him the correct answers to his myriad of questions.

Dinner ended too soon and, leaving Grandpa to do the dishes at his insistence, we said our goodbyes and turned the Camaro toward the Springs. We rode in silence until we reached the state highway.

"He likes you. I knew he would."

"Who likes who?" I said, downshifting to slide into a turn.

"Grandpa. He likes you and he's very discriminating." She smiled and turned to me as if looking for a reaction.

"Well, I wasn't so sure some of the time. What makes you think I'm approved?"

"Grandpa used to have a dog named Sadie. He said she had a sixth sense about people. She'd growl at some folks and make right up to others. There was nothing half-way about Sadie. She liked you or she didn't. She never liked Brian."

"Brian?"

"Oh, sorry. Brian Evans, a guy I dated for a while in Boulder. Anyway, Sadie saw him a couple of times gave a low growl and slipped away each time. Sadie couldn't stand Brian. She was a wonderful dog and a good judge of character. Do you know what Grandpa told me just before we left?"

I shook my head as she placed her hand over mine on the floor shift knob.

"He said Sadie would have liked this boy. And I knew exactly what he meant."

Stephen J. Dennis

Chapter Fourteen

Sunday Evening
Hey Sis,

Well, I took your advice. I tried the "granola type" girl as you so artfully phrased it. So far I like what I've seen. Time will tell if they are "lower maintenance" as you suggested.

My "granola" girl is named Maggie. I actually met her the first day I arrived in the Springs when she slid into my car in a snow storm, but that's another story. Anyway, I've seen her a few times and we seem to hit it off. Not sure where it's going so don't even mention it to mom but she's a fun gal and I think you two would hit it off.

I continue to put in a good word for you with Mom. I tell her you're responsible, mature, thoughtful, etc, etc. Don't let me down. I only believe half of what I tell her but I'm laying it on so thick half should be enuf! (Just kidding.)

Take care and behave. If you can't be good, be careful!!!!
Rog

P.S.: Thanks for your offer to fix me up with your "granola" roommate. She must be a nice gal to come with your recommendation. I'd better let my Colorado "granola" girl play out before I consider an Oregon version!

***

Monday morning dawned like so many mornings before. But this one was different. I was still euphoric from the weekend. It wasn't just the sex. I mean, that was great and all but it was more. It was the blissful, whimsical, happy memory of just being with Maggie, tossing a Frisbee, pulling a cinnamon twist apart, spreading pizza dough. Lost in such delightful thoughts, I'd just lathered my face when the phone clattered.

I glanced at my watch—a bit before 7:00. No one ever called me a bit before 7:00, except my time zone challenged mother. I cleared the lather from my left cheek and answered it on the third ring.

"Hi there, sailor," whispered a so familiar voice. "Did I get you up?"

"Maggie?"

"Excuse me, do you get lots of girls calling you at this hour?"

"No, no, of course not. It's just such a surprise to hear your voice this early. A pleasant surprise."

"That sounds better. Anyway I missed you and wanted to tell you that before this house wakes up and you head off to the mountain."

That sounded wonderful to giddy me. "I'm glad you did. Say, about this weekend, are you OK with it? With us, with everything I mean."

"Why you naughty man," she chirped with a feigned southern accent, "I just might tell my daddy about you, you devil."

"No, really Maggie. I mean it was really special and I ...."

"Lieutenant, I couldn't agree more. And I'm very much looking forward to a time very soon when we can talk about it and try to figure out what it all means. I'm actually a little confused, confused in a good way though. Now someone's coming. I need to go."

"Maggie?"

"Yes?"

"Call anytime."

***

"The colonel's going to be a bit late," said Cory, entering and taking his regular staff meeting seat next to the colonel's empty chair. "He got called up to General Jackson's office a few minutes ago. Shouldn't be long so, to kill time, we can do show and tell; everyone can tell about their weekend."

I may have blushed. If so, no one noticed.

Lutz grimaced and reached into his jacket pocket for the black rock.

"Bob could tell us about the little Grand Prix tour he took yesterday, couldn't you Bob?" Gruber asked with a laugh.

Bob Kirkwood smiled and gave Gruber a "you-son-of-a-bitch" glare.

"OK, let's hear it," said Cory.

Kirkwood smiled, shaking his head. "I've got nothing to say. My weekend is classified...."

"Since the captain's a little shy," Gruber continued, "let me explain. Seems he was trying his little baby out on some corners near Cripple Creek and she decides to leave the road."

"Oh cripes," winced Cory. "Really Bob? Did you mess up the Porsche?"

"The car is fine, thank you very much. I just got onto a soft shoulder and needed a little tow to get out. It was no big deal. By the end of the day, Gruber will have this story so embellished that even I won't recognize it."

"I'm only trying to...."

"Dammit, George," bellowed Colonel Hahn, bursting into the room. "Dammit to hell." He stopped short of Lutz, turned and leaned over with his ass inches from Lutz's surprised expression. "See that, can you see that?" he sputtered, pointing in the area of his hip pocket.

With a disgusted look on his face Lutz leaned back to distance himself from the south end of his north-facing colonel. "See what sir? What am I supposed to see?"

"The hunk missing from my back side, that's what. I've just had the ass chewing of my life and there must be a piece missing back there. I've never seen General Jackson so fired up, and that Major Wiser just stood there soaking it all in, the shithead." The Colonel moved to his place by Cory and, before sitting, leaned toward Lutz, hands on the table and reading glasses dangling from their chain around his neck. "How could you have set me up like this?"

While the rest of us eagerly awaited the next salvo, Lutz picked up his black stone and gave it a rub before responding. "This wouldn't have anything to do with that congressman who tried to get in the mountain Saturday night, would it?"

"It has everything to do with Congressman Bickle and his very influential wife. You knew he was a congressman. And you knew Wiser was with them. What more could you want?"

"I want them to go through the same procedures that

every other visitor goes through. He wasn't on the access list. We had no prior notification. Wiser had no business trying to bring him in."

The colonel's complexion turned from ruddy to scarlet. "Can't you ever show any initiative, any flexibility? Bickle is not only a congressman but he comes from Wiser's home town and their families have been friends for years. And that wife of his has more Washington connections than the White House switchboard. If that's not enough, you have to pick a member of the Armed Services Sub-Committee. His hand is on our purse strings and he is the man you decide to lock out of the mountain."

"This is rich," tossed in Gruber. "You fuckin' turned Wiser and his buddy away. Nice move, George."

"I don't see anything funny about this, Andy. This is serious shit," said the colonel, switching his glare to Gruber.

"Sorry sir."

"Now George, why can't your guys use their heads once in a while? They could surely have made an exception for a congressman escorted by Wiser," pressed Hahn.

Staring at the black stone in his hand Lutz seemed to be measuring his response. After a painful pause he turned to Hahn. "Sir, my security detachment is made up of kids; some haven't even seen their 20th birthday. I ask them to follow the rules. In fact, I order them to follow the rules. I don't ask them to use their own judgment. The rules are black and white. They work. They work if people like Wiser follow them. I take full responsibility for what happened. My guys followed the correct procedures. The guard stopped Wiser. The duty NCO called me when Wiser and his friends got lippy. I concurred with the guard's action. He did the right thing."

Hahn leaned forward, resting his head on his hands. "George, George, George, why do you do this to me?"

Eyes darted from Lutz to Hahn and back again. You could almost hear the colonel's pounding pulse in the silent room.

Finally Hahn sat upright and surveyed the meeting attendees. "I need to deal with this. Is there anything hot on the agenda that can't be put off until next week?"

That was an amusing question since there was rarely anything other than routine reports on the agenda and the world would get along just fine if they were never given or placed in some musty file for posterity.

Seeing a chorus of negative nods, Hahn gathered his papers and rose from the chair. "Good. See you all next Monday. George, you come with me."

***

The others gathered their papers and shuffled from the room, picking up the Porsche discussion where they'd left it. I sat in a sort of a daze trying to sort out the whole Lutz discussion. Now Lutz was not my favorite person, but I couldn't help but think his persecution was unwarranted. What he said made sense in a Lutz "by the book" sense. Now his ass was in a sling.

"Hey, the meeting's over. You can go now," quipped Cory, returning to gather the left-over reports.

"Oh hi. I was just trying to digest this whole Lutz-Wiser thing."

"Don't lose any sleep over it. Lutz will recover. He always does. He may be a bit bruised when Wiser gets through with him but he's a survivor and a smart one at that. Now, do you want to grab a cup?"

I was surprised by how causal Cory was about the whole incident but his suggestion was welcomed. "Sure, but you're buying after that Patti O'Neal thing."

"Oh, that. Sorry. Jessie made me do it, honest," he pleaded with a guilty smile as he fell into step beside me. "But it turned out OK didn't it. I mean, didn't I see Maggie's car in the lot Saturday?"

"There are other yellow VWs in the Springs."

"And on Sunday morning?"

I couldn't help but smile. "And I'm the one being accused of spying. You're a natural. But this isn't hallway talk. Let's wait until we get to the mess hall before you interrogate me."

We took the stairs two at a time, arriving at the coffee urn short of breath. Cups in hand we retired to our favorite corner table, far from the main crowd.

"OK, talk. Did Maggie spend another night on the sofa?"

"Her regular spot. But I'm not sure how much to tell you. Everyone seems to be spying on everyone else around here," I responded with a smile I couldn't restrain. "I do think we're back together but I don't want Jessie to know. She'll get too cocky about her matchmaking ability and who knows what she'll try next."

He laughed, swirling cream around his cup. "You seem to know my wife pretty well. Anyway, it's too late; she's the one that spotted the VW. But I think it's great if Maggie is back on the scene. She's a neat girl. Not sure she's your type but she's a fascinating girl all the same. As for the 'Patti' dinner, I was not for that at all. Jessie told me all I had to do was get you there and she would do the rest. I guess she did, the rest I mean."

"Maggie and I had our awkward moments at the club but, in the end, I think things worked out for the best. I'll tell you what. You tell Jessie that, if this Maggie thing works out, we'll name our first child after her."

"You and Maggie are that serious?"

"Hmm. Better strike that from the record. You can forget that last part." Now I felt a little exposed. I shouldn't have said that. We were a long way from that kind of conversation. Marriage? Children? Oddly I hadn't even thought about it until that morning and now this kind of talk was passing my lips. Perhaps I was getting ahead of myself, ahead of our relationship. Perhaps....

***

I sailed into my office, greeting Lopez and the three NCOs with a hardy "Good morning everyone," settled into my chair and began shuffling the papers scattered over the gray desk. My concentration was interrupted by a figure looming over the desk.

"Begging your pardon, sir. You said you wanted those performance reports on your desk this morning but Gruber, I mean Lt. Gruber, gave me a rush job and I wasn't able to do your stuff. I can work through lunch if you like but ...."

"No problem. The end of today will be fine. Thanks for the update. Now how was your weekend?"

"Good sir, real good. And thank you sir." He turned and

walked back to his desk. Out of the corner of my eye I could see him exchange glances and "what was with that" shoulder shrugs with Sgt. Roberts.

My curiosity couldn't let the moment pass. "OK you two. What's the secret joke here? Did someone win a bet?"

Lopez and Roberts exchanged an "oh shit, we've been discovered" look but neither of them spoke.

"What's wrong with you two," piped up Sgt Lawson, from across the aisle. "I told you the lieutenant wouldn't bite. You see, sir," he said, turning to me, "poor Lopez has been quaking in his little black boots all morning fearing a Lt. Munson ass chewing, if you'll pardon the expression. When Gruber insisted his work get done before yours, poor Lopez nearly had a shit fit."

I found myself offering an embarrassed laugh. "Oh, that Munson left town. You're looking at a new and improved version. I guess I've had a little burr under my saddle lately. Anyway, I'm feeling like my old self again so you can stop putting road flares around my desk."

With that brief exchange it was as if a balloon of tension had burst in the office. The word spread fast. As the day progressed, a parade of personnel stopped by with questions or comments they'd been afraid to offer during my time of terror in the office. I felt a little silly about the whole thing but was as glad my self generated inquisition was over as I suspect they were.

At the end of the day I left the mountain again feeling like one of the guys; Roberts and Lopez actually walked to the bus with me. I hadn't realized how much I'd missed being connected with those I worked with and depended on.

Alone in the car I was able to put work out of my mind and concentrate on Maggie. I wanted to see her dreadfully but, short of sitting in on her evening class, that was not going to happen. Instead I tried to grasp what the weekend had really meant. She was clearly disrupting the ordered life I thought I wanted. My plan to avoid women and focus on sports was now in shambles. I would need to redo the chart I'd so carefully drawn.

As I settled into traffic I found myself thinking of

Maggie as a wife and mother. She certainly didn't fit my image of the happy, apron-clad homemaker. And yet being with her was exhilarating. I didn't want to stop seeing her and that path seemed to lead toward marriage and all that goes with it. Perhaps I'd need to alter my image of the perfect "Betty Crocker" type of wife and mother. Maggie was not a country club girl and I couldn't picture her with an apron on, standing by a hot stove. And yet all of that seemed to be diminished in importance as the thought of being with Maggie anywhere, doing anything, filled my consciousness.

But all that would have to be in the future, I thought, as I rolled into my parking space. Now I needed to figure out what I was having for dinner.

***

"Well, it's hump day," said Capt. Kirkwood by way of a greeting as he fell in step with me near the tunnel mouth. "If I can make it through hump Wednesday, the rest of the week seems to go fast."

"Oh hi, Bob. I thought you usually rode the bus."

"You looked so healthy walking I thought I'd join you. Besides, the colonel wants to scrap the carts and walk the course tomorrow so this is my conditioning program," he responded with a laugh which I barely heard with the bus grumbling past our narrow sidewalk.

We walked silently, dodging occasional puddles, while we waited for the bus noise to subside. It still amazed me that water could find its way through 800 feet of granite and end up forming puddles on the walk and dripping on my uniform jacket. I guessed the "solid" rock wasn't so solid after all.

"Big plans for the weekend?" I asked to break the silence. I usually skipped the "sir" with Kirkwood. While he was the same rank as Lutz he never made a big deal about protocol and it was easy to forget he was my commanding officer.

"Not this weekend. But next Saturday Gail and I are going to Denver to take in a play and celebrate our first anniversary."

"Isn't that the same day the peaceniks plan to take over City Hall Plaza and generally screw up traffic? According to the Denver Post it...."

200

"Shouldn't be an issue," he interrupted. "We're stopping to see her folks first. By the time we get downtown they'll all be off in a park somewhere sniffing whatever it is they sniff these days."

The returning bus stifled further conversation as we passed through the giant blast doors, merged with the bus crowd and entered our building. Kirkwood ducked into his office and I continued down the hall to mine where I was greeted by an anxious Airman Lopez.

"Morning sir. Say, did you forget your meeting with the colonel? He just called and seemed to be in a ...."

"Oh shit. Indeed I did." With that I tossed my hat on a shelf, briefcase on my desk, grabbed a pad and black pen and hastened to the forgotten meeting.

"Sorry, sir," I panted, rushing past his clerk and joining Cory who was already seated opposite Hahn's desk. "Got caught up in a little issue with the road crew and time got away from me."

Cory rolled his eyes and smiled as I took a seat.

Hahn closed one file and pulled a second from a stack on the edge of his cluttered desk. "No problem, Roger. It gave Cory and me a chance to tie off some loose ends, if you know what I mean. Now the reason I wanted to see you two boys was to ...."

"What in holy hell is going on around here Colonel?" exclaimed George Lutz, bursting unannounced into the office and tossing a bundle of clipped pages onto Hahn's desk. "Did you know about this Thule order?"

"Perhaps we should come back later," said Cory, beginning to rise from his chair.

Hahn stopped him with a hand gesture and turned his attention to Lutz who was standing, feet apart, fists clenched just inches from the desk. "Of course I knew about the order. But if the final decision was mine they'd be for a two-year stint, not two weeks."

"But sir, Thule, Greenland? And I'll be out of country next weekend when the shit's scheduled to hit the fan. I can't do it. This assignment's got to be put off or delayed or something. I can't leave at a time like this. I won't leave at a ...."

Lutz spun and slammed the half open door, rattling the

colonel's framed collection of diplomas and good conduct certificates.

"Oh George, don't be so dramatic and be damn glad it's only for two weeks. According to Wiser, Gen. Jackson wanted you out of here for good. But the base security guy, what's his name, Rawlings ...."

"Roland, sir, Colonel Roland," offered Lutz, retrieving his black stone from a coat pocket.

"Rawlings, Roland, whatever. Anyway he seems to think you're worth keeping around here. He figures that a cooling-off period might do some good. You know, out of sight, out of mind. That might give last Saturday's incident time to blow over and Wiser can tell his congressman buddy that 'decisive action' was taken."

"Roland's a good man sir," Lutz replied. He seemed to relax a bit and began pacing behind my chair. "But can't it be delayed a few days, a week? What's so important about these particular dates?"

"I don't know the details but Roland said there is a security team scheduled to inspect the Thule set up. The guy that was supposed to lead it went and had his appendix removed last week. So you're an ideal substitute. Timing couldn't be better. So don't make waves. Lay low, get your ass out of here and hope Jackson gets distracted before you get back."

Still pacing Lutz said, "Yes, with Wiser whispering in his ear that's not likely to happen. But who'll take over for me while I'm gone?"

"Your senior NCO, what's his name?"

"Sgt. Larson."

"Right, Larson. Well, he seems like a capable guy. He can report to me while you're gone and I'll look after things. It can't be too difficult."

Lutz took on a stunned expression but stifled his tongue. Cory gave me a "this is going to be good" eye roll while I squirmed in the chair. I was glad we were there to witness the proceedings, but it was painful to see Lutz suffer so and not be able to fight back, restrained by rank and tradition.

"So here," said Hahn, handing the bundle of orders back to Lutz. "Now you'd better get yourself organized. You're supposed to be on that plane Friday morning. And I suggest you throw in your parka. It's colder than a well-digger's ass up there. Now that will be all, George."

Lutz paused, giving the colonel an ice melting stare, before replying, "Yes sir." He snatched the packet from Hahn's outstretched hand, whirled and stormed from the room, slamming the door as he departed.

Chapter Fifteen

May 15th
Lt. Hunk,

First, let apologize for any typos you may detect. I'm using my clerk's electric and it's very sensitive, unlike the clunky portable I used in school. At least you don't have to deal with my handwriting. I have three bottles of correction fluid so should be OK!!!!

Second, your last letter was a bit morose. Sounds like that place is getting to you, for good reason judging from some of the shit you've been through. My suggestion: get the hell out as soon as you can. When are they going to recognize your great mind and pull you up to HQ where you can really impress people?

Seriously, you are making me feel guilty sitting here in the mountains, safe and sound. I do suspect they will snatch me out of here after a year or so and send me for my tour in the jungle but, even then, I imagine it will be cushy compared to the crap you're dealing with.

Most of the older guys in my unit have done a tour in Nam. But sitting in a protected airbase keeping the lights on and water systems working is a far cry from humping in the bush. One NCO in our squadron said his grunt buddy actually spent his R&R with him at Da Nang airbase sleeping in his hootch. The hootch was four-star compared to the conditions the grunt had been living in.

So I feel guilty with me here and you there and, when I go, I'll still feel guilty living in relative comfort. Maybe I'll get over it. In any case I should feel less guilt than the boneheads marching on the campuses.

OK, enough of war shit. Now to my social life; I actually have one! If you recall I said I wasn't going to get serious about anyone until I was out of the service. Well, that resolve lasted all of two months. Despite my best intentions I've met someone I really like. Not sure where it's going but I'm sure enjoying the ride. I'll let you know if it keeps moving but, for now, Lt. Munson is smitten, if that's a word.

I'd best sign off. The cleaners have arrived and want to wax the floors. I'm in the way.

Keep your head down. Some special people are counting on you.

Rog

***

The Saturday morning Dunkin's crowd ebbed and flowed through the lobby like an ocean tide. Two booths behind me a group of retired Army guys discussed politics and medications while a bible study group held court in the far corner. They were all Saturday morning regulars. In some ways I'd become a regular as well. Dunkin's had become my "thinking" place, a place where I could watch the world go by while my mind worked over whatever seemed important at that moment. Again today I was thinking about Maggie.

Last night our relationship reached a new plateau of sorts; we went on what could really be called a date. At least it was the first real date since we'd come to the realization that we might be more than "just friends."

At Capt. Kirkwood's recommendation I'd made dinner reservations at an Italian place in the foothills north of town near the Air Force Academy. It was a romantic little spot with checkered tablecloths, candles set in old wicker covered Chianti bottles and a strolling violinist. However, it was clear from the first glance at the menu that captains could afford fancier dinners than second lieutenants. The evening cost me a weeks pay. It was worth it.

Maggie had looked delectable in a loose fitting greenish wool jumper and a white sweater. Her clothing choice struck me as falling somewhere between campus wear and officer's club standards. At some level I didn't care what she wore. As far as I was concerned she looked good in anything, or nothing at all. Maybe it was just her.

The setting was romantic. The meal was exquisite. The wine was expensive.

We talked about us: things we might want to do

together, places to go, dreams, wishes and fears. She learned things about me I'd never shared with a girl before, not even Penny. It felt like I was cruising in uncharted waters, being so open with my thoughts. At first I was feeling a bit vulnerable but, as she opened up, it seemed OK, somehow safe.

Then I asked if she'd like to come back to my place for the night. After last weekend it seemed like a fair question. "No," she'd said. "I don't think I should. It was very special. Don't get me wrong but I want it to remain special, not routine."

So we talked about it, very matter-of-factly. But the answer remained "no." At some level I suspected she was right. But at another level I just couldn't get enough of Maggie Meyers. It was clearly more than lust, though lust was likely a factor. It was all very confusing and only reinforced my repressed belief that I would never understand women.

So we ended the evening with a shared tiramisu, agreed on a hike this morning, necked for a while outside her place and then I meandered toward my apartment, alone.

And I couldn't wait to see her again.

I finished up my old-fashion, snapped a lid on the coffee and headed off to Maggie's with a bag of twists and donuts in my hand. She saw me climbing from the Camaro and leaned out of her bedroom window. "Let yourself in. I'll be down in a minute."

The living room was empty but, hearing voices in the kitchen, I wandered that way hoping to find Val. Instead I surprised Len, Doggie and a third guy who slipped from the room, out the back door before we could be introduced. Both Len and Doggie were sitting at the table in paint-stained jeans and t-shirts, nursing hot beverages.

"Good morning. Hope I didn't interrupt anything," I offered.

"Oh shit. Who let you in?" Len sneered.

"Sorry, Leonard. Didn't know I needed your permission."

"You bastard," he spat, beginning to rise.

"Oh back off Len," said Doggie, grabbing Leonard and pushing him back into his chair. "Don't be so testy. The last thing we need right now is a brawl." Turning to me he continued.

"Don't mind him. How you doing? The water's still hot and the tea's in that canister. Help yourself."

I displayed my Dunkin cup. "Thanks, I'm covered. Looks like someone's been doing a little painting."

"Welcome to Leonard's sign shop," replied Doggie, gesturing to the detached garage across the lawn in back of the house.

I walked to the window over the sink and surveyed the scene. Luke was busy sawing big pieces of plywood into small pieces of plywood. Two other guys, including the one who'd escaped the kitchen, were busy painting on a table of some sort, sitting on wooden saw horses. Leaning against the garage wall, apparently drying, were samples of the morning's work. The messages varied but the themes were consistent: Peace Now, No More War, Nixon's War No More.

"We've got an extra brush. Want to help?" sneered Len.

"No, art wasn't my best subject. I'll pass."

"Or were you sent to keep and eye on us. Is that a button on your shirt or a little microphone?"

I turned toward them and pushed my chest out. "Actually, it's a miniature camera. Now if you'll turn toward me I can get a better picture."

Doggie grinned. Len glared.

Maggie bound into the kitchen, taking my hand in hers. "What are you boys up to?" The activity in the backyard caught her attention and she walked to the sink, leaning forward to gain a better view. "You've got quite a production line set up. How long till we get our garage back?"

"One more week. Just one more week." Len rose and set his cup on the counter near the sink. "We've plenty of signs if you two would care to join the rally. You could even wear your uniform if you like. The cameras would like that. I can see the headline now. 'Air Force Officer Sees the Light.' Think about it."

He ambled out the back door with Doggie close behind.

Maggie shook her head, kissed me on the cheek and led the way to the front door.

***

"Where to m'lady?" I quipped as we curved through

207

Manitou Springs on our way west, into the mountains. Maggie was curled in the seat beside me with her window down and an old straw hat holding her short hair in place.

"Why don't we go back to our picnic spot on the east face of Pikes Peak? It shouldn't be so snowy now."

"The last time we were there you blew me off."

"Oh, I did not. Besides, that was months ago. I was just, well, just concerned that's all. But I think I'm over it now so let's give it a try. It will be a good test of our relationship." She flashed a smile that overcame my weak resistance and we were soon coasting into the trailhead lot and rolling to a stop.

The hike proved to be different in every respect from our first traverse of this ground. My lungs had clearly adjusted to the thin mountain air; I was not panting like before. The snow was gone and the first signs of emerald spring green were creeping across sunny patches on the slope. The crisp winter air had given way to a radiant warmth. I was glad I'd chosen to wear shorts. Our light jackets were stashed in my pack at our first water stop. And we were different; our relationship was different. As I struggled to maintain her pace, with her firm, denim covered bottom just a few feet in front of me, I couldn't think of any place on earth I'd rather be at that moment in time.

Too soon we found our way to the previous picnic spot, a sun-warmed flat rock with a view of the prairie below. Maggie had made giant hoagies loaded with cheese, pickles and some sort of sausage. We shared one, saved the second and moved to my part of the meal, dessert.

Her smile brightened when my offering emerged from the pack. "How did you know? Oreos are my favorite." She hovered over me as I struggled to open the package without scattering cookies all over our granite seat.

"Intuition I guess. You just seemed like an Oreo kind of girl." Actually she'd told me of her Oreo affection during our first hike. But I didn't see any reason to remind her of that.

She took her first cookie, carefully twisted the halves apart and began savoring the frosting off of the coated side.

"This is great. We have one more thing in common. We both know the right way to eat an Oreo." I successfully mimicked her movements and licked the frosting from the coated side.

"Absolutely," she laughed, stuffing the now bare cookie into her mouth. "As far as I'm concerned the cookie part is only there as a carrier for the frosting."

"You shouldn't talk with your mouth full."

"Now you're sounding like my mother."

She took another cookie and settled on the rock, leaning against me. Taking it apart she offered me the half with frosting. "I want you to know you're special. I don't usually give up the frosting."

Gallantry suggested I refuse the frosting offering. I didn't. I simply enjoyed it, the moment and the girl sitting beside me in the sun.

Only the crackle of unseen insects broke the silence of the windless place. It was easy to let the mind drift into another world. After two more cookies Maggie brought me back with a question that revealed the path of her always-busy mind.

"Do you find all the stuff in the news confusing? I mean all the talk about the war, the people yelling at each other in D.C., the civil rights stuff.... I don't know, all of it. At times it seems the whole country is coming apart. Then I drive around town and everything seems to be normal. Are we living in some sort of fantasy land or are we normal and all the other places abnormal? I find it very confusing." She slid across the rock and turned to face me. "Am I making any sense?"

Of course she was making sense but I was sufficiently surprised by the introduction of such a serious topic that I was slow responding. "Maybe things aren't as screwed up as they seem. You know, the press likes to cover the bad news; good news doesn't sell papers."

"Maybe, but don't you think some of it's real? I mean, this war has a lot of people riled up. It's not just Len. There are lots of Lens on the campus. And some of the professors say really awful things about Nixon and the war. But then Grandpa Meyers has a completely different view and you met him; he is a thoughtful guy. I get confused."

She took another cookie, carefully extracting the cream filling, before continuing. "I wish there was a place, like this one, where we could go and be away from it all. Isn't that selfish of me?"

"Selfish? Maybe, but it sounds good to me. If you find such a place I hope you'll take me with you."

She snuggled closer without a reply. I could tell she was still twisting the world's problems through her mind as she savored the white coating. Then she tacked the conversation onto a new course.

"Did you have to join up or could you have pulled a deferment?"

"It was join or be drafted. Joining seemed like a better idea to me."

"I know kids that dodged the draft by having a baby. Did you ever consider doing that?"

"Now that's an interesting idea. But in case you didn't notice, I'm not plumbed to have a baby so ...."

"Oh, you know what I mean, you and Penny. You were a serious item, weren't you?"

"Not that serious. Besides, it seems like a dumb reason to have a baby. One of my frat brothers deliberately went the marriage/baby route. I hope the marriage lasts but I wouldn't put money on it."

"What about your friend, Hunk? Could he have pulled a baby deferment?" she continued.

"Not sure. But he is or was committed. He wouldn't have tried to dodge, baby or not. I'm not sure what he'd do if he could do it over though. From the tone of his letters he's not as sure about the whole Vietnam thing now as he was last summer."

She slipped from our perch and took a few steps down slope before pursuing the subject from a new angle. "Did you consider going to Canada?"

"Why all the questions?"

"I don't know. I'm just trying to understand you or me or I don't know."

"I didn't consider going to Canada. I figured I had some obligation to my country. And besides, I suspected I'd meet someone like you and I didn't want to miss that opportunity."

She absorbed the answer with a skeptical eye. "I'm glad you joined up. And I'm glad you met me too."

She stepped forward and gave me a delightfully brief

kiss. "Now, enough of this serious talk. We should pack up and head down. I don't like the looks of those clouds coming over the peak."

***

We turned into my apartment parking lot and spotted Jessie and Cory working at the open trunk of their car.

"My God, look how big she is. I can't believe she has a month to go," exclaimed Maggie as we glided past. "Since she's short to begin with that baby looks all the bigger. It looks so uncomfortable…"

I eased into my space and the two of us hopped from the Camaro and headed their way.

"You're not going to have the baby here in the lot are you? It's not permitted in the lease," I hailed.

"Hey, you two," responded Cory, pulling his head from the trunk. "Well, isn't this nice, an able-bodied man to help carry the groceries. Why don't you and Maggie go on in, honey? Smart-mouth Roger can help me with the boxes."

"Suits me." Jessie took Maggie's arm and steered her toward the door. "Come on Maggie; we've got lots to catch up on."

By the time Cory and I lumbered into their apartment, burdened by loaded grocery boxes, Jessie was seated in a big rocker and Maggie was busy emptying an ice cube tray into four tall glasses on the counter. "We've been invited in for a Coke and I said 'yes.' Hope that's OK."

"Suits me," I replied setting my box on the table and taking a seat on the sofa near Jessie. "Well, how's Miss Cupid doing today?"

"Just fine, thank you. Say, why don't you and Maggie come for dinner? I feel like I haven't talked to her for ages. You've been hiding her from me."

"That's a laugh. You seem to find her when you need to. Anyway, no on dinner. It looks like you need to be spending your time sitting in that rocker thinking up baby names. But that reminds me. I owe you a dozen dinners. Why don't you come to dinner at my place, say next Friday. I have no idea what we'll have but I'll dredge up something spectacular just for you two and little Cory Jr."

"That's a wonderful idea," chimed in Maggie, delivering a Coke to Jessie. "Assuming Roger invites me too I'll keep an eye on things and make sure you get a decent meal."

"Works for me," chimed in Cory. "She's suppose to stay off her feet so I've been doing the evening cooking and the results have been disappointing."

The banter continued until the sun's descent behind Pikes Peak signaled the coming of evening. "Oops, it's getting late and Roger needs to get this student home," said Maggie, gathering up empty bottles and glasses. "Let's leave these love birds alone."

We said our "goodbyes" and headed up to my apartment. "Do you really have to go right now? Couldn't you stay? Stay for dinner I mean?"

"Of course I can stay. You can't get rid of me that easy," she said, closing the apartment door as she squeezed my hand. "Now what's for dinner?"

An hour later, as I put the leftover waffle batter in the refrigerator, Maggie sat at the table, nursing a cup of coffee. "You are truly a superb waffle baker Lieutenant. Is that what you're serving Jessie next Friday?"

"Oh Geez, that's a good question. I've already done my steak and baked potato option with them. I'll have to be a little more creative this time."

Maggie looked thoughtful as she tore a napkin into small strips. "How about fondue?"

"Fondue? You've got to be kidding. That takes a bunch of paraphernalia that I don't have: pots, oils and I don't know what all. I'm afraid that may be beyond my creative comfort level."

"Nonsense. Mother did it when I was home at Christmas. It didn't look that hard. And, as for the 'paraphernalia,' as you call it, she also gave me a fondue kit: pot, sterno, forks, recipe book, the works. So, if you invite me to the dinner, I'll help you pull it off. Come on, let's give it a try. It will give me an excuse to get it out of its box for the first time."

"I'm game, if you're up to it. I guess that means you're invited to dinner as well," I said, coming up behind, leaning down and kissing her on the neck. "Now I suppose I have to get my student home."

She rose, turned and pinned me against the wall with lovely embrace. "Or you could invite me to spend the night."

Nibbling on her ear I pondered that delicious thought. I extricated myself from her embrace and held her away so I could look into her luminous eyes. "Miss Maggie, there was a time when you could sleep on my sofa with impunity. But the way I feel about you now I can't make any guarantees of good behavior."

"Who said anything about a sofa or good behavior? Just be yourself."

***

"Fondue! Oh this will be fun," exclaimed Jessie, seeing the table set with the stainless steel pot stand in the middle and fondue forks at each place setting. "All the magazines rave about it but I've never done it."

I turned to Maggie, who was busy cutting chicken breast into uniform cubes. "You can thank my cook here. It was her idea. She's been making sauces and chopping meat for hours. I can't even spell 'fondue.' I nearly flunked French."

Maggie pushed the hair from her eyes with the back of her hand with the look of an exhausted cook. "You are all part of a grand experiment. I just got the thing out of its box," she said, nodding toward the gleaming new fondue pot.

"What inspired you to buy it?" asked Jessie.

"Good grief, I didn't buy it. It was a Christmas gift from my mom. She's always buying things for my hope chest. This didn't fit so I brought it to school with me. But, as Roger knows, I don't live in a 'fondue' kind of house."

Cory gave the table set up a cursory look. "What's with women and this hope chest thing anyway? As far as I'm concerned Jessie's chest is just a good place to store tablecloths and to sit when I'm tying my shoes."

"Good question. And why just hope chests for daughters?" I added. "God, it seems to me sons are being left out."

Cory laughed and picked up the theme. "How about a tool chest for men? Instead of linens and fondue pots, we could fill it with saws and drills and other really useful stuff. This hope chest thing is damned unfair if you ask me."

Jessie responded as Cory helped her with her chair. "Oh put a sock in it, dear. It's because mothers know their sons will find talented women like me and Maggie to take care of them." Reaching for a fork she continued. "Now what do we have here and how do we do it?"

I carefully placed the stainless steel fondue pot, half filled with peanut oil, over the sterno flame which served as table center piece. "Now be careful with this thing. That oil is hotter than hell. I'm not so sure this cooking at the table thing is such a wise idea."

"Oh Roger, sit down. People do this all the time. Now, as I said, this is a grand experiment. We have chicken and beef. Those little bowls are the dipping sauces; Teriyaki, béarnaise and mustard. You put the sauce into the little...."

The meal was a great adventure and resounding success. The evening was topped off with a chocolate fondue dessert.

"That angel food cake dipped in chocolate was so good," exclaimed Jessie, sitting alone at the table while the rest of us cleared the dishes. "I'm sure to flunk my weigh-in on Tuesday."

"For now, little mother, we need to get you home. It's been a long day." Cory helped her up before turning to me. "Well, we'll see you Monday if not before."

"Are you on standby or anything for tomorrow, you know, the student protest threat and all of that Lutz stuff?" I asked.

"Not really. The colonel doesn't take the thing very seriously, thinks Lutz was just seeing commies under every rock, so to speak. No, he and Sgt. Larson have spoken a few times but he seems to think Larson is doing a great job filling in for Lutz. Are you planning to go up?"

"Not to work."

Maggie came up and wrapped her arm in mine. "Roger's being a hero. At sunrise he's taking me up to the Cheyenne Mountain parking lot to do some serious picture taking. I'm hoping for morning clouds again tomorrow to give me a nice pink sunrise."

"You two have a good time," chipped in Jessie. "I don't do sunrise; it comes too early."

Maggie and I each gave Jessie a gentle hug before sending her lumbering way.

I closed the door and turned to Maggie. "You did a fabulous job with dinner, Miss Meyers. I'll have to have you back again sometime."

"I'd like that, Lieutenant. I'd like that very much. Now let's get to those dishes."

Chapter Sixteen

May 15; Madigan General Hospital, Ft. Lewis WA
Rog,

    I survived! Madigan General Hospital; three of the most beautiful words I can think of!!! I'm back in the World and loving it! I see Sally everyday and I've gotten to hold my son. What a boy!

    Sorry about the chicken scratch again but the typewriter hasn't caught up with me so you'll have to decipher my handwriting again.

    As you may have heard, I'm here doing the last of my PT on the way to near full recovery. I say near because I may end up with a slight limp; time will tell. Maybe I can get a job as Chester, Marshal Dillon's peg-legged sidekick on Gunsmoke! The leg may be my ticket to an early out.

    Remember I said I thought some gook had my number? Well, he almost collected. Details are fuzzy but we were humping up this ridge when all hell broke loose. I took a round in the thigh and was roughed up a bit by a nearby mortar round but our doc patched me up and I got a medivac chopper out. That started me on a multi-week trip through a series of clean, cool, white hospital rooms that ended up with a flight to McChord and bed here in the Madigan Orthopedic ward. The bullet shattered my femur, which has caused the most complications, but my manhood is intact (though unused to date) and the healing is coming along fine.

    As I look around the ward, I realize how lucky I am; I've got all my limbs to work with. Some of these poor grunts were not so lucky.

    Sally broke into tears when she saw me. I thought it was from happiness but she later said it was because I looked so shitty (my words) that she hardly recognized me. But the hospital food and inactivity are putting my weight back on so there will be more of me to love. Jeff Jr. can't come into the ward so they

*wheel me down to the lobby and I can hold the little "hunk." He
is the best looking baby I've ever seen. But, hey, look at his
parents!*

*Sally's here now and says "hi." I need to sign off so she
can mail it when she leaves. Take care and watch for falling
rocks. I know your assignment must be harrowing!*

*Write, you blue-suited bastard. Use our Anacortes
address. Ciao.*
Hunk

FIGMO COUNTDOWN: ZERO!!!!!

***

It was still inky black outside when the alarm jarred me
awake. I rolled to the side of the bed trying to sort out what the
wailing tone meant. Was it a work day? Had I set it by mistake?
Then my sleep-fogged mind settled on the solution. I was
supposed to pick up Maggie for our sunrise photo trip. It was
Saturday.

I found old jeans on the closet floor, a gray sweatshirt in
the back of a drawer and my well-worn sneakers under the bed.
It wasn't fancy but it would do. I ran a comb through my tousled
hair, covered the evidence with a baseball cap, skipped my
shave, grabbed an old parka and headed off to Dunkin's. I could
skip a shave but not a coffee.

The big V8 violated the morning quiet as I eased from
the lot while reflecting on the last week with Maggie. Never far
from my mind, she was an endless source of surprise. Last
Sunday, when I didn't expect her to stay over, she did. Last
night, when I thought she might stay, she didn't. I gently pressed
the matter, but to no avail. She wanted to keep our times together
"special" and I could respect that, even if I didn't understand it.
A cold shower had provided but scant relief.

I rolled into the nearly empty Dunkin lot, grabbed a fiver
from my mad money stash in the ashtray and made my hasty
purchase. Then the trusty Camaro made its way to Maggie's
carrying drowsy me, two coffees and a bag of assorted donuts.

"Oh you dear man," said Maggie, seeing the coffees as
she opened the door. She rose to her toes and gave me a

delightful "good morning" kiss before leading me to the living room.

She stopped by a pile of coats, camera bags and tripods. "Do you mind if Val joins us? She thought it would be fun. She took the same photography class fall quarter."

Val walked into the room as I surveyed the pile. "It works for me but it's going to be a little crowded in the back seat with all this stuff."

"How about the trunk?" Maggie asked.

"Full of junk. I suppose I could leave the big stuff here and…."

"Why don't we take Len's van?" Val interjected. "I've got the keys. He won't mind as long as I don't tell him Roger was with us."

"I don't know if that's a good idea," I began. "What will he use? I'm not loaning him the Camaro."

"Chill out, Roger. He borrowed the new kid's jeep-like thing. You know the one, Maggie, 'Borky's Bronco.'"

"Oh, that's choice," laughed Maggie. "Roger, you should see this thing. It's a giant Ford Bronco with this picture of a bucking bronco and the name, 'Borky's Bronco' painted on the driver's door. It reminds me of the nose art they put on bombers in the old days."

"I don't care. I'm not riding in that heap. Besides, it would stand out like a sore thumb in the parking lot. No sense attracting attention to our little photo shoot," I said, heading for the front door.

"What's the big deal?" asked Val as she gathered her equipment. "Aren't we supposed to be there?"

I paused and turned to face the confused gaze of two women. "It's not that exactly. It's just that I don't want to have anyone asking questions, especially with me looking like this," I concluded, gesturing to my rumpled attire.

"Oh Roger, you look fine for taking pictures. It's not like you're going to work or anything," said Maggie, with a laugh.

"That's your opinion. Just give me a second to empty the trunk. I'd prefer to drive my own car." I turned, took the two steps from the porch in a single bound and ran toward the Camaro, fumbling for my keys as I went. Val was close on my heels.

"Ah, Roger. You may want to take a look at this. Seems this front tire is a bit out of round"

I stepped to where Val was gazing at my beautiful right front Goodyear radial. "Now how the hell did that happen? I didn't notice anything five minutes ago," I said, kneeling and rubbing my hand over the tread surface. I couldn't feel anything but the tire was flatter than a flounder.

"Doesn't matter how it happened. This rig's not going anywhere for a while. I'll go get Len's ...."

"Wait, I can change it. It'll only take a minute."

"Val's right," said Maggie, taking my arm. "I'm sure you're fast but the sunrise won't wait. We need to go. It's already getting light. Come on, I'm sure Len's van isn't all that bad."

So that's how I ended up sitting on a carpet covered plywood box that served as a bench seat in the back of Leonard's decrepit van. As Val drove up the access road, with Maggie riding shotgun, I just hoped no one recognized me,

***

Maggie had picked an ideal morning. As we coasted to a stop at the outer edge of the parking lot the first hints of light were piercing the thin horizontal layers of clouds hovering on the eastern horizon.

I directed Val to the perimeter of the lot avoiding the cluster of vehicles near the security building. There was no sense in attracting attention to our little photo shoot. Cars, which I assumed belonged to the night shift, were scattered in the lot near the entrance and an early morning stillness hung over the place. The next major activity would likely be the arrival of the day crew around 8:00 o'clock, an hour from now.

While the girls busied themselves with film, filters and tripods, I settled into the passenger seat to enjoy my coffee and survey the fragrant interior of Leonard's rolling hemp house. It was as disgusting on the inside as on the outside. It had the look of a former, well-used, delivery van. The interior was bare metal except for the two front buckets, the wooden bench and a few carpet scraps scattered around the cold floor. The only cargo area windows were in the two rear doors giving the back of the van a cave-like atmosphere. I had the uneasy feeling that I should wash my hands well before handling a donut.

The dim light was suddenly pierced by a pair of headlights curving along the edge of the lot, heading straight for the van. Whatever it was stopped a few feet from the van's bumper and two large forms emerged from the blinding beams. There was no mistaking their current occupations; both wore helmets with the letters "MP" stenciled in black on a white background. In case we missed the helmets the same "MP" message appeared on large patches on their arms. Their olive-drab uniforms were starchy crisp, covered with patches, pins and symbols I didn't recognize. I did recognize their web belts which were holding up giant holsters concealing what I suspected were giant guns. But at the moment their hands were occupied by sinister looking wooden batons. They appeared to be all business.

Army military police, what the hell were they doing here?

"You there, out of the van and over with the others."

I stole a glance at the girls who were standing by their tripods shielding their eyes from the headlight glare. For the first time I noticed a second pair of headlights at the rear of the van and two more MPs coming out of that glare. The posse had us surrounded.

"You deaf? Now get your sorry ass out of there." With that, the bigger of the two grabbed my coat collar and yanked me from the seat.

The sudden movement wrenched the paper coffee cup from my hands and onto his thigh where it released its contents down a bloused pant leg and onto his gleaming boots.

"Ah shit, you bastard," I heard as he encouraged me along with the baton poking the center of my back.

"Hey guys, easy now," I pleaded, trying to turn around. "I work here. I'm Air Force."

"Yes, and I'm General Patton," snarled Mr. Coffee Pants.

"No, really," I said, reaching for my wallet. "I can show you my ID card." At least I thought I could. But the pocket was empty. I never left without my wallet. At least not until this morning as I raced around the apartment with Dunkin's on my mind.

"Watch him, Harry. He may have something," shouted a voice from the left while someone grabbed my wallet hand, bending it behind my back. "Now, you two, down on the curb, hands where we can see them."

"OK," said the voice inches from my ear, "I'm going to release your arm and you're going to reach for your wallet real slow like."

In slow motion I patted my pants and coat pockets in the vain hope the wallet was there. "Ah, I seem to have left it at home. But if we go over to security they can ID me."

"Yes, right," responded the one called Harry. "We'll get right on that. Now, in the meantime you just sit your little ass down by your lady friends there." He concluded the instruction with a push that sent me stumbling toward the curb.

"Now just what the hell is going on cowboy?" shouted an angry Val, stepping toward Coffee Pants. "Who do you think you are, swooping down on us like this? Why don't you bug off and leave us alone."

I was the guy. I was supposed to do the heroic deeds so I decided to join Val's protest movement. I moved toward Val. "OK guys, this is ridiculous. I'm an officer in the United States Air Force. I have every right to…."

"Cuff'em," said a deep voice from the left. "Garrett, search the van."

"Hey, you can't do that," continued Val. "The Constitution prohibits…."

"You don't read too good, do you lady? The sign at the entrance says you are on a military reservation and all vehicles are subject to search. So do as you're told before…."

Despite our protestations, or perhaps because of them, the three of us were soon sitting on the low curb with our hands cuffed ignobly in front and the glorious sun rising at our backs. Looking around, I could see why they were having trouble with my claim to be an officer. First, I looked like hell; I looked like I belonged in that van. Maggie and Val fit the "van" image as well. Maggie was wearing an old denim jacket over her flannel shirt and well-worn jeans. Her floppy pink hat topped off her

Stephen J. Dennis

ensemble. Val was all campus attire with a wool sweater over a baggy cotton shift which billowed in the breeze to reveal her leather sandals. Even with the wool stocking cap I thought she must be freezing her ass in the morning chill.

In the growing light our captors gained a clearer identity. They had arrived in matching little Jeeps with "Military Police" in bold letters beneath their windshield glass. Their headlights were now off but little red lights still revolved from a position above the windshield. Why they were even at the mountain was a mystery to me. Perhaps it was some Lutz joint operation agreement that he'd alluded to at a staff meeting. But they were here, I was cuffed and I was pissed.

The leader, the one they called "Sarge," was sitting in the left Jeep talking on some sort of radio trying to figure out what to do with us. He looked the part. Lutz would have appreciated him. His uniform was impeccable, moustache neatly trimmed and he wore those aviator type sunglasses, even in the dark. His sidekick, Mr. Coffee Pants, tried to look sharp as well but had trouble pulling it off with a beer belly hanging over his web belt.

I was telling Val and Maggie not to worry as this would all work out when there was a shout from the back of the Van.

"Hey Sarge, I think we've got something."

Harry, the solidly built little redhead, stepped from behind the rear doors holding a small plastic bag. "Found it in the side panel. Looks like...."

"I know what it looks like," said Sarge, raising his sunglasses to examine the bag. "So we got us some dopers. Nice work, Preston."

"Hey, that's not ours. It's not even our van," implored Maggie, rising from the curb.

The redhead reached out and pushed her back down. "Never is ma'am. Nope, nobody can ever figure how this shit gets in their vehicle. It always appears like magic."

"Keep your hands off her, Mr. Macho," I pressed, rising and moving toward him.

Beer Belly stepped between us, pressing his baton horizontally against my chest, stopping my progress. "Sit back down, boy. Don't want nobody to get hurt here."

222

We stood eyeball to eyeball for a moment while he shifted a wad of gum from side to side in his mouth. I was about to continue my protest when the morning quiet was rent by the strange sound of a distant bugle.

I pushed the club away and moved to the front of the van, gazed toward the sound of the bugle and was greeted with a strange sight. A half a dozen figures appeared suspended from ropes on the flat rock face maybe 100 feet above the tunnel entrance. The sound was coming from that general area.

Sarg sprang into action. "Garrett, you stay with the prisoners. You two come with me. Let's roll."

Coffee Pants and Red Head tumbled into the Jeep at our front bumper which rumbled to life and careened across the parking lot making more noise than speed.

Our remaining guard was a tall skinny kid built like a basketball center. He fidgeted with his wooden club, as if he was not comfortable with the three-to-one odds. I decided to take advantage of his confusion and press our case.

"OK, this is it. We're going over to the gate and clear up this misunderstanding."

"Sit. Sit back down or I'll…."

"Or you'll follow us to the gate. Come on, ladies. Let's get out of here." I walked past the front of the van and headed toward the gate.

"Roger, a gun," came Maggie's panicked voice. "Roger he has a gun."

I stopped and turned to face the business end of a big assed government issue "45."

"Sit…sit back down. I mean it now…sit, pronto," said the skinny kid, with a breaking voice.

"Oh shit." I turned and walked slowly back toward Maggie. "OK, OK. Put that gun away. Someone could get hurt with a thing like that."

He looked at me. He looked at the gun. He looked at me again. "OK, but no funny stuff. Now back on the curb."

He holstered the gun and snapped its cover back into place.

***

I don't know how long we sat on the stony curb. Time

seemed frozen. I was unable to dwell on our hapless situation as our attention was focused on the unfolding drama at the mountain entrance.

News vans from Channels Four and Seven had rolled into the lot shortly after the bugle blast. They had to have been tipped off. There was no way they could have just "heard the news" and rushed to the mountain. I could see them in their distinctive wind breakers, red for Channel Seven and yellow for Channel Four, racing around, setting up cameras and trying to look important for on-camera spots.

Other cars, some in Air Force blue, had begun to cluster near the gate house. Then there was a collection of olive-colored Jeeps which were later joined by a truck containing a dozen or more olive-clad Army-looking troops.

Clearly the event had attracted some attention.

On the rock wall the situation was both amusing and interesting. The little dangling figures had successfully unfurled a banner, about 20 feet square, emblazed with a peace symbol above the words "Peace Now." Actually the symbol was below the words since the banner was unfurled upside down. The dangling figures were now in the middle of a supreme effort to correct the error and turn the banner right side up, not an easy task hanging on a rock wall.

All this time our guard paced back and forth between us and the mountain to prevent another escape attempt.

"Hey kid, what's your name," called Maggie.

"Garrett, ma'am."

"Well Garrett, how about a donut? There's a bag beside the front seat. There's plenty for everyone. Why don't you grab it?"

He eyed her suspiciously then backed to the van, never taking his eyes off of his prisoners. He recovered the bag and tossed it to Maggie, underhand. She opened it and held it out so he could select one before she shared with us.

I was enjoying mine, trying to think of a way to get through to this young man when Val broke the impasse.

"All right, this is it," she said rising to her feet. "I've got to pee. Shoot me if you wish but I'm going to walk over to that building and pee. Anyone want to join me?"

"Wait, you can't," said nervous Garrett, gripping his club. "You've got to stay here. I've got my orders."

Maggie and I rose and caught up with Val and her pursuing guard.

"Garrett," I said, coming abreast of him. "The girl's got to pee. We'll all stay together so you can still guard us and you don't catch hell. You're just showing initiative. Nothing wrong with that."

His eyes skittered from me, to the cluster of Jeeps, to Val, to the TV vans and back to me. He didn't know what to do but by that time we were nearly at the security building and I was busy looking for a familiar face, any familiar face.

"Munson! What the hell are you doing?"

I turned, delighted to hear the voice of Col. Hahn standing with binoculars dangling from his neck with his reading glasses. "Colonel, am I ever glad to see you. Would you please explain to…?"

"What, are you in handcuffs? What the hell kind of a mess have you gotten yourself into?"

"It's a mistake sir, a big mistake," I shouted over another blast from the bugle. "Now if you'll just explain who I am to Private Garrett here I can get out of these things."

Garrett looked like a dog trying to herd squirrels. Val was drifting toward the security building, Maggie and I had stopped and now this colonel was talking to his prisoners.

"Yes, right, private. He's one of my officers. Get those things off of him."

"Sorry sir, I can't do that. You see, he's under arrest and…."

"Oh balls," the colonel growled. He turned to the security building and shouted, "Larson, Sgt. Larson, get your ass out here."

With the ruckus I didn't notice the official blue Chevrolet staff car pull up and stop just a few feet behind us. Suddenly a new voice joined the cacophony. "Maggie, what on earth are you doing here?"

I spun to be greeted by the sight of General Jackson, all six feet two of him, striding from the car toward a handcuffed Maggie Meyers.

"Oh, hi Manny," she said, with an embarrassed shuffle. "It's not as bad as it looks, really it isn't. I can explain."

He stopped in front of her, placed his hands on her shoulders examining her from floppy hat to boots. "Someone get these God damned cuffs off of her. This is ridiculous."

"I'm taking care of it sir," said Col. Hahn in his best groveling manner as Sgt. Larson pushed through the crowd and began unlocking the handcuffs.

Private Garrett, overwhelmed by rank, melted into the crowd. Perhaps he'd return with reinforcements. In any case he'd have a hell of a story to tell his boss.

"And who are these other people?" asked the General, gesturing toward me and Val.

"That is Val over there, one of my roommates; you've met her before. And this is my boyfriend, Roger Munson. Roger, I'd like you to meet my stepfather."

Stepfather! General Maynard Jackson was Maggie's stepfather? Unbelievable. Despite the shock and confusion, instinct took over and the right words passed my lips. "Pleased to meet you, sir," I said, while trying to digest what I'd just heard. My first instinct was to salute but he offered his hand before I could make a bigger fool of myself.

"Hmmm, you look familiar. Have we met before?" he asked, with a skeptical look that seemed to burn through my shabby parka.

"Yes sir. You see, sir, I'm actually Lt. Munson, U. S. Air Force. I work for Col. Hahn here in the engineering group, sir." Instinctively I'd come to full attention while offering that explanation.

He studied me from top to bottom with a look that I did not classify as approving.

"Am I to assume you're not on duty at this time?"

"Yes sir. I mean no, sir. I mean yes, I'm not on duty. I just brought Maggie up here to take some pictures and…."

Maggie, sensing my discomfort, came to my side and took my arm. "It's OK Roger. Manny won't bite."

From his pinched glare I wasn't too sure and her "bite" remark seemed to elevate his frustration level. But the general quickly recovered his composure. "Well, why don't you kids wait in my car here? I've got to get this mess straightened out."

"Oh, my God. I think that's Len up there, the one on the left," shrieked Val.

In unison we turned our gaze to the little cluster of figures on the left side of the ill fated banner. It was now on its side and scrunched so the words were unreadable. Five figures were struggling against a slight morning breeze to turn it, while a sixth, the one that Val was gesturing toward, shouted orders between discordant bugle blasts.

"Let me see those things," said Val, deftly removing Hahn's binoculars from around his neck, knocking his hat askew. "Oh shit, that cretin. It's him. And I think Doggie is the one in the red cap on his left."

The general moved close to Val and squinted at the bodies swinging on long ropes along the rugged granite wall. "Friends of yours?"

"Leonard? He's just a...."

"He's a guy we see on campus," Maggie interrupted, taking the binoculars from Val and turning them to the rock face. "I've seen him at the Commons passing out anti-war stuff."

"Hmmm, well, he's picked the wrong rock to play on. Hahn, get those bastards down before someone gets hurt. And, as for you three, you can wait this one out in the backseat of my car. We can talk later," he ordered, looking directly at Maggie.

His driver opened the rear door and I was about to follow what I considered to be an order and join the girls in the car when Maggie paused. "Manny, could Val and I run to the rest room first? You see we…"

"What? Oh, of course. But then you'd best stay out of the way. Things are confusing enough as it is," General Jackson replied.

"And sir, I need him. I need Lt. Munson," said Col. Hahn, looking nervously from me to the general.

I paused by the open car door.

"Him?" he replied, again looking me over head to scruffy shoes. "Looking like that?"

"Well, yes. I'm sorry about his appearance but, you see, he's not on duty exactly. In any case, I need his engineers to roll out and man their fire-fighting pumps.'

"You expecting a fire?"

"No sir. I intend to use the high pressure water to hose them off the hill like ants. They should be down in no time and then we can deal with these trespassers," shouted Hahn, over the background chaos of bugles and shouting reporters.

The general turned again and studied the rock face.

I moved toward Colonel Hahn trying to absorb what I'd just heard against the carnival-like scene around us. The intermittent bugle blaring continued. A cordon of MPs surrounded our party, at Sgt. Larson's insistence, to ward off reporters who were trying to reach General Jackson. At that moment Larson was on the other side of the staff car trying to block the view of a newly arrived TV camera whose operator was talking about his constitutional rights. Above it all I could hear the faint "wop, wop, wop" of a helicopter.

The words "hose them off like ants" tumbled through my mind as I approached the colonel. "Sir," I began to either or both of them. "Sir, I wonder if there's a better way."

In unison the general and the colonel turned skeptical looks towards me. I suddenly wished I was still sitting on the curb with Private Garrett.

"Ah, perhaps we should move into the security building where it will be a little quieter, where I can lay out my idea for this thing." I gestured toward the building and, without a word, they both turned and, with a moving cordon cutting the crowd ahead of us, walked toward the safety and relative quiet of Lutz's office.

The move to the building bought me much needed time. My mind was tapioca. I didn't have a plan. Leonard was on the wall. The general was Maggie's stepfather. I was dressed like a tramp. Trying to override Hahn's idea, without making him look like an ass, would be a challenge. This was not a good place for a fresh face second lieutenant. Of that much I was certain.

We met Val and Maggie in the building lobby and, without asking, they joined the entourage and made themselves inconspicuous in a corner of the now-crowded office.

***

"Well, it's a damn sight quieter in here. Now what's your big plan for ending this embarrassing charade, Lieutenant?"

General Jackson turned and sat on a corner of Lutz's desktop, which was clear of everything but a desk top blotter, nameplate, ashtray, desk lamp and phone.

The trouble was, I didn't have a plan. I just didn't like Hahn's. While the climbing protesters were now only about 50 feet above the asphalt drive I didn't relish the thought of scraping one of them off the paving. My mind went into overdrive and my lips began spewing words almost before my mind formed them.

"Well, sir, it's the publicity thing I'm concerned about. Yes, that's it, the publicity thing."

The general rolled his eyes and reached inside his uniform jacket for a cigarette. Hahn's eyes flitted from Jackson to me as if not sure how to react.

"I'm wondering what those guys on ropes think they can accomplish hanging up there. They can't shut us down. They can't end the war. But they can garner publicity for their cause. They can get on the evening news. I know that…or I mean I've seen that bugle blower on campus. I'd be willing to bet it's publicity for his cause that he's after. And he'd welcome anything we do that helps achieve that goal."

The general gave me an impatient look. "So what are you suggesting, that we turn the hoses on the reporters? Now that would look good on the news."

"Oh, we'd never do that sir. Hose the reporters I mean," offered Hahn. "But the boy may be on to something. I could just have security round up the press guys and escort them off the mountain. It's government property and I could do that. No sense having them around. No reporters and no cameras means no publicity."

"Works for me. Make it happen." Jackson flicked his ash into Lutz's ashtray and made a move toward the door.

"That wasn't exactly what I had in mind, Colonel," I said, rushing to block their path. "Running them off the mountain I mean. I mean, I can hear them shouting 'freedom of the press' and all that as we round them up. That might not produce the kind of press we want."

The general stopped and turned to me. "Well then, exactly what did you have in mind Lieutenant?"

My mind was a kaleidoscope of dead end ideas. I was conscious of perspiration forming on my tousled brow. I caught Maggie's eye in the background. She appeared relaxed and seemed to be enjoying the whole tableau. Then an idea took the shape of words. "Well sir, what if we didn't do anything? I mean, what if we just leave them alone, hanging up there in the sun. Six guys hanging on ropes may make the news but that's it. End of story. But six guys getting hosed off the mountain, and possibly injured, would be news with staying power." I was beginning to warm to the subject and the idea began to take form.

"We could even have the mess hall bring out a coffee urn for the news types and try to make them real comfortable. When nothing more happens they'll likely toddle off to cover some real news.

The general returned to the desk.

"I appreciate your concern, Roger, but the general can hardly be seen as simply sitting around while these guys threaten to compromise the security of this mountain. No, we need to be more proactive than that."

General Jackson held up a hand to silence Hahn, taking a long draw on his smoke. He walked slowly to the window and peered up at the protesters suspended on the sun-splashed rock face.

Hahn fidgeted with his binocular strap and paced the far wall.

For the first time I could study this man, this man who was Maggie's stepfather. That shock was still settling in. Why the big secret? Why hadn't she told me? What was her relationship with him, this general in the U.S. Air Force? There had never even been a hint that her stepfather and, most likely, her mother lived right in Colorado Springs. What would this revelation do to my Maggie relationship? I wanted to join Hahn in his pacing but had an aversion to anything that looked like I was emulating his dithering manner.

As the general turned, his smoldering ash fell to the tile floor. "Interesting idea, son. What did you say your name was again?"

"Munson, sir. Lieutenant Roger Munson."

"Well Munson, you have an interesting idea if, as you suggest, publicity is their game. It's at least worth a try. Hahn, let's launch a charm campaign. Coffee, access to the rest room, the whole bit and anything else you can think of to make the press guys as comfortable as possible."

"Yes, sir. Right away, sir." Hahn bolted for the door and nearly ran into Major Wiser, the general's aide, as he pushed past the guard and squeezed into the office.

Wiser, clad in golf attire, ignored Hahn and rushed to his boss. "Sir, I'm glad I found you. Those yokels outside didn't seem to have any idea where you'd gone. Got here as soon as I could. What's the situation?"

Jackson pushed the door shut while explaining the charm offensive to his obviously skeptical aide.

"So we're going to feed the press and let the goons just hang on the wall?" A spark of recognition crossed Wiser's face while examining me from head to toe. His surprised gaze then shifted to the two girls huddled beside the file cabinet.

Jackson smiled. "Not exactly. That's where you come in. I want you to contact General Collin's boys down at Fort Carson. I'd like some of his chopper jockies in the air on the back side of this mountain to find out where these 'goons,' as you call them, came from. It's a long hike in so I suspect there are vehicles waiting for them up on one of the old mining roads. Then we can arrange a welcoming committee for them when they decide to go back to wherever they came from."

"Sir, about the press ramifications of...," I began.

"Don't worry Muncy. I'm not going to rough them up or anything. Just want to know who they are and put the fear of God in their little souls."

Wiser gave me a "how dare you speak to the general like that look" and headed for the phone. "I'll get right on it, sir."

"That will be all, Lieutenant. Why don't you and the girls wait out in the lobby for a few minutes? When things quiet down I'd like to have a word with Maggie. For now I need to make some calls."

"Yes, sir," I said, relieved at the chance to escape the scene.

"And Muncy," he added as I followed the girls out of the

room.

I stopped and turned. "It's Munson, sir."

"Right. Whatever. Next time, before you come up here, I suggest you stand a little closer to your razor." He finished with a subtle grin and nodded for me to go.

Rubbing my stubbled chin I never looked back.

Chapter Seventeen

May 29th
My Dear (and only) Sister,

Have I had a couple of interesting weeks!! Not sure where to begin.

First, last weekend we had a big anti-war demonstration at the mountain. You'd have felt right at home. Unwashed people chanting and waving signs etc; it was quite the scene. I didn't make the news but, if I had, mother would have been proud. Won't go into details now but, suffice to say, one minute I was about to be arrested and the next I was sort of a hero (at least in some eyes.) Anyway, it was a bit of Saturday excitement I can do without.

The next news scoop concerns a young lady named Maggie. The enclosed photo was taken on a recent hike. Not a bad-looking girl, don't you think?

I took your advice and bypassed the sorority set and went for granola. So far I have to say I'm liking granola. She's a very interesting young lady who I think you will enjoy meeting. Gorgeous, smart, full of surprises and she seems to be attracted to me. How good is that? She is pursuing an art major which is about as far from engineering as you can be but you might say we complement each other.

Mother doesn't know and I'm not sure when I'll tell her. For now she is just happy to know "I'm making new friends." Keep the Maggie thing under your hat for now. But I have a feeling she will be part of the family in the not too distant future.

There, I've told you all my secrets. Now it's your turn to tell me about your love life. Take care and write soon.
Rog

***

"You should have seen him Grandpa. He was magnificent."

I was more than a little embarrassed by Maggie's

retelling of my role in putting down what the press had labeled "The Cheyenne Mountain Incident." Now, as I sat on Grandpa Meyer's front porch swing with Maggie at my side and a cool lemonade in hand, my time in Army handcuffs seemed like a strange dream from long, long ago. Yet it had happened, much as she described it, just one week before.

"God, I'd have loved to see that. Manny had to call the Army in to help him out. That must have bugged the hell out of a dyed-in-the-wool Air Force guy. So this Colonel Hahn wants to hose them off the rocks and you suggest a charm campaign. What happened then?" Grandpa asked, leaning forward to refill our glasses from a frosty pitcher.

"Nothing happened," continued Maggie. "That's what was so cool about it. Nothing happened. So, while Leonard and his buddies are hanging on that hot rock face, the TV guys are hanging around the security building drinking coffee, eating Air Force issue cinnamon rolls and chatting like they were at a cocktail party or something. Meantime Len and his boys are struggling to get their banner turned right-side-up."

"And Leonard kept blowing that infernal bugle," I added.

"Yes, that bugle. God, that was annoying."

"Did they ever get the banner turned over?" Grandpa asked.

"Eventually," I responded. "In retrospect, that was the only TV worthy part of the event. I was afraid that alone would make the news. After they managed to get it right-side-up, there wasn't much for them to do so the six of them just hung there trying to look defiant, listening to Len's occasional bugle blast."

"Oh, that was great," exclaimed Maggie, moving from the swing to the table beside Grandpa's chair. "Now you have to understand that Manny had taken over Captain Lutz's office and was using it like a headquarters or command post or something; people were rushing in and out, looking very important. Val and I are sitting outside the office trying to be inconspicuous and, of course, Roger's there too. He still looks like a bum, not a clever young officer, so they didn't want him out trying to charm the press."

She gave me a smile and a wink before continuing.

"When Roger notices the climbers are beginning to ascend the wall he suggests to Col. Hahn that they come up with something to distract the press. When Hahn suggests it to Manny his first reaction is, 'A diversion? What the hell do you suggest, blow up a car in the parking lot or something?' Well, Roger steps up and suggests Manny hold an impromptu question and answer session to keep the cameras busy for a while. The aide, a guy named Wiser, jumps all over the idea and the next thing you know Manny is holding court for the reporters. He seemed nervous at first but was soon giving them great material for the evening news. Of course, at Roger's suggestion, they held the conference outside the security building where the press could focus on Manny and not see the guys on the mountain."

I moved from the swing and eased onto the porch railing, waiting for her to take a breath. Hearing her version of the incident, I couldn't help but smile.

"I have to say I was amazed at how well it worked," she continued. "The press was all over him like piranhas but he effortlessly shifted the message away from the protest to the important mission of Cheyenne Mountain. Pretty soon they were asking how many of those huge steel springs were holding up the buildings, how many tons of rock was excavated to dig the tunnels, all sorts of irrelevant but interesting stuff that had nothing to do with Leonard and his buddies hanging on the rock wall."

Grandpa was enjoying the whole story, chortling from time to time, his left hand clutching Maggie's and his right holding his lemonade. "Whatever you did to the TV guys it seemed to work. The two broadcasts I saw showed the banner and then switched to Manny jabbering about Cheyenne Mountain. But what happened to the mountain men?"

I took up the telling of the story as Maggie returned to the heavy wooden swing. "At the time we didn't know. But I saw the final incident report in the office on Friday. Turns out the call to the Army brought out two choppers which located their vehicles on an old mining road west of the mountain."

"Ha, the Army again. I knew it. Maybe I should give Manny a call just to rub it in."

"Now, Grandpa...."

"Anyway, they found a place to set down, blocked the only road and nabbed the mountain men as they drove out. No press, no trouble. They held them until the sheriff could get some guys up there to take them off Army hands."

Grandpa pushed himself from the chair and walked slowly down the porch gleefully rubbing his hands together. "Man, I'd have loved to have seen it, seen the whole thing, Manny, the rock boys, you two, the whole thing."

He paused at the end of the porch and turned back, fixing me in his gaze. "You know Roger, you did a remarkable job. Your idea for the peace offensive with the press, the diversionary press conference, those were great ideas. Maggie's right; you should be proud of yourself for the way you responded under pretty stressful conditions. I mean, people could have been hurt."

I squirmed and, most likely, blushed.

Perhaps sensing my discomfort, Maggie pushed from the swing and joined me on the railing taking my arm and snuggling against my shoulder. "He's too modest Grandpa but I'm proud of my second lieutenant. He was very cool under pressure."

Grandpa seemed to light up when she put emphasis on "my second lieutenant" as if reading something into her message.

"And Manny was impressed too," she added.

"Have you talked with him since?" Grandpa asked, easing onto the swing across from us.

"Have we talked to him? Mother invited me and Roger to dinner last night. That's why we couldn't get up here sooner. So we've talked to him, I've talked to him and Manny even cornered Roger in his den for a little man-to-man talk. So, yes, we've spoken with him."

"Wonderful. And they were impressed with this young man I assume," he said, nodding toward me.

"Mother was beside herself with joy. She thinks Roger is 'the finest boy I've ever brought home,' as she puts it. I didn't tell you this before, Roger, but she even changed the menu after she met you."

"She what?"

"True story. Do you remember she excused herself after

we arrived and were sitting in the living room talking with Manny and Aunt Ruth? Well, I joined her in the kitchen later and she was busy making her signature baking powder biscuits just for you. She doesn't do that for everyone, you know. And paired with her homemade grape jelly the biscuits are usually quite a hit."

"They were good."

"And when you told her that at dinner, I thought she was going to adopt you on the spot. Didn't you notice that adoring look she gave you?"

"OK, OK," Grandpa interjected. "But how was Manny?"

"I thought he was great. Roger kept 'siring' him every other breath and there was a little of that lieutenant vs. general tension, but he and Roger got along fine."

"That's because you have no idea how stressed I was. Even out of uniform he has a general's air about him."

"Oh pooh. I saw you two in the den looking over his airplane photo collection. You were chumming like old fraternity brothers. Trust me, I've seen him with other people. He was relaxed with you. And Grandpa, he even told Mother and Aunt Ruth about Roger's suggestions during the protest. He remembered. Of course, he wasn't so complimentary about your appearance that day but...."

***

The afternoon warmed and flew by. Maggie and Grandpa retired to the house to go over some family albums he'd found in the attic. He was intent on explaining to Maggie who was who in the old photos as she was the only link from his past to the future.

To keep me occupied he checked me out on a newly purchased riding mower and turned me loose in the grassy area between the house and the road. He called it his lawn but it was more weeds and wild grasses than the rich green lawns I'd grown up with in the rainy Pacific Northwest. Nonetheless it needed mowing so I cranked up the nine horse power Briggs & Stratton and drove that little green machine like a Grand Prix racer.

With the lengthening shadows, dinner time arrived. I parked the mower and found Maggie in the kitchen watching over the stove while Grandpa shuttled between there and the front porch barbeque.

A slamming screen door announced his arrival with a platter of oversized steaks. "You did a mighty fine job on that lawn, Roger. If this Air Force thing doesn't work out, you can always find work as a landscaper."

He set the platter on the dining room table while Maggie retrieved the rest of the food from the kitchen. "I cooked them all to my version of 'medium.' If they're too bloody let me know and I'll pop them back on the grill. The coals have plenty of life left. If they're too done, too bad."

"This is an impressive spread, Chef Meyers," said Maggie, arriving with the last of the serving dishes. "You've grown into quite a cook; baked potatoes, corn and even a salad. I think you've covered all the food groups."

"Yes, well, you'll notice the rolls are from the bakery. No baking powder biscuits at this restaurant. Now load that plate and then I want to hear more about the intrigues of Cheyenne Mountain. As I think about it there are some things that don't add up."

"Like what?" I asked as I prepared my baked potato.

"Like what were the MP's doing at the mountain when they nabbed you. That's Air Force turf, not Army. There not normally there, are they?"

"That was Lutz's doing."

"But I thought he was in Greenland or somewhere. Pass the jelly there, will you Sweetie?"

"In retrospect you've got to hand it to Lutz. You see, he tried and failed to get more staff for his security operation. So he headed down the hill to Fort Carson and cut a mutual aid agreement with the head of security, a you-help-us and we'll-help-you sort of thing. Of course, it was a one-sided deal since the grunt...or excuse me...the Army guy has hundreds of men and a fleet of vehicles and we have a handful of each. But he was happy to do it since it kept his guys busy and out of trouble."

Grandpa studied me while absorbing my story and savoring his steak. "But why was the Army there that Saturday. Nothing had happened."

"Roger, you'd better quit talking and start eating. Your

food's getting cold," offered Maggie. I had to smile since the guidance reminded me of my mother's typical admonitions.

"Yes dear," I replied, drawing a smile from Grandpa.

"Now, why were they there?" I continued. "It turns out you can take the man from the mountain but not the mountain from the man. Lutz may have been in Greenland but he was burning up the phone lines with calls to his senior NCO, Sgt. Larson. Lutz was certain something was going to happen so had Larson invoke the aid agreement. That way the MP's would be at the mountain just in case. In hindsight it was a good call."

"That should be a real feather in Lutz's cap," said Grandpa. "Good planning and good execution and all that."

"Maybe, maybe not. Don't forget, he wasn't there and Hahn appears to have been in charge. So Hahn may claim whatever credit there is to claim and the Lutz involvement will slip between the cracks. Then there is the little matter of setting up the aid agreement without even telling his boss. I'm sure when Hahn thinks about that, he'll not be too happy."

"Ah, palace intrigue. How I miss my days of playing politics in the Army. One more thing. Has anyone found a spy or mole or whatever Lutz called it when he was recruiting you into his 'spy' operation?"

"Actually yes."

"Really?" questioned Maggie, setting her fork down to focus on me. "I haven't heard this part."

"Remember the new kid you said was hanging out with Leonard, the one with the car Val said was called Borky's Bronco?"

She nodded.

"Well, it turns out the owner is none other than Lutz's clerk typist, Airman Borkowski." I settled back to let the revelation sink in.

"No way," she exclaimed, leaning forward and nearly getting her blouse into her sour cream. "His own clerk was a mole?"

"That may be generous where Borkowski's concerned. I think he's just a naive kid who got mixed up with the wrong crowd. The story they've pieced together is that he likes music, wandered into that record shop where Len works and fell under his spell. Lutz wants to hang him but, in his case, I think there's a fine line between spying and just talking too much. I suspect Len did learn some stuff from him, innocently or not. It may even have been something Bork heard or saw at work that led him to the conclusion that I was one of Lutz's spies. In any case he was at a concert in Denver last weekend, not with Leonard, though Leonard was driving 'Borky's Bronco' when they nabbed him."

Grandpa appeared to be savoring the tale as much as his steak. "Hell, I've seen this kind of thing before. It's hard to . prove intent in a case like this. I suspect they'll ship him to some backwater post where he keeps quiet and can't get in too much trouble."

"Or send him home," I added. "He's due to get out in a few months. But you can bet they'll keep him out of Lutz's cross-hairs until then. I think the good captain would disembowel him given a chance."

"That's a pleasant thought, Roger," grimaced Maggie as she resumed eating.

"Sorry."

"What about Maggie's roommate, this Leonard person?" Grandpa smiled at Maggie, anticipating her reaction.

"You stop that. You sound just like Roger. He's not my roommate. He rents a room in the same house."

"OK, OK," he responded, patting her arm.

I smiled, enjoying the way her grandfather could tease her. "I don't know. They were booked and released. I guess it depends on the Air Force. They were trespassing and as the signs on the security gate say, 'trespassers will be prosecuted to the fullest extent of the law.' But no damage was done and I doubt anyone wants to make martyrs out of these guys. They're small fish in the big picture."

"Hmm, you're probably right. Anyway, it makes for a good story. Bad guy gets captured. Good guy gets the girl." With the last comment his eyes flashed from Maggie to me and back again, as if waiting for a reaction. He didn't get one.

Moving on, he took his last bite of steak and began gathering empty serving dishes. "Hope you all got enough to eat. Let me tidy the table up a bit."

"Nonsense," said Maggie, reaching for his arm as if to restrain him. "I can do that. Why don't you and Roger go to your den or outside and do some guy thing. I can handle this mess. After all, you did most of the cooking."

He considered resisting and then relaxed back in his chair. "You're just like your grandmother, bossy and strong-willed. I guess that's why I love you so. And I do have a guy thing for us to do. But it's not in the den. It's in my wood shop. Come on, Roger. Let the little lady have her space."

***

Grandpa and I wandered across the yard in the fading glow of dusk. The fragrance of wood chips and shavings engulfed us as he pushed open the door and found the pull string on the ceiling-mounted light. Proudly he gave a quick tour of his works in progress. On the left, a work bench was covered with small blocks of wood that would soon be converted into a laminated chess board. Leaning in the corner were slats of various lengths destined for two Adirondack chairs he was preparing for a charity auction. Finally we stopped before a boxy-shaped object on the main work bench, covered with an old bed sheet.

"OK, here's the surprise. I didn't think Maggie could keep to herself," he began. "Tell me what you think."

He pulled off the sheet, like a game show host, revealing a contemporary looking coffee table, about four feet long. "It's cherry," he offered, rubbing the unfinished surface with affection. "What do you think?"

"It's beautiful," I replied, running my fingers over the neatly made corner joints. "For Maggie?"

"Nope. For you. She said you could use some furniture so she gave me a picture of one she thought you'd like and here it is. It's nothing fancy but …."

"You've got to be kidding. This is beautiful. I don't know what to say. This is great."

"Well then, don't say anything. Now that you've seen it you can pick the stain color. I've tried a few on the underside. We can turn it over before you leave and see what you like. In the meantime, how about a little snort?"

He produced a pint of scotch and two coffee cups and

gestured toward a pair of paint spattered chairs arrayed around the unlit wood stove. I took a seat while he set the cups down on an upturned wooden apple crate that served as his fireside table. He poured a shot in each and then handed me a cup emblazoned with the Colorado state flag.

"Nice refuge you have here," I offered, more to break the silence than to start a conversation.

"Hmmm, it is that all right. It is that."

We slipped back into silence, both staring at the unlit wood stove. He took a slow sip before he began in a serious tone. "Roger, I want you to know how glad I am you're back with Maggie. She was up here after that spy breakup thing you had and she was not a happy girl. I love the girl dearly and almost drove down to the Springs to personally wring your neck for hurting her but...."

"But sir...."

"Don't 'sir' me and I know it was all a misunderstanding but I just wanted to tell you what I felt like doing. Just as well. You'd likely have kicked my old butt." He looked toward me, smiled and softened his gaze.

"Anyway, I'm glad you're back on the scene. She seems happy when she's with you. She's all I have and this granddad's fondest wish is to see his little girl happy and with someone she loves. An old man can't ask for more than that."

Now my mind was racing again. Like that protest morning my mouth began to form words before my mind could form thoughts. This was an ideal time, a time to ask a question that had been pinballing around my mind for weeks. But how to say it?

"Sir...."

The word earned me a stern look.

"I mean, Grandpa...do you mind if I call you Grandpa?" He smiled and nodded approval. "Suit yourself."

"Grandpa, since you're so important to her and, like, very close to her I thought you'd be the right person to ask." At that point I believe he knew where I was going with the conversation but he didn't give me any help. Well, in a way he helped. He poured a bit more Scotch into my cup.

"I'd like to ask your permission to marry Maggie."

I think I detected the hint of a satisfied smile but he restrained its full bloom. "Do you love her?"

"With all my heart."

He offered me his hand. "Well then, welcome to the family, Roger Munson. Nothing you could say would make me happier. I've always wanted a grandson. So, if Maggie will share you, I'll have one. What does she think of the idea?" he concluded, relaxing his grip on my right hand.

"I haven't asked her."

"Well, what are we sitting around here for? Finish that drink and let's get back to the house."

***

As he left the shop Grandpa flipped on a yard light which revealed Maggie, heading our way across the darkened drive.

"That's better," she called out. "Man, it was black out here before you turned that on. Say, what have you two been doing out there. We need to get on the road home."

"Oh, take it easy, young lady. What's the rush? In fact, why don't you and Roger stay the night? I've gotten Roger all liquored up so he's not fit to drive. Your old room is always ready and we can put Roger on the sofa in the den. What do you say?"

By now Maggie was between us taking hold of Grandpa's arm and mine.

"Fine with me," I replied. "My Sunday schedule is wide open and I can't think of a better place to spend the day."

"It's done then. Now Maggie, why don't you grab a flashlight from the basket by the door and take this young man for a walk up the creek to the little spot you always liked. Meantime I'll get the den cleaned up for Roger."

"I can help," Maggie insisted.

"I'm not crippled. Now scoot. I think your young man may want to have you alone for a bit, right Roger?"

I was glad she couldn't see me blushing in the dim light. "Right sir...err, I mean Grandpa. That would be nice."

Maggie looked from Grandpa to me and back again, shrugging in confusion. "I think there's a conspiracy afoot. Grandma always said strange things happened in that workshop

243

of yours."

Without a word he retrieved a flashlight from the house, pressed it into my hand and waved us off.

"Men! I guess everything they say about them is true," she said, looking from Grandpa to me and back again. Finally, taking my hand Maggie led me from the porch and off toward the creek side path. "Oh well; come on sailor. Let's go for a walk."

THE END

Reading Group Questions and Topics for Discussion

1. What themes did the author emphasize throughout the novel? What do you believe the author was trying to get across to the reader?

2. Did the characters seem real and believable? Can you relate to their predicaments? Do they remind you of someone you know or knew and, if so, in what ways?

3. How do the characters views evolve throughout the course of the story? What events trigger the changes?

4. If you recall the Vietnam era, how do your recollections compare to the experiences of Roger and Maggie?

5. Maggie had been burned by a bad relationship? How understandable is her reluctance to begin a new one in Colorado Springs?

6. How does Roger's attitude toward the Vietnam War evolve as he learns more about it from his friend "Hunk" and others?

7. The author utilizes letters to introduce characters we never meet (Mother, Sister, Hunk.) How effective were the letters in incorporating those characters into the broader story fabric?"

8. Maggie and Roger seem to give credence to the adage, opposites attract one another?" What real life

examples (without incriminating anyone) of opposites attracting opposites can you recall? How successful were the matches?

9. Maggie is vague about her mother and stepfather. Why do you suppose she wished to keep them in the background?

10. If you were the casting director for a movie version of "The Girl With the Cinnamon Twist" who might you cast in Roger and Maggie's roles? Why?

11. Which character do you most relate to and why?

Would you like to hear of other work by the same author? Simply send an e-mail to

Simonereads@comcast.net

21318602R00152

Made in the USA
San Bernardino, CA
15 May 2015